Happy Summer!! xo Jen Calonita

Summer State of Mind

by Jen Calonita

poppy

Little, Brown and Company
New York • Boston

Poppy

Hachette Book Group
237 Park Avenue, New York, NY 10017
Visit us at lb-teens.com

Poppy is an imprint of Little, Brown and Company.
The Poppy name and logo are trademarks of Hachette Book Group, Inc.

The publisher is not responsible for websites (or their content)
that are not owned by the publisher.

First Edition: April 2014

Library of Congress Cataloging-in-Publication Data

Calonita, Jen.
Summer state of mind / by Jen Calonita. — First edition.
pages cm
Summary: "Spoiled, yet lovable fifteen-year-old Harper McCallister is sent to sleepaway camp where she is an outcast at first but eventually finds a way to make her mark, gaining new perspectives on friendship and life in general"— Provided by publisher.
ISBN 978-0-316-09115-2 (pbk) — ISBN 978-0-316-32342-0 (ebook) [1. Camps—Fiction. 2. Self-actualization (Psychology)— Fiction. 3. Interpersonal relations—Fiction. 4. Brothers and sisters—Fiction. 5. Twins—Fiction. 6. Catskill Mountains Region (N.Y.)—Fiction.] I. Title.
PZ7.C1364Sum 2014   [Fic]—dc23   2013019009

10 9 8 7 6 5 4 3 2 1

RRD-C

Printed in the United States of America

For Brooke Katherine, the newest member of our family.
I look forward to the day we can read this book together.

1

CONFESSIONS OF a SHOPaHOLIC

Harper McAllister @HarperMc
SCHOOL. IS. OVER! Can't wait to hang w/ my friends
@KatetheGreat & @MargoDivine at our home away
from home...the Americana!

THIS IS HOW I WaS MEANT to spend my afternoons. Standing in the middle of a big, bright store filled with all my favorite people—Emilio Pucci, Stella McCartney, and Chloé.

Not behind a Bunsen burner wearing supertight plastic goggles that leave red marks on my tender skin.

As I flip through the racks at Intermix, I can feel my stress level drop, much like that piece of plastic that accidentally fell into my Bunsen burner during my second-to-last science lab. (The lab *still* smelled this morning, even after I secretly spritzed Vera Wang Princess perfume in the air.)

"Eeee!" I look up and see Margo racing toward me waving a long electric-blue halter top like a flag. The glittery straps are so blinding I shield my eyes. "This is that top I saw in *Lucky*!" Margo pins it to her tiny torso and spins, which sends her long black hair flying. "I've been looking for it everywhere! Isn't it cute? I could wear it as a shirt! Or a minidress! Or as a beach cover-up if we go to Cancun!"

When Margo is excited she talks so fast that I wish I could rewind her. The girl loves to shop even more than I do. "It looks like something you'd wear for a dance competition," I say with a laugh. Margo starts to pout, so I add, "But if we do go to Cancun, we'll just have to go dancing so you can wear it."

Margo squeezes me like a lemon.

"What do you mean *if* we go to Cancun?" Kate teeters over on four-inch cork wedges, towering over us like a giant. She practically trips into me, and her dirty blond hair smacks me in the face. "I thought the trip was a done deal."

I backpedal. "Did I say *if*? I meant *when*."

Kate looks at me harder. "Are you sure?"

Sometimes Kate cross-examines me like they do on those legal shows my grandma watches in the middle of the afternoon. "Yes!" I say brightly. She continues to stare me down, and I crack. "The thing is I haven't exactly asked McDaddy about a date yet." Kate gives me a look. "I tried to bring it up the other night, but he was meeting Rihanna for dinner and was stressed 'cause he couldn't find his keys. I'll sort it all out tonight."

Kate smiles with satisfaction. "Okay. I don't mean to hound you. I just want to tell my parents when I'm going to Atlantis so they can go to Barbados the same week." She wrinkles her nose as if she just got a whiff of rancid sushi. "I hate Barbados."

"Atlantis?" Margo and I repeat at the same time.

"Harper's dad said he is taking us to Cancun," Margo reminds Kate, speaking slowly in case the fumes from my Bunsen burner incident the other day are having some lasting effect on Kate's memory.

"That's right!" Kate hits her forehead. "*I* was the one who suggested Atlantis." She thumbs the fabric of a pair of dark wash jeans on a table next to her. "I just thought it would be more fun to swim with sharks and celebrity watch than worry about being kidnapped in Mexico." She sighs. "But it's your choice, Harper. Margo picked last time."

"Yeah, because my dad paid." Margo's mood goes from a shopping high to a discount-bin low, and I feel my heart race with alarm. Kate and Margo step toward each other, and my thumbnail goes to my mouth. I start to bite it. "I don't recall you being that bent out of shape about skiing in Park City, Utah, Harper!" Margo swats my hand away from my mouth. "Stop biting your nails!"

"Sorry," I say sheepishly. I asked Margo to keep me in check about my nail biting. My disgusting habit seems to get worse in high-stress moments like this.

"Actually, now that I think about it, we picked Park City because Harper wanted to go there. I suggested Aspen, remember?" Kate clicks the heels on her cork wedges loudly and looks at me.

Okay, I did say I've always wanted to ski the white powder in Utah, but I didn't know Margo was going to book our winter break trip around something I said. We usually do what Kate wants. She picks what table we sit at for lunch, what movie we see on a Friday night, whose party is worthy of us attending. The three of us have been tighter than super-skinny jeans since I arrived at Friends Prep almost two years ago, but sometimes I still feel like I'm on friend probation with Kate. Margo says that's because Kate thinks I've moved above her in the hierarchy of our friendship. All because a few people—including the lunch lady—have started asking for my advice instead of hers.

"Should I get the Greek yogurt or Yoplait for lunch today, Harper?"

"Would you button this top or leave it unbuttoned, Harper?"

"Harper, what is the square root of 364?"

Honestly, I have no clue what the answer is to that last one.

I don't want Kate to feel threatened by me. If it wasn't for her, I wouldn't even be popular. When my family moved to Brookville almost two years ago, I didn't know a soul. Thankfully, Kate rescued me from lunch-table no-man's-land. She spied me in line wearing my pink Hunter rain boots and said she knew I was "one of them," which in Kate's book meant "destined to be popular." I was an overnight success, just like my dad when his wedding video company produced an unknown rap star's low-budget music video and the song became record of the year. McDaddy Productions was born soon afterward, and we went from a tiny house in middle-class Mineola to a mansion in JLo country (she and Marc Anthony used to own the house across the street from ours). Some days I am still getting used to how different my life is here.

"My dad has his heart set on Cancun," I tell Kate apologetically. "But the good news is he said the resort is secluded and five-star. I think Beyoncé told him about it."

That makes Kate smile. "Well, if Beyoncé goes there . . . You're *sure* we're going?"

"Absolutely!" I insist, but the truth is, I'm not sure McDaddy remembers promising to take my friends and me away for my fifteenth birthday. He was shooting a video with the hottest pop star on the charts, London Blue, on my actual birthday and promised to make it up to me. He also arranged for me to get a shout-out from London Blue online that got over a hundred thousand hits on YouTube. I don't want to disappoint my friends, though. Margo has taken us away twice, and Kate keeps promising to bring us on a trip next winter. Mom finds the group-trip tradition kind of strange, but she chalks it up to being a North Shore thing. Going from the middle of Long Island to the North Shore really was like moving from Antarctica to Los Angeles. There are a lot of cultural differences. Don't even get me started on the Truvia versus real sugar debate.

"And the best part about Cancun is that we don't have to worry about getting eaten alive on an excursion," I tell Kate. "Swimming with sharks at Atlantis has *Good Morning America* lifestyle piece written all over it. 'Almost high school sophomore eaten by sharks on summer break,'" I say using my best reporter voice. "I'll be darned if Josh Elliott reports on me, and I'm not alive to see it."

"Amen," seconds Margo, folding her hands in prayer for a moment before slipping the blue halter over her head to try it on, much to the chagrin of the nearby saleswoman.

"I guess you're right. Again." Kate pulls off the cork wedges dejectedly.

I quickly look around the store of brightly colored designer pieces to find something that will cheer her up. "Ooh, Kate! Isn't that the Chloé shirt you were looking for the other day? They must have gotten more in."

Kate rushes over to the rack and squeals. I breathe a sigh of relief.

"It's the shirt!" she announces, a smile replacing the scowl on her face. She holds up the tee. It has nylon flowers around the collar, the Chloé logo written across the front, and a stick figure drawing of a girl on it. I don't think it's anything special, but Kate is acting like she won a private fitting with the designer herself. "Isn't it sweet?"

"Yeah," I say, because that's what she wants to hear.

"If we each get one, we'll look like triplets!" Kate pulls me in front of the nearest mirror and holds the tee up under my chin. She and I do look somewhat related. We have the same dirty blond hair and brown eyes, but she towers over me in the height department while I have her beat in the bra-size category. "We have to buy them. This will look great on you even if it is a bit snug in the chest." She opens her slouchy leather bag and retrieves her wallet. I open my mouth to protest and watch her eyes widen in horror. "Seriously! My credit card is in my other wallet." She sits down on one of the velvet ottomans in the store, and Margo walks up next to her. "I was going to buy them for us as last-day-of-school gifts. They'll be gone tomorrow." She drops her bag on the floor in disgust. Her eyes narrow as she stares at the front door. "Cassie Anderson is probably hiding behind one of the racks trying to steal them from us as we speak. Some last day of school this is turning out to be. First no Atlantis, now no Chloé tee that I have wanted forever."

She's laying the guilt on thick. "I'll buy them for us." I gently pry the shirt from Kate's hands, and the saleswoman swoops in to take the tees up to the register.

Margo follows us. "H, no! You bought us the Swarovski crystal flip-flops last week and MAC makeup the week before that. It's too much."

"So? You bought us facials at Red Door Spa a few weeks back." I pull my credit card out and hand it to the salesgirl. "Friends do things for each other, right?"

"Right!" Kate seconds. I notice she's still holding the cork wedges she tried on earlier. She stops a salesgirl walking by, and I hear her whisper: "Can I put these on hold for tomorrow?"

On hold. I suddenly wonder why Kate didn't do that with these shirts, too.

"That will be three hundred sixty-eight dollars and forty-two cents," my salesgirl says and swipes my credit card before I even have time to hesitate.

Three hundred and sixty-eight dollars isn't that bad, is it? I sign the receipt with a whimsical signature I have been perfecting, making a giant loop around the *H* and *A* for Harper Avery McAllister. Usually signing my name and getting handed a cute bag full of new clothes is my favorite part of shopping. But when the salesgirl hands me my receipt this time, I can't help but think about everything I've bought lately. There was that Nikon 1 camera I needed because for a split second I wanted to become a photographer, the pair of skis I've never used but had to have because they were on sale, and the Prada dress for the spring fling that looked like the one Amanda Seyfried wore to an awards ceremony. Those three items add up to about eight hundred dollars and that doesn't include any of my Starbucks runs or dinners out with the girls. Gulp.

I'm sure I have nothing to worry about, though. McDaddy is the one who gave me the AMEX and told me to consider it my "fun money."

"Here you go." The saleswoman walks around the counter and hands me three bags. One for each of us. I start to cheer up as I pass them out like candy.

Kate throws her arms around me. "Thanks, H!" She's always more pleasant after she gets a present. "Let's celebrate the last day of school over dinner."

"Intermezzo?" we say at the same time. "Lobster mac and cheese!" We both burst out laughing, and Kate links arms with me. Things are so much easier when Kate and I are on the same page.

"I thought you didn't have your credit card," Margo grumbles, but Kate ignores her. When we step outside, the humidity hits us in the face. The sidewalk is crowded with people carrying designer shopping bags as they hurry from one store to the next. Margo walks alongside us to the restaurant area, and I give her hand a squeeze.

"Thanks for getting us those shirts," Kate says as we walk the short distance to Intermezzo, which is nestled between Prada and Gucci in the outdoor mall. "We have to think of a really great place to wear them together."

"July Fourth on Hallie's boat?" Margo suggests. "My beach club for the opening weekend party? Ooh! Ooh!" She grips my arm tightly as she rattles off several other suggestions and then, "Or the week we go to my house on the Jersey Shore? We could wait until Cancun, but that is over a month away."

"I don't want to wait till August to wear this shirt," Kate moans.

My head is spinning. Summer hasn't even started yet, and I can already tell I'm not going to have a minute to just be lazy. "Wow! Do we have that many plans already? What about time to chill?"

"Downtime?" Kate looks at me as if I've sniffed glue. "To do what? Read a book?" She cracks herself up.

I laugh along with her, but really I am thinking, *Yeah, to read a book or go for a run or do nothing at all.* I bite my nails again. "I just hate schedules in the summer."

"Me too, but look at the alternative," Kate says. "If you didn't have plans, you'd be stuck hanging out in a parking lot like these losers." Kate motions to a group of teens milling outside Intermezzo.

I want to say not everyone chooses to get a table at a place where a soda is four bucks, but I don't. The truth is some of these people go to Friends Prep with us. As we pass by the crowd, two girls wave and say, "Hi, Harper!" I wave back as Kate ushers me inside so we can get a table . . . outside. The patio has the best seating and, as Kate always points out, a great view for people watching. Mary, the regular hostess, is standing at the check-in desk when we walk in. She waves me over.

"Hey, Harper!" She ignores Kate, probably because Kate refused to give her a tip last week when Mary subbed in as our waitress ("Hostesses don't get tips!"). "Last day of school, huh?" Mary says, looking directly at me and only me. "Any big plans?"

"Dinner," Kate says bluntly. "Is there a table open on the patio?"

Mary looks around the crowded restaurant and then at me again. "Anything for *Harper*. Just give me a few minutes to turn over a table." She gives me a little wink.

Yep, she hasn't gotten over the no-tip thing yet.

Fifteen minutes later we're settled at a table in the ivy-covered garden. The fountain nearby is gurgling, the bright yellow umbrellas are shading us from the eighty-five-degree heat, and we're all studying the menu as if we've never eaten here before.

Kate sighs impatiently. "Where are our drinks? The waitress should have gotten them by now." She snaps her fingers at a guy who just finished cleaning the table next to ours. "Hey! You!" He stops so suddenly I'm afraid he's going to drop the plastic bucket full of dirty dishes. "Can you get us our drinks? We've been waiting forever."

Margo and I look at each other. Doesn't Kate realize he isn't a waiter? Besides the fact that he is carting dirty dishes, he looks to be around our age. He must be a busboy. He looks at Kate strangely. "Sorry, I'm not a waiter. Notice the messy apron?" He smiles. "I'll call one over for you."

10

I feel my stomach do a little flip. I know this busboy! He is in our grade at Friends Prep. What is his name? Ethan! That's it. Ethan Thompson! How could I forget this cute face? Dark brown hair, big brown eyes, and lashes I only get when I buy those glue-on ones at CVS. Even his stained light blue T-shirt looks adorable on him.

I notice Kate isn't giving him the same adoring look. "We can't wait for a waiter to come over. It's hot out, and we're parched!" She snaps her fingers. "Can't you just bring us our usual drinks?"

I rearrange the silverware in front of me to avoid looking like I share Kate's attitude and opinion. When I finally sneak a peek at Ethan, I notice he's staring at Kate in annoyance.

"I couldn't even get your drinks if I wanted to." He motions to the bucket in his hands as proof. "Besides, knowing Kate Harrison's usual drink order is not one of my job requirements."

"Excuse me?" Kate's voice is so low I can barely hear it over the fountain.

Margo and I shoot each other warning looks. Ethan is not afraid of Kate, which makes me even more in awe of him. It's rare for anybody to stand up to her unless they don't care about their social standing at Friends Prep.

"I said it's not my job to know Kate Harrison's drink order," Ethan says matter-of-factly. "So if you want me to pass along your order, you're going to have to tell me whether you drink Diet Coke, Coke, or spring water."

I laugh, and Margo hits me. There's that famous glare again from Kate. She hates being the butt of jokes, even if they are harmless and funny. This is definitely funny.

"If you want to even *think* about keeping your job, you'll ask someone our drink order." Kate loves to act as if she owns the place. I think her dad is an investor. "And if you want a tip, you'll bring it over with a smile on your pasty face and your lips sealed."

I wouldn't call Ethan's face pasty at all. It actually has a slight glow to it.

Ethan shrugs. "I've already heard you don't tip, so I'll take my chances."

Snap!

"A Diet Coke, a Perrier, and a Coke," I blurt out before Kate can lunge across the table and stab him with her fork. "You don't have to get them, either. If you could just tell our waiter— that would be great." I smile, but he doesn't smile back. Instead he walks away without asking if we want the complimentary bread basket. (Sadly, the answer is no. On the North Shore, eating bread is as taboo as revealing your true weight.)

"Who was that jerk?" Kate asks.

Margo looks at Kate incredulously. "Uh, he goes to our school."

"He's going to be a sophomore, too," I clarify. "That's Ethan Thompson."

"And you know that why?" Kate's never bothered to learn the names of people we don't hang out with.

I blink. "He sits at a table near us in the cafeteria every day."

Thud! Ethan returns with our drinks and angrily begins placing the glasses on the table. I'm so surprised, I forget to say thank you.

"Hey, Harper," says a girl walking by our table.

"Hey!" I say pleasantly because I don't know her name.

"Why'd you just say hi to her?" Kate snaps at me. Margo secretly rolls her eyes.

"She goes to our school, too." I can't believe I'm back on Kate's bad side so quickly. "She's going into eighth grade."

"She's in *middle* school," Kate says. "You're in high school."

I don't point out that when we were in middle school, Kate tried to talk to all the high school boys.

Ethan snickers, and we all look up. "Sorry," he says as he places Kate's water on the table. "Something in my throat. Must be that sixth grader I ate for breakfast."

Kate looks like one of those Monster High dolls with her creepy smile. "I want our waiter. *Now.* I'm going to make sure you get fired for the way you're acting."

"Try it," Ethan dares her, and I blink fast. "Why do you think nobody has come over yet? No one wants to deal with you three." He gives each of us a dirty look, and I suddenly feel as if I've been blasted with air-conditioning.

Kate pushes her chair away from the table, and people turn to look at us. "I'm not going to sit here and listen to this. I want the manager."

"No need." Ethan's incredibly calm for someone about to have his head handed to him. Margo and I look at each other. "Today is my last day, anyway. Thankfully, where I'm going, I don't have to deal with the spoiled, popular girls of the world like you three."

Is he calling me a mean girl? I'm anything but, especially at

Intermezzo. I even tip the lady in the bathroom who hands me a towel after I wash my hands!

"I..." It's too late. Ethan is already walking away.

Kate throws down her napkin. "I don't care if it's his last day!" she tells us. "I'm going to tell the manager how he spoke to us." She stomps off.

"Kate's ego is so big I'll be shocked if she fits through the door," Margo says, watching Kate go. "Poor guy. I thought he was cool for trying to take her down a peg. No one ever starts with her."

"I have to go to the bathroom." I rush inside after Ethan.

I'm not sure what I'm going to do, or why I even think I need to prove myself to a boy I don't know, but I can't stop myself. I'm not that girl he's describing. By the time I get through the pack of people waiting for an outdoor table, Ethan's already got a beat-up backpack slung over his arm, and he's hugging Mary good-bye. "Wait!" They both turn and look at me. Now I can't remember what I was going to say.

"I wanted to give you a tip for all your trouble." I reach inside my Tory Burch bag and pull out two twenties. I try to hand them to him. "Here."

"Usually the waiter gets a tip *after* you drop the check," he says, staring at my outstretched hand. "Not the busboy your spoiled friend just tried to get fired."

"About that..." I fumble over the words. Mary looks sympathetic.

"I don't want your money." Ethan sticks his hands in his jeans. "See ya, Mary." I watch him walk out the front door and head straight to the parking lot, where he begins talking to all the other kids milling about. I can see his hands going wildly, and I just know he's talking about me. I groan inwardly.

The phone at the hostess stand rings, and Mary picks it up before I can try to explain myself to her, too. I give up and trudge back to the table, my thoughts alternating between anger at myself and anger at Ethan. *Who is he to call us spoiled? I'm not spoiled! I just have money. There's a difference!*

The phone in my bag vibrates, and I pull it out to see the text. I'm assuming it's Kate to see what's taking me so long, but when I look at the phone, my bag slides down my arm in defeat. The worst kind of text is waiting for me.

The mad McDaddy variety.

McDaddy's Cell: H, just got home and saw your latest AMEX bill. We need to talk. Pronto.

Harper McAllister @HarperMc
What's scarier than a zombie apocalypse and an alien invasion combined? A daddy who has just seen your credit card bill. #deadmeat

2

IF IT AIN'T BROKE, DON'T FIX IT

"READY TO FACE THE MUSIC?" Margo asks me as her Land Rover turns down my long, tree-lined driveway. The music is pumping so loud I can barely hear her. Margo loves a good drive-time tune, and Harold, her driver, is hard of hearing, so it's all good. Margo doesn't drive yet, but she got a car and a driver in her parents' divorce. I guess having a professional ballplayer dad who is never home has its benefits.

I stare at our Dutch Colonial warily as the car comes to a stop in the circular driveway. "I think McDaddy is really mad at me this time."

"He'll get over it," Margo assures me. I was glad Harold dropped Kate off first tonight. I know we're all friends, but sometimes I feel weird telling Kate family drama. Since Margo has plenty of her own, she's always sympathetic. "My dad yells at me about my credit card bill all the time. He usually freezes my card in a block of ice to teach me a lesson." She points to her noggin. "He forgets that I have the numbers memorized. I just do all my ordering online instead!"

I start to bite one of my nails, then stop myself. "I don't use my AMEX *that* often, so maybe he'll go easy on me. I really only charge when it's an emergency."

Margo snorts. "Yeah, those Chloé tops you bought us today were a *real* emergency." I pale. "Just remember my motto: Deny, deny, deny!" Harold coughs.

"Margo, he's seen the bill," I remind her. "He knows what I've charged."

"Oh." Margo thinks for a second and then grins. "Say everything was for charity!"

I feel guilty even considering that lie. "I'll think of something. I'll call you after—if I'm alive." I shut the car door behind me and watch her car pull all the way out of our driveway to delay going into the house for a few more seconds. Then I make my way up the path and use my key instead of ringing the bell. Our housekeeper/personal chef Marisol works full-time, so she usually lets me in, but today I want the element of surprise. If I can show off some of those B-pluses I got on my report card, maybe he'll forget about those salsa lessons I charged after watching *Step Up 4*.

"Harper?" My dad calls my name before I even shut the door. Darn. His voice bounces off the marble tiles in the two-story foyer. "Could you come into the kitchen, please?"

"Coming, McDaddy!" I yell pleasantly. I've called my dad McDaddy forever. McAllister, McDaddy, get it? Mom says I started calling him that when I was three. (I tried McMommy for a while, too, but that didn't stick.) Dad took to it so well, he named his company McDaddy Productions. It has a cool rap-music vibe going for it, even though the three-year-old in me never planned it that way. I guess I'm very forward thinking.

I slowly walk past the walls of family portraits and original works of art that are hung under warmly lit sconces in the hall-way that leads from the foyer to the kitchen. It's amazing how much my mom has done with the house in two years. She threw herself into decorating the minute we moved in and hasn't stopped doing DIY projects ever since. She's so obsessed with home renovations she started her own blog, HomeBody. She's got over forty thousand subscribers. When I walk into our spa-cious kitchen, with the Sub-Zero fridge and Viking stove Mom never cooks on, I see everyone is in their usual spots. Mom is at her custom mini office tucked into the corner of the room, Marisol is washing dishes, and McDaddy is at the table, eating sushi. He and I used to cook together all the time, but now that we have a personal chef and eat out so much, there's no need.

"Happy Friday!" I drop my bag in the corner of the room, and Marisol frowns. I watch her shut off the water and pick up my bag, presumably to bring it back to its proper resting place in the foyer. I always forget those sorts of details.

I lean over to give Mom a kiss. "He's itemized the bill," she whispers. "Run." Mom has her studious, dark brown glasses on. She wears them for blogging purposes (she was going to get LASIK until market research showed her fans preferred her in specs).

I smile at McDaddy while I talk to Mom. "Oh, is that today's post? You turned an old hair dryer into a planter? Cool!" Then I whisper in her ear, "How bad was the bill?"

"Bad." Mom turns the volume up on the iPod dock next to her desk in the hope that our conversation can be drowned out, even though McDaddy is less than five feet away. "Tuba lessons, Harper? Really?"

"It sounded fun at the time." I took one lesson and realized my lungs didn't have the strength to support such an activity. I also didn't like how I looked holding a tuba. Maybe I should have held one in front of a mirror before I signed up. "I gave the lessons to Kyle and now he's in the band, so it all worked out." I flash an upbeat smile.

"Yes, but as part of the marching band, your brother could have had lessons for *free*," Mom reminds me. "He didn't need private ones that cost a thousand dollars."

Darn. She's got me there.

Mom has always been a defender of my need to fit in to this very privileged community that is as different from Mineola as Earth is from Mars. When we moved, my twin brother, Kyle, had it easy. His life has always been sports—soccer in the fall, basketball in the winter, and lacrosse in the spring—so he's supremely busy year-round and only has time to hang out with other sports people. Thanks to his various teams, he instantly had a whole new group of friends. But me? I sit out gym class whenever I possibly can. (If you need someone to raise money for children in Syria, I'm your girl. If you want an extra player for the volleyball team, I can't help you.) And all the other non-lame activities I had my eye on were already full. Where was I supposed to meet people? During *class*? Who knows what would have happened if Kate hadn't rescued me that day at lunch. So if she wants to take tuba lessons, then we take tuba lessons. Okay, Kate did cancel hers before our first class and never told me, but five other girls signed up so at least I wasn't alone. And look at all the girls I introduced to the tuba! The school should thank me for the wealth of musicians they have to choose from now.

"Girls, you know I can hear you, right?" McDaddy eats another piece of sashimi, a look of amusement on his face. He's dressed in his standard uniform: jeans and a black V-neck. Jeans are to a video producer what tuxes are to James Bond.

I drop into the seat next to him and catch a whiff of his woodsy cologne. It reminds me of camping in our backyard when I was a kid. He's worn the same cologne since I was a baby. Mom says McDaddy is a creature of habit. "Your mom and I want to talk to you about your spending and your behavior lately," he says seriously.

I groan. "You're not going to give me the 'you're not the girl you were in Mineola' speech again, are you?" I ask. Now is not the time to bring up Cancun, that's for sure.

"Bingo!" McDaddy drops his chopsticks in frustration. He wastes no time getting to the point. "You're going to be in college in three years and the way you've been acting lately makes me think you're completely unprepared." His brown eyes get squinty. "I hate to say this, but since you've moved here, you've become completely spoiled, Harper."

"Rick!" my mom scolds. "That was harsh."

I try not to look as hurt as I feel. That's what Ethan called me earlier, too. *Spoiled*. I'm not spoiled! I pull my report card out from behind my back and slide it across the table toward him. "Look at this lineup of beautiful Bs. I did great this year."

"Your grades are not the problem," he says with a sigh. "It's your friends. You're different with them."

"I thought you liked Margo and Kate," I say. I feel my stomach lurch. I hate conflict and try to avoid it.

McDaddy looks twisted like a salt-free pretzel. "Margo is a good kid, but Kyle says Kate is one step down from being a character in *Mean Girls*."

"That's not true," I say, even though now that he mentions it, Kate does have a Regina George thing going on.

"You were never this preoccupied with money till you met her." Mom steps away from her computer and joins us at the table. "I've tried to be supportive because I know how hard the move was for you, but we're worried." She looks at McDaddy before continuing. "You've become—how do I say it?—superficial since you started hanging out with Kate."

"You think I'm a poseur?" I feel like I've been slapped.

"We didn't say that," McDaddy says quickly. "We're all a little different in Brookville. Who knew how much one video shoot would change our lives?"

None of us did, but that's exactly what happened. Within a year, McDaddy Productions was getting calls from everyone who is anyone in the music industry. McDaddy himself was getting invites to things like the Grammys and bringing Mom to *Rolling Stone* parties. Jay Z suddenly knew our home number.

Carrie Underwood sent him Edible Arrangements as thank-you gifts. London Blue thanked my dad in her American Music Award speech. It only made sense that we upgrade our lifestyle along with all of that.

"The problem is your spending," he says. "Before we moved here, you were happy to spend a Friday night at Chili's. Now, you think it's okay to pop into the Gucci store and buy yourself a new bag and key rings for all your friends."

"Some people would say that makes me generous," I say defensively.

He slides my credit card statement in front of me. I am ashamed to admit the charges are two pages long. "Generous is one thing. Excessive is another. Your brother only uses his AMEX to buy sports equipment, and he asks me first, but you . . ." He points to a charge. "An espresso cart rental for seven hundred dollars?"

"The basketball team lost five games in a row. Kyle and his friends needed a pick-me-up." And I needed a way to get Pat St. James to notice me. It didn't work.

"Six hundred dollars at Red Door Spa?" he asks.

"We had tension headaches before midterms." Because Kate didn't study, and I was stressed knowing she didn't prep. It was a nightmare.

Mom gives me a look. "Three hundred fifty dollars on school spirit wear?"

"I thought it would be cute if our entire English class had matching T-shirts to wear to the Long Island Poetry Slam," I explain.

"While I appreciate that you want to share the wealth, this is insane. I can afford a Porsche, but I didn't run out and get one. I still drive my '94 BMW because I love it, and you shouldn't buy half the school just so they'll like you. I've been so busy that I didn't see this earlier, but…" McDaddy seems so hesitant I'm not sure what to make of it. "You need a dose of reality, and I'm going to give it to you whether you like it or not."

He passes me a faded pamphlet that has a picture of a cabin with pine trees on it.

I'm not sure what I'm staring at. Is he doing an ad for Pine-Sol?

"You're spending your summer at Whispering Pines sleep-away camp," he says, and for a minute I think he's speaking a foreign language.

Sleepaway camp? Me?

I burst out laughing. "Where's the camera?" My parents look baffled. "Is this for that new TV show you're producing? This prank has kind of been done before, but that's okay. I'll go along with it." I sit back down. "Say it again, and this time I'll cry." I take a deep breath, push my hair out of my eyes, and smile big and wide.

"Harper, this is not a joke." My mom is looking at me like I inhaled some of her aerosol craft sprays. "Your father is driving you up himself. You leave tomorrow."

"Tomorrow?" I feel slightly dizzy. "I have the beach club opening tomorrow."

"Actually, you have camp orientation at ten o'clock." He points to the flyer again and smiles cheerily.

"You can't be serious." They both nod, and that's when I

feel the gravity of the situation. He's not joking. "I'm not going to camp! I already have plans for the summer!" They don't look moved. "Do you know what will happen if I'm not here?"

"Yes. You might remember who the real Harper is," McDaddy says calmly. He pushes the rest of the uneaten sushi away, and Marisol swoops in to pick up the tray.

"I know who I am." I pull at the front of my Stella McCartney sundress self-consciously. "Mom." I stare at my mom with the widest eyes I can muster. Mom is like my own personal on-staff lawyer. She can't turn her back on me.

Her face tells a different story. "I'm with your father," she says quietly. "We miss the down-to-earth Harper we used to know. I think camp is the way to help you find her again."

"I can't believe you're doing this to me," I whisper, feeling my hands begin to shake. "You're just going to abandon me in the middle of nowhere's-land?"

"The Catskills are hardly the middle of nowhere," McDaddy says. "And you won't be alone. Your brother is going, too. Whispering Pines has an excellent reputation for sports, and Kyle's always wanted to see where I went to camp."

A swirl of images comes charging at me like a freight train. Wood cabins, muddy trails, a musty dining hall, and way too much nature. McDaddy took Kyle and me there when we were eight because he had a camp reunion. Even when we couldn't afford the thousands of dollars it would cost to go to sleepaway camp, I had no desire to go there. They don't even have central air! How is a person supposed to survive without that most basic of needs? "So that's it?" I sound shrill. "I don't get a say at all?"

McDaddy smiles. I have a feeling he is enjoying this. "Registration is past due, but my college buddy is squeezing you guys in. When I went there, if you were fifteen you had to apply to be a CIT—counselor-in-training—but Hitch says they changed the policy two years ago, so you'll still get to be a camper this year. Hitch says you're going to love it there."

"Hitch?" I repeat, unable to keep the disdain out of my voice.

"Yes, Alan Hitchens. We went there together as kids. He runs the place now with his new wife, Pam. His stepdaughter is a counselor." Dad makes this sound like a major accomplishment. "He says there is a zip line now, but otherwise the place is still pretty much the same as it was when we were kids."

"Lucky me," I deadpan.

He stands up and pulls me in for a hug. His mood has improved big time since I walked in, whereas mine has gone steadily downhill. I refuse to make eye contact. "This is going to be the best summer of your life, kiddo. You might be mad at us now, but in a few weeks you're going to be thanking me for kicking you out of here. You'll see."

I see all right. I see that McDaddy has ruined my summer before it even started.

Harper McAllister @HarperMc
Sending a frizz-hating, Prada-wearing girl like me to
CAMP? You know how this will end! I'll be eaten by a bear.
#wishsummerwasoveralready

3

OH, a-camping we will go

I HEAR McDADDY KNOCKING SOFTLY on my door, and I jump up. I look at my piggy alarm clock. It's 5:32 a.m.! Is McDaddy insane? We didn't even leave this early when we flew to Tahiti!

McDaddy knocks louder. "You up? We need to be at Whispering Pines by nine."

Whispering Pines.

Sleepaway camp.

Last night's conversation comes back to me like a bad dream. The Louis Vuitton luggage overflowing with clothes and beauty products in the corner of my bedroom is not a mirage. Neither is the wastebasket full of tissues I used while I cried about the fact that my father expected me to sleep on a cot all summer.

I'm leaving Brookville.

To go to sleepaway camp.

For four weeks.

Starting today.

"H?" McDaddy's voice is louder now. "Okay, you've left me no choice."

London Blue's latest song comes blasting through the speakers in the ceiling at full volume. It is one of my faves, but at five in the morning it is giving me a migraine! I grab my pillow and wrap it around my head. "I surrender!" The music shuts off just as quickly. McDaddy is never without his remote phone app, which controls everything from the garage doors to the dishwasher disposal.

"Just making sure," McDaddy says, and I hear Kyle laughing. He is probably dressed and has eaten already. Sports people are so punctual. "We leave at six fifteen."

I roll out of bed with a heavy sigh and walk straight to my spacious, private bathroom. The two of us need a moment before parting ways for the next four weeks. I couldn't find anything about shower habits or dining menus on the Whispering Pines website. All I found were pictures of guys and girls canoeing (never!), playing sports (blech!), and doing lots of hugging (personal space, please!). The official camp tee was a downer, too. They were boxy red things that looked like undershirts. I am not wearing an undershirt in public! Not that anyone I know will see me in it. I three-way called Margo and Kate last night after the McDaddy powwow to break the bad news.

"We're not going to Cancun?" Kate cried. I tried not to be offended (even though I was). I'd made Kate pause her favorite show to talk to me, so I should have known she'd be cranky.

"Kate! Harper is upset!" Margo sounded as unnerved as I

27

was. "There's nothing we can do to change your dad's mind? I can't imagine you not being here."

"I can't, either," I whined. "I wish you guys were coming to camp with me. I bet my dad could get you in if I asked him."

Hint, hint.

"You know I would come if I could, but the custody arrangement says I have to stay with Daddy every other week during the summer," Margo said mournfully.

"I understand." We waited to hear Kate's response. "Kate?"

"What?" I heard her turn down the volume on the TV. "Oh, yeah, that stinks about camp. Why don't you just ask your dad if you can intern at his office instead? That will show him you're responsible! Hanging with Kanye is way better than dealing with mosquitoes."

"Yes! Do that!" Margo encouraged me.

"He won't go for that," I said dejectedly. "His mind is made up." I felt so alone all of a sudden. My besties were not coming with me. For the past two years, I hadn't done a thing without them.

"If he won't budge, remember it's only four weeks," Kate said brightly. "That's shorter than a season of *Pretty Little Liars*. And when you get back—Cancun!"

Kate sounded a little too upbeat for someone who was losing her best friend for half the summer. Was she trying to get rid of me? Now I had another thing to add to my list of worries that included being eaten by bears and contracting West Nile virus.

"You're right. It will be like I'm not even gone," I assured them. "And we'll text and call each other every day so we can plan Cancun." If I could hack four weeks at camp, McDaddy had to agree to take us to Cancun. Camping is as unspoiled as you can get!

"You'll be back in Brookville before you know it," Margo agreed.

As I took a long, last lingering look around my room, I prayed Margo was right. Then I headed downstairs and found Mom waiting for me in the kitchen in her pj's.

"I'm sorry I'm not going on the drive up." She envelops me in her arms. I can still smell her perfume from the night before. "I have the contractor coming at nine this morning about the mudroom, and it was too late to call him last night and cancel after...the talk."

I'm not really mad at my mom. She may have agreed with McDaddy, but it's not like camp was her idea. Besides, she promised to send awesome care packages from Philosophy and Kiehl's. She also convinced McDaddy that I only had to go to camp for the first session, which runs through July. Kyle has to stick it out until late August. "It's okay," I tell her. "I don't think I'm going to do much talking on the drive up, anyway."

Mom pulls away and stares at me intently. I hope I have her skin when I'm her age. Even without makeup she still looks dewy at six a.m. "Don't be too hard on your dad. He's trying to do right by you. He always said what he learned at camp got him where he is today."

I am not sure what learning how to start a fire has to do with shooting music videos, but my last few minutes with my mom is not the time to ask.

She kisses my cheek and pushes a stray curl behind my ear.

"You are the life of every party, Harper. I'm sure you'll find a way to have fun at camp, too."

I snort. "I doubt that. I'm going to be sending texts begging you to rescue me."

"It is not going to be that bad," Mom insists. "But do text and post online." She gave me a knowing look. "I'll be reading your Twitter feed so I can keep track of what you and Kyle are up to. I'm counting on you to be the family mouthpiece. Your brother will never post anything."

"I will." Kyle doesn't even have a Twitter account. He calls Twitter a "time suck." I give Mom another hug and then go outside to face McDaddy.

I find him in the driveway in the early morning air, humming a Justin Timberlake tune as he stuffs my Louis bags in the back of the Land Rover for their drive to isolation. Kyle's sports gear is waiting to go in there, too, including two of his lacrosse sticks and his lucky basketball.

Kyle is humming along as he picks up a giant sports bag and tosses it in the back. The sun casts Kyle in an amber light that makes his light brown hair look red and the muscles in his arms practically glow. My fraternal twin is the crush of almost every girl in our grade, much to my annoyance. When I first became friends with Kate, she claimed Kyle as her own. I didn't have the heart to tell her Kyle wouldn't be interested. Kate's idea of physical activity is getting a tan at the outdoor mall, while Kyle wants a girl who can keep up with him on the basketball court.

There aren't many of those at our school.

Kyle sees me and grins. "Morning, sunshine!"

I'm too cranky to come up with a comeback, so I just ignore him. It's amazing to think how much my mood has changed in under twelve hours. I'm generally the happiest person I know. See what camp is doing to me already? I haven't even left yet!

"The last time I saw you up this early was the year we drove to the Outer Banks on vacation," Kyle says. "You cried the whole drive down there."

"I had a stomachache," I insist. Caused by the early morning wake-up. I don't do mornings. I'm almost late to school on a daily basis, and we get the bus. Kyle shakes his head at me. "What?" I grumble. Twins are supposed to have some sort of sixth sense when it comes to each other. This skill seems to have skipped the two of us.

Kyle smirks. "I'm wondering how you're going to handle being woken up by a bugle, showering with lukewarm water, cleaning a fish and eating it, and camping outdoors." His laugh sounds strange in the quiet of morning. "When Dad mentioned sending us to Whispering Pines, I half wanted to go just to see you try to hack it."

I didn't see anything on their website about mandatory fish guttings! "Camp isn't just about sports, you know. Wait till you have to weave a basket," I threaten, desperate to say something that will freak him out even though I have no idea if basket weaving is an actual elective. "Or do your own laundry."

"I already do my own laundry," Kyle says, grinning as he wins back the upper hand. "And I know how to make dinner if I have to." He gives me a look. "Not all of us wait around for Marisol to do everything."

"I don't expect Marisol to do everything!" Okay, so maybe I let Marisol iron my Laundry dresses, clean my room, and make me new foods to try (like quinoa, which is Kate's new favorite grain), but isn't that what we pay her for?

"Well, there is no Marisol at camp," Kyle reminds me.

"I can handle it," I lie. "What I can't handle is anyone I know seeing me at the Pines. Thank God no one we know goes there." I lean against the Land Rover, exhausted at the thought. "The last thing I want is for someone to see me looking frizzy in a boxy tee wearing half-melted makeup."

"Ethan Thompson might," Kyle says, and my head almost spins off. Ethan Thompson? As in, the Ethan who Kate tried to get fired from Intermezzo? I feel my eyes widen.

"You know, Ethan, right? He was on the basketball team with me. He's gone to the Pines for years. I should text him to say we're going." Kyle pulls his phone out of his pocket.

"Don't!" I knock Kyle's phone out of his hand. He looks at me like I'm deranged, and I bend down to pick it up. "I mean, we should surprise him." I smile nervously. "I'm sure he'll be happy to see us." *Happy to see you. Not me.*

"Ready?" McDaddy asks.

Kyle slides into the front seat next to McDaddy and I jump in the back, but I can't stop thinking about Ethan. I do not want to run into him at camp after what happened yesterday. He hates me! Hopefully the Pines is a big camp and we'll never even run into each other.

"So, who is ready for an awesome summer?" McDaddy looks at me.

Kyle gives a halfhearted holler (I think the fear of having to go to a basket-weaving class got to him), while I give the silent treatment. My father gets the hint and pulls out of the driveway. Within minutes, Kyle is snoring (how is that possible?) and I am staring out the window at the 495 expressway exits as they fly by. I should probably be tweeting my demise, or texting my friends before I hit a dead spot on the highway, but I don't want to miss how pretty the island looks in the early morning light. Too soon we're driving over the Throgs Neck Bridge, and New York City looks like an oasis in the distant background. I watch as the large buildings fade away and the exits become less frequent. All I can see now are trees, rock formations, the occasional rest stop, and open air. I suddenly wonder when the last time was that we took a drive up north like this.

We cruise almost the first two hours in silence with the occasional interruption of a snore from Kyle or the volume on McDaddy's CD increasing during a song's chorus. He's playing a song by a band that isn't famous yet. McDaddy always works extra hard on a new group's videos. He's all about the underdog, I realize, and listening to him hum along to an unknown band's music makes me feel guilty for being mad at him.

"What's the group's name?" I ask quietly. The two of us shared a love of music even before he got into the business.

"Hudson Street." McDaddy turns the music up slightly so I can hear the pop-friendly voices and the chorus that will probably make the song a hit. "It's the name of the block they grew up on. They played in the garage of one of the band members until they could get someone to listen to their demo. I admire how industrious they are." He looks at me in the rearview mirror.

"You and I are the same way, you know. When we love something, we throw ourselves into it. I'm hoping you'll give Whispering Pines the chance to grow on you."

"It's hard to feel open when you're forcing me to go there." I feel the gruffness return to my voice. "And saying I have to go because I need a personality makeover doesn't make me feel too warm and fuzzy about going to camp, either."

"I said a *reality* makeover, not personality," McDaddy corrects me. "I don't want you to forget who you are, Harper, because you are a great kid. I don't want our new life to change that." I don't say anything. Out the window, I see a big green sign that says WELCOME TO MASSACHUSETTS. We can't be far from camp now. "Give the Pines a shot. If you do, I bet you'll be begging me to let you stay for the second session."

"I doubt that," I say. "What you should worry about is me surviving four weeks in the wild without being eaten by a large animal."

McDaddy turns off the I-95 exit into the middle of nowhere. I don't see a sign for camp anywhere, just more wilderness.

"You will not be eaten by anything," he assures me. "I only saw a bear once in all my years there."

"You saw one?" I screech, jolting Kyle awake. "You said they didn't have bears!"

"Bears? Cool," Kyle says with a yawn, stretching his arms wide.

"They don't," McDaddy backpedals. "I'm sure that one was just lost. Besides we just took some metal trashcan tops and banged them and he ran away. No big deal."

Soon the GPS has us heading off the main road and doing a

series of twists and turns past small streams and bridges. We pass a small convenience store, then a half hour later a deli called Slim Jim's, and finally a run-down gas station. "I haven't seen a single Starbucks in hours," I tell them, staring at miles and miles of wilderness out the window. "Or a Target. How do they survive up here?"

"I know!" Kyle turns around in his seat and mocks me. "I haven't seen a nail salon, either. I hope you got an industrial mani-pedi before we left."

I glare at him. "I didn't have time, but I did get a gel manicure and pedicure this week, so that should last me almost a month if I'm careful. And I can survive if it doesn't," I add so I don't sound vain. "Buff nails are very in right now."

His light brown eyes seem skeptical. "Mineola Harper could survive no manicures. Brookville Harper is a bit high maintenance."

I'm about to argue with him when McDaddy makes another sharp turn, and Kyle is forced to turn back around and hold on. My stomach lurches. It feels like we're climbing a mountain. I see a wood sign, red with white lettering, that says WHISPERING PINES just as my ears pop.

"We made it!" McDaddy shouts. He pulls up to a red-and-green guard booth that makes me think we've arrived at some odd little Christmas village. "Look at this place! It hasn't changed a bit since we visited when you were kids." A man in a red T-shirt waves us past the camp guard station.

Kyle and I stare out the windows as we make the winding drive down a tree-lined road. A few minutes later, the drive opens up to a giant, blacktopped parking lot that is half full with cars. WELCOME (BACK) TO THE PINES! a large banner says.

Several red tarps and tents are set up along the grass on the other side of the lot. Banners and signs hang on them with slogans like THE GREEN MACHINES—2012 COLOR WAR CHAMPIONS! and RED ROVERS RULE THE PINES—COLOR WAR VICTORS (2013)! If I squint, I can see a line of cabins beyond the tents, painted red with accents of white and green. I wrinkle my nose. I hope that's not the kind of cabin I'll be sleeping in. It looks ancient. The only thing I don't see is people.

"Are you sure this place is still in business?" I ask skeptically. I feel like I'm trapped in a horror movie from the seventies.

"We're just early." McDaddy parks in a spot near the entrance. "Hitch says the first buses pull in at nine thirty."

"I got up at five forty-five for nothing?" I cry as I get out of the car.

McDaddy presses the button to open the back lift gate and starts unloading our bags. "It's good practice. Here you'll rise to the sound of the bugle every day at eight."

"Eight?" I feel my feet superglue to the car floor. I am not going somewhere I have to wake with the sun. "On my summer vacation?"

"Aww, Dad, look at her!" Kyle teases. "Maybe you should take her home with you. She's not going to last a week here."

I punch Kyle in the arm. I may not want to stay here, but if I am stuck here, I will not quit. I am a survivor who knows that Karma comes around. I'm a survivor who is going to shock this town (to quote lines from my favorite London Blue song). "You wish. You're just afraid I'll be better at camp than you are."

Kyle pretends to look offended. "Have you met the Harper I know?" I give him a look. "You don't play sports, you don't do bugs, and you certainly don't do camping."

"What I do is make friends easily," I brag. "They're going to love me here whether I like bugs and outdoorsy stuff or not. You'll see."

Kyle's grin widens. "Is that a challenge, Camping Barbie?"

I hold out my pinkie like we used to do when we dared each other as kids. Kyle links his own pinkie with mine. "Oh, it's a challenge all right. What's the prize?"

Our bets are always better when there is a prize. One time, Kyle bet me he could list more movie stars whose names start with *M* than I could. He lost and had to clean our joint bathroom in Mineola all summer.

Kyle thinks for a moment, then grins. "Loser has to wear whatever the winner says for the first week of school."

Gulp. If I lose, Kyle will dress me in lacrosse shorts, baggy shirts, and no-name clothes. Shudder! I have to win. "Deal." We pinkie shake. "May the best camper win."

McDaddy continues hauling bags out of the car and placing them in a pile. "You know, I could use some help here," he prompts.

Kyle and I get out of the car and Kyle begins unloading. He drops one of my duffels on top of the pile. "Geez, how much did you pack? You must have eight bags!"

"This is everything I need to survive," I point out. Except nail files! I forgot to pack those! I must text Mom to send a pack.

"I can survive with three bags and sports gear," Kyle gloats. "One point for me."

Grrr...

"Hot Pants McAllister!" someone bellows in a deep voice.

Kyle and I look at each other. "Hot Pants McAllister?" we repeat.

McDaddy flushes. "My camp nickname. Long story."

"Oh, this I have to hear." I watch as a guy in camo fatigues jogs toward us. He's unusually tan and has shorn, military-style white hair. For a moment I wonder if McDaddy has secretly signed Kyle and me up for military boot camp.

"Who you calling Hot Pants, Skivvies?" McDaddy shoots back. The two burst out laughing and do some strange handshake that includes yelling out the words "Pines! Pines! Pines!" The two men hug while Kyle and I observe them in their natural habitat.

"Never gets any less lame the more times I see it," someone says, and I realize an older girl is standing next to me. Her smirk is identical to my brother's. "Do either of you know why my stepdad is called 'Skivvies'?" she asks us.

"Nope," Kyle says. "We were hoping you could tell us why our dad is 'Hot Pants.'"

"Sorry," she says and adjusts the ponytail holder in her light brown hair. "In my stepdad's case, I have a suspicion Hitch was left stranded in a canoe in the middle of the night in just his skivvies. He won't confirm or deny that scenario."

A pretty woman walks up behind her. "Sam, I married the man, and I still don't know why his camp friends call him 'Skivvies.'" She looks at Kyle and me and smiles. "Hi, I'm Pam Hitchens, Hitch's wife and the head of camp publicity and recreation. It's nice to meet you two. Hitch has told me many stories about your dad."

"I'm Harper, and this is my brother, Kyle," I say. I can't help staring at what Pam is wearing. She has on a white button-down shirt over a camouflage tank top. Maybe camouflage is the official camp uniform. I could work with that.

"I see you've met my daughter, Sam," Pam says, putting an arm around her. "She's a senior counselor. She started here when she was your age as a CIT. Of course, we changed the policy since then so kids can be campers a year longer now."

Sam nudges me. "Lucky! Nothing beats being a camper here, and if you like the place enough, you can come back and get a job as a CIT next year."

"Of course they're going to like it!" Pam says indignantly. I bite my tongue.

Behind Sam, I see a few older girls and guys starting to congregate by the large pop-up tents. I bet they're counselors. They're wearing the red Pines T-shirts I saw in the catalog. My dreams of wearing a cute camo top and a pink skirt go out the window.

"Thanks for taking the twins in on short notice," McDaddy tells Pam, finally rejoining the conversation. "I don't know why I didn't think of it before."

"Not a problem." Hitch hits McDaddy on the back. "Anything for Hot Pants."

"Are you two going to tell us why you call him that?" Kyle asks.

Hitch laughs. "Nope! But I will tell you one of his other nicknames: Richie Rick. Even back then we knew this guy was destined to be a CEO. He always had all these grand ideas for the camp and ways to improve it. Who would have thought I would be the one someday running this place and you'd be hanging out with P. Ditzy?"

Sam, Kyle, and I laugh. "It's P. *Diddy*, Hitch," Sam says.

"This is why I am handling the pop culture and the publicity stuff," Pam tells McDaddy. "We're actually participating in a few nationwide camp contests this summer, and one has a pretty big-name talent attached to it. Do you know London Blue?"

Kyle and I look at McDaddy. "I've done all her music videos," he says.

"I love London Blue!" Sam sounds a lot less composed than she was a moment ago. Sam looks at me in awe. "So, have you met London?"

I always feel awkward name-dropping when McDaddy's job comes up with new people. I just hope Sam doesn't tell everyone. I want the girls to like me because I am fantabulous, not because I've met London. I nod yes, anyway. "She's really cool and surprisingly normal," I say. "She also wears a lot of orange on tour, which I'm in favor of. The shade looks great with her coloring." Sam blinks.

"Who needs celebrities when you can have the Pines?" Hitch spreads his arms wide to showcase the whole camp. "We have great facilities and awesome activities—like giant trampolines, canoeing, sailing, and a new rock-climbing wall."

"A rock-climbing wall? Nice!" Kyle says, while I try to remain steady. I hope they don't expect me to give that thing a whirl. Have they seen these wedges I'm wearing? Kyle winks at me. "I can't wait to see you climb it!"

I ignore him. "What kind of nonphysical activities do you have?" I ask. "I'm a genius when it comes to party planning. I once whipped up a Fourth of July party in under an hour with only Cool Whip and orange juice in the house."

I hear tires screeching, and the rest of my story gets drowned out by cheers. The first of several yellow buses is pulling into the parking lot.

Hitch holds up a megaphone, and Sam holds her ears. "Troops!" he yells into it, and all the counselors by the tents stop what they're doing and look at us. "The first campers are here! Let's give them a warm Pines welcome!" The guys and girls in red shirts immediately spring into action, picking up clipboards and walkie-talkies and yelling out commands as the first bus pulls up to the tent. "Sam!" Hitch yells, forgetting she's standing right there. "Oh!" He drops his megaphone. "Let's get to work." He looks at my father. "Hot Pants, I'll call you tonight and let you know how the kids are doing."

"I'll be waiting, Skivvies!" McDaddy tells him.

Sam looks at us. "I've got to run, but I'll introduce you guys to your counselors first."

"You're not mine?" I'm disappointed.

"No, but you'll love Courtney," Sam says, "and we will see each other all the time because I'm in the adjoining bunk. It's more like one large cabin with two rooms." She looks at Kyle. "And you're with my friend Cole. He's a total wiseass, but in a good way."

I feel like I'm at a London Blue concert the way the campers are carrying on all around us. Girls getting off buses are screaming when they see a friend, kids are crying as they say good-bye to parents who drove them up, and people are running around saying hi to everyone they know. The place has gone from tranquil to pandemonium in moments.

"You know what? You should probably say good-bye to your dad," Sam says gently. "Then you can meet me at that red tent. It will be a half hour till we're ready to go zip-lining."

I blanch. "Zip-lining?"

Sam grins. "Great, right? The older campers—we call them marshmallows—are doing trust-building exercises on it."

"Marshmallows?" Kyle and I repeat. We seem to have gained a new twin power at camp—saying the same thing at the same time.

Sam shakes her head. "Corny, right? The Pines has used the same names for campers since the Stone Age. Marshmallows are the oldest, then there are pez, who are all between nine and eleven years old, and the youngest, who are under eight, are called peeps." A group of tearful campers gets off a bus near us. "I should go deal with that. See you soon."

"I've entered a real-life version of Candy Land," I tell Kyle. "I can't believe people are going to be referring to me as a marshmallow."

He shrugs and turns to our dad. "This place looks cool. I'll call you when I can."

What kind of good-bye was that? I look at McDaddy. He reaches out to hug me, and I feel a little misty, especially since things have been so stormy between us. "I love you, kiddo. Try to enjoy it here."

"I'll try to." I sigh. "And I'll text you every day if I'm not."

"About that…," McDaddy starts to say but trails off. "Never mind. You'll figure everything out in your own time." I look at him strangely, and he gives me a kiss. "Talk to you soon."

I watch him get in the car and slowly make his way out of the lot, getting in line with the other cars of parents that are inching their way toward the exit…and freedom. I resist the urge to run after the car and throw myself on it to get back home—if only because I don't want to make a fool out of myself. I tend to make a good first impression, but I start to worry as I notice that the campers getting off the buses look a lot different from the girls at my school. Only a few of the girls are wearing nail polish. No one has her hair blown out. Some of them are even in sweat shorts!

Kyle has left me in the dust, so I begin making my way over to the tent where Sam told me to meet her. I am held up by a security guy letting another bus pull in. This bus is the rowdiest one I've heard yet. They're singing some strange song as the bus doors open. Then a group of guys start pushing one another off.

Hello, boys!

Each guy who gets off the bus is cuter than the last. The grungy look works so much better on boys than it does on girls. And that's when I see him emerge from the pack.

Ethan.

The cute busboy from my school Kate almost got fired.

My stomach twists and growls like it's about to stage an

exodus from my body. I'm not sure what to do. I know he sees me. Oh God. He's looking right at me!

In a panic, I smile and give a small wave.

Ethan doesn't return the smile. Or the wave. Instead he heads off with his friends and doesn't bother looking back.

Harper McAllister @HarperMc
Survived drive to no-man's-land but won't last 24 hours. Natives are not friendly. Plus, there isn't a Starbucks for miles! #roughingit

4

WELCOME HOME

"UM, YOU'RE NOT SUPPOSED TO bring that to camp."

I look up from where I'm sitting under a red tent wedged in between two duffel bags while I wait for Sam to introduce me to Courtney. I was about to text Margo about my Ethan sighting when I notice that a girl who looks like Merida in *Brave* is staring at me. I'm instantly envious of her curls.

"Hi!" I say in my friendliest voice. "I'm Harper." I try to get up and realize I'm stuck. How embarrassing. The girl stares at me as I struggle to pull myself out of the bag pile and stand to greet her. "There! Took me a minute!" I laugh. "As I was saying, I'm Harper, and I'm new here." I lean in closer. "Wow, you have amazing hair."

Merida backs away. "*I said* you're not supposed to have that here."

I look down at my silver nails. "Nail polish?" Really? Seems like a strange rule, but I guess I can handle that. My nails could kind of use a break from all those gel manicures. "I only found out I was coming here yesterday, so I didn't know." I scratch at a nail. "I'm not sure I can get it off. Gel manicures are like Krazy Glue! Do you know where the nearest nail salon is around here?" I look around as if expecting to see some sort of map to off-site activities. "We do get to leave the camp, don't we?"

"I meant your phone," the girl repeats, wrapping a perfect curl around her finger.

"Oh!" I hold it up. The glitter case on my phone is bright green and silver, my two favorite colors. "Cute, right? The gems keep falling off whenever I drop it, which is often, but at least I can still get on Safari. I just read on Twitter that Alexis Holden is getting married! Isn't she, like, twenty?" I play with my necklace. It's a diamond nameplate my mom begged me not to take to camp, but I never take it off, so I wouldn't leave it home. "I know her boyfriend is cute and all, but couldn't she just travel the world with him instead—like she's already doing—instead of getting hitched?"

The girl lets out something resembling a growl. "I meant you're not supposed to bring a cell phone to camp!" Her voice is loud now. "They're not allowed."

I stand corrected: This girl could *not* be Merida in *Brave*. Despite the gorgeous long, red, curly hair and ivory skin she seems way too tense to star in a Disney movie. I don't think we're going to be friends after all. Especially now that she's threatening to take away my lifeline, my crutch, my only link to the civilized world.

Time to try a new tactic with her. I smile. "I'm sorry, I didn't catch your name."

She folds her arms across her chest, hiding her Snoopy character tank top that she is wearing as a statement of…I'm not sure. She could be trying to be cool or retro, or she is just completely out of touch with fashion. I'm thinking option B. "It's Jeanie."

"Are you in bunk 10A, too?" I ask. "This is my first time here—"

"I know." She runs a hand through her perfect hair. "You're the *only* new girl in 10A. We got stuck with you because 10B was already at its max."

Am I really the only new girl my age? Well, that's never stopped me from fitting in before. It actually works to my advantage. "Their loss is your gain," I say.

Sam appears with her clipboard. "Hey, Jeanie, I see you've met Harper."

"Yep." Jeanie sounds unimpressed. I see her look at my hand again, and I slip my phone in my pocket.

"Jeanie is the perfect person to show you around the Pines, Harper," says Sam, giving Jeanie the classic "you got me?" mom look. "She's been coming to the Pines since she was six, just like—"

"Camilla!" For the first time, I see Jeanie smile. She throws her arms around a pixie of a girl with short blond hair. The two scream and pull each other around and around, Jeanie's hair whipping in a circle.

Maybe this is not a military camp. It's a Disney Princess training camp! If so, I wonder who I get to be. What princess has a great wardrobe, bubbly personality, and curly (but not as curly as Jeanie's), dirty blond hair? Hmm. I'm stumped.

Jeanie stops spinning and whispers something in Camilla's ear. Jeanie and the pixie stare at me, giving me plenty of time to check out their clothes. Neither is wearing a particularly remarkable outfit for the first day of camp. Jeanie has on a Snoopy shirt, and Camilla is wearing what I think are sweat shorts and a school tee that says TIGER POWER! Yet they are staring at my killer green sundress with the bike shorts underneath as if I'm from another planet. Jeanie whispers something in Camilla's ear again.

"Oh, you're the new girl," Camilla says, and I watch her size me up.

"And you're Camilla," I say, trying to be cute. "Can I call you Cami?"

"No," she says, and looks at me like I'm a little strange.

How picky. You could call me H, Harp, Harpie (although that one would be kind of mean), or Harper and I'd still answer. "Nice to meet you." I look at Jeanie again. "Do you use Kérastase treatments on your hair?" I touch a strand and she jumps back.

"Kéra-what?" Jeanie sounds confused.

"Kérastase. It's a hair treatment. I have some in one of my bags. I can let you try it one night. Ooh!" I grab her forearm. "We can do hair makeovers. There is nothing I like more in this world than white chocolate peppermint M&M'S and makeovers. Are you in 10A with Jeanie and me?"

"*You're* in 10A with *us*," Jeanie corrects me, glossing over my awesome makeover offer. "But only for the first session, right?"

Wow, word travels faster at camp than it does in homeroom.

"Jeanie Beanie and I have been in the same bunk since we were six," Camilla brags, linking arms with her friend. I wonder if I'm supposed to give her a medal.

Suddenly a few girls push past me and race over to Camilla

and Jeanie Beanie (it's going to be hard not to call her that). They do the same squeal I've heard all morning and hug one another, forming a Jeanie/Camilla sandwich.

"All right! Break it up already!" a tall African American girl says as she makes her way into the tent. She looks at Sam. "Were we this annoying every season when we first saw each other?"

Sam laughs. "No, but that's because you've never been the touchy-feely type."

The first thing I notice about the older girl is her Pines T-shirt. She's bunched it up so it is not so boxy, and she's also fringed the bottom and added beads. Even though she's still talking to Sam, I can't help but interrupt her. "Can you do my camp tee the same way you did yours?" I beg. Everyone stops and looks at me. "I love it! Did you see this look in *Vogue*? Of course you did! It isn't summer without an issue of *Vogue*! Stella McCartney is doing the exact same thing this season."

The girl turns to look at me curiously. "Let me guess. You're my new girl."

Sam clears her throat. "Courtney, Harper. Harper, Courtney. You two are going to love each other, I just know it." I notice Courtney giving her a look. Sam claps her hands. "Okay, 10A and 10B! Let's get to the zip line for our first trust exercise before lunch."

"After that, it's free periods all day, people," Courtney adds, and the girls cheer.

Suddenly I have a headache. People aren't this peppy at pep rallies!

I am frozen as the girls take off around me. Zip line time

already? I'm left staring at the back of Jeanie's beautiful head. God, I want her hair.

"Come on, New Girl," Courtney tells me.

"My name is Harper," I say, watching the girls walk ahead. No one asked me to join them.

"For now, it's New Girl," Courtney says.

Sam whispers in my ear. "Don't let her scare you. She's a total teddy bear."

Courtney laughs. "I heard that! Do not repeat that teddy bear thing. So have you had a proper tour of this place yet, New Girl?"

"I haven't—" I start to say, perking up at the offer.

"Well, no time for one now," Courtney cuts me off. Sam gives her a look. "But I will point stuff out along the way. This, for example, is the upper campus."

She gestures to the long row of cabins surrounding us. The creepy cabins I saw in the distance look even older close up. Please don't say we're sleeping in one of those.

"The only reason you'll have to come up here is if you break your arm on the zip line, get written up for bad behavior, or get a nasty case of poison ivy. Watch where you're walking," she warns as we pass the nurse's office and the post office. We head farther down the trail, and I notice the buildings get bigger and look newer.

Courtney points out a large cabin with a wraparound porch and a sign that says mess hall. "Most of your meals will be eaten in here—no food fights—and over there," she says, pointing to another cabin, "is the theater. Last summer we did *Guys and Dolls*. Again. Sam, didn't we do that the summer you started, too?"

"Yes." Sam groans. "We've got to get some new plays in here. I can't sit through *The Pajama Game* again."

We pass another two rows of smaller cabins. They look as creepy as the ones on the upper campus. "What are those for?"

"Indoor activities," Courtney explains. "We have art, photography, dance, yoga, the camp newspaper, and cooking classes. You name it, they probably have a class for it here. Since you're older you can pick and choose most of your electives. There are only a few sessions a day that you'll do as a group."

This place can't be that archaic if they have yoga. "Where are our cabins?"

"Over that hill." Courtney points to large cabins with porches that surround a lake. From here, the cabins look like tiny red, green, and white dollhouses. I've seen them before! McDaddy has a picture of himself and a group of very muddy-looking guys in front of them in his office. I bet Hitch is one of them. "The porches are my favorite part of the cabin," Courtney adds. "They give you a great view of the lake."

Lakefront living! That's cushy.

But it also means being a mosquito's snack. Yuck.

"There is an upper and lower campus to divide the age groups, but all the bunks are housed together with boys and girls in the same area." Courtney gives me a stern look. "Don't get any ideas." Sam bursts out laughing. "What?" Courtney demands.

"You're telling someone to stay away from the boys' bunks," Sam says and shakes her head.

Courtney colors. "Tour paused while I talk to my best friend about counselor dos and don'ts." Courtney grabs Sam, and the two walk ahead, their heads close together as they whisper to each other.

Their closeness makes me miss my friends. I look at the group of girls walking way ahead of me but choose not to run over and join them. The way they are jabbering about a sleepover in Atlanta and a New Year's party in New York makes me think I wouldn't be welcome. I miss Margo and Kate. I wonder what they are doing at the beach club right now. Since Courtney isn't looking, I pull my phone out of my pocket to try to text Margo. "OEUF!" Someone bumps into me, and I fall.

"Are you okay?" A girl bends down to help me up. "I guess testing out my I-could-find-my-way-around-this-place-blindfolded theory was not a good idea." The girl's wearing funky black glasses, and her hair has pink tips that are the same color as the Bubblicious gum vintage T-shirt she's paired with bright yellow shorts. We definitely do not have a dress code here.

"No biggie," I say, dusting off the dirt on the bottom of my dress. "I have the opposite problem—I have no clue where I'm going."

"Give it three hours and you'll know the whole camp backward and forward." She reaches down and spots my cell phone before I do. "Is this yours?"

An alarm goes off inside my head, and I practically pull it out of her hands. She looks at me strangely. "Sorry." I feel my face flush. "Lifeline." I hold up the phone. "I've already gotten the 'you can't have one of those' speech from another camper, so I'm a little paranoid about having my phone confiscated."

She pushes a loose strand of pink hair behind her ear. No

one I know has ever dyed her hair anything other than auburn or honey-colored brown (my favorite highlight color, natch, which closely resembles actress Kaitlin Burke's).

She looks around, then pulls a phone from her back pocket. It has a bright pink, zebra-stripe case on it. "I can't live without mine, either."

I like her already! "I'm Harper," I introduce myself.

"Angelina," she tells me, "but everyone calls me Lina. Where are you from?"

"Long Island. You?"

"Pennsylvania, but I'm on Long Island all the time. My grandparents live in Westbury."

"Brookville," I say.

Angelina's eyes widen. "Isn't that where JLo lived?"

And she knows celebrity stuff! Yep, we're going to be friends.

"Supposedly, when she was married to Marc Anthony she had the house near ours," I confide. "We just moved there two years ago. I actually grew up in Mineola."

Lina seems to be studying my clothes, hair, and shoes, the same as I just did hers. From the outside at least, we are nothing alike. "If I lived in Brookville, I would spend my whole summer floating in my pool," she says. "How'd you wind up here?"

I sigh. "My father forced me after seeing my credit card statement. I've got a *teeny* shopping habit, and he says I need a shot of reality." I've been holding in that secret all morning. For some reason, it feels better to tell someone, especially when Lina doesn't judge me. "My dad came here when he was a kid and it changed his life, so he's hoping it will do the same thing for me. I doubt it," I tell her. "I'm homesick already, which is why I need to hold on to my phone. If I can't text my friends or phone my mom, I think I would have a complete breakdown."

"I don't text that much," she says to my surprise. "I wanted to keep my phone so I can go on YouTube." She types something in, then shows me the screen. XTREME SPORTS NUT, the website says. "I'm a total junkie when it comes to sports stunts, and this guy does them all. I'm addicted to his videos. I'm dying to sky-dive, but I haven't gotten up the nerve." Her cheeks flush. "Most people find my obsession weird."

"I won't be skydiving with you, if that's what you're asking," I say. "My hair looks horrible windswept. But it's not weird. My brother is a sports freak, too."

Wait a minute... matchmaker! Scratch that. Kyle is the enemy during competition. I will not wear Kmart to school! Finding him a girlfriend would help him win.

I see a familiar app on Lina's phone. "Is that the London Blue My Mind app?"

Lina's face turns as pink as the tips of her hair. "No. Maybe. Why do you ask?"

I remember when London was testing that app. I was on McDaddy's shoot, and she wanted to know if girls would want an app about her videos, blog, Twitter feed, favorite websites, and so on. "Self-absorbed, no?" she asked me. *Me!* And I said, "If your fans are asking you where you buy your sparkly Converse, then why not give them a link to it?" I think she really liked that answer. She called me McCool for the rest of the shoot.

But I am not telling Lina that story. If she's a Londonophile then that will make her want to talk to me about London all the time. So instead I just say. "I like London, too. I have that app."

Lina blushes. "Sorry. My friends at home make fun of how into London I am. I never miss her blog posts. She gives away prizes, like VIP passes to her concerts. I'm dying to meet her." She sounds so animated. "You think I'm completely cheesy now, don't you? Cool girl with pink hair likes pop tart."

"I'm the one who showed up at camp wearing cork wedges." We look at my feet. "I couldn't leave them home alone for a month. They are too cute to go unworn."

Lina frowns. "They are cute, but not the best footwear for zip-lining."

"Oh, I'm not zip-lining. I'm more of a spectator."

"What? Zip-lining is awesome!" she says, getting really excited again. "Flying through the air with the wind in your face and the ground zipping by is such an incredible high. I zip-line every day while I'm here if I can."

"My stomach hurts just thinking about getting up there *once*," I say, and Lina laughs. "But I will happily watch you. Any chance you're in bunk 10A?" I ask hopefully.

"Yep! I'm a Courtney girl," Lina says, and I breathe a sigh of relief. "She has a bark, but she will always have your back. She doesn't favor the Lifers, either."

"Lifers?" I ask.

Lina rolls her eyes. "The ones who think they own the place because they were practically born here." She gestures toward Jeanie, Camilla, and a bunch of other girls I haven't met yet. "Our bunk is all Lifers except for Addison." She points to a blonde talking a mile a minute in a very animated voice. "She's in because her brother, Hunter, was a god here before he gave up being a counselor to run a surf clinic in Malibu."

I hear a burst of laughter from the girls' cluster, which is moving at warp speed ahead of us. "How long have you been coming here?" I ask.

"This is my third year." Lina plays with her funky black-rope necklace. "I love the sports program, so I ignore the bunk nonsense. I've made friends with some of the guys. They are much easier to get along with." Lina smiles, and I notice the gap between her two front teeth. On me it would look strange, but it gives her character.

Courtney walks back to us. "You've met Lina. The girl is crazy daring, and she can draw, too. You should see the murals she did for last summer's *Guys and Dolls*."

I've been so busy talking to Lina, I stopped looking around. We've reached a grassy area that is surrounded by trees. The lake is to my left, and to the right you can see for miles. It's hilly, too, which is something we don't have on our flat-as-a-pancake island back home. I'll get a good leg workout as I go up and down these hills and in the...woods! Wow, that's like a real forest back there. The basketball courts are right near it, along with a baseball diamond with a turf field and lights.

We go around a bend, and my heart stops along with my feet. In front of me is the scariest sight I have ever seen (even scarier than the year wearing feathers was in style again): It's a rock wall—and I suspect they're going to force me to climb it.

I turn around and prepare to run.

5

IN THE LINE OF FIRE

LINA GRABS ME SO FAST that I almost twist my ankle. "Where's the fire?"

"I am not climbing that rock wall!" I say, hyperventilating.

"Relax," Lina says calmly. "We're passing through on our way to the zip line. Although I wish I were staying. I'm dying to test out the new rock wall!"

"You test it and let me know how it is," I say.

The rock wall must tower twenty-five feet in the air. I've seen rock walls before, but watching people scurry up and down it like they're being offered a free Red Mango yogurt is bizarre. A group of boys in helmets and gear are waiting to go up.

"Yes!" I hear someone yell as they reach the top and hit the bell. Everyone cheers, and the guys hanging from the wall by harnesses high-five the guy. Hey, that's Kyle! He rappels off the side and swings around even as a counselor reprimands him. When he sees me, he hollers, "Top that, Harper!"

I blush as everyone turns and stares at me. God, he's such a show-off. I can't even do a chin-up. Not one! Ms. Schnarz wrote that on my gym report card to prove that I'm slacking. I've got to find a way to show him who is boss.

"That's your brother?" Addison says in astonishment. This is the first time any of the other girls have actually spoken to me.

"Yeah, we're twins," I say.

"Your brother is hot," Addison says, and the girls start whispering. "Is he single?"

I watch my brother continue to swing like an ape. Or a toddler. "What do you think?" I ask dryly. Addison just blinks. "Yes, totally single."

I can tell the girls suddenly see me in a whole new way. They move closer, and one tries to push Lina out of the way. Eww!

"Um, excuse me," Lina says. They ignore her.

"Are you close?" Jeanie asks me, playing with a strand of her beautiful red hair.

"Harper is going to lose!" my brother sings, completely unembarrassed by his public display. "Let's see you try to zipline in heels, Camping Barbie!"

Grr... "Two points for me if I do!" I yell back before I realize what I'm doing.

Oh man, did I just commit to getting up there? Why do I open my big mouth? Kyle always does this to me! Winds me up and then I make a fool of myself.

Jeanie is still looking at me. "No," I say angrily. "We're not close at all."

That's all the girls have to hear. They back away and re-form their own circle.

"Your popularity certainly was short-lived," Lina whispers to me sarcastically.

"Well, it looks like we've got some competition," says a guy counselor with short, wavy brown hair, wearing a red tank top. Wow, he's really cute. "What do you say, bunk 11A? Want to give the girls a run for their money?"

The guys in line for the rock wall cheer as Kyle is lowered back to the ground.

"Cole," Sam says through gritted teeth, "you're not starting a rivalry between the guy and girl bunks already, are you? They've been here an hour!"

Cole's green eyes glint mischievously. "It's never too early to start. What do you say, Court? Guys versus girls on the zip line? Whoever has the shorter group time has to clear the other bunk's plates at dinner for a week?"

"Court...," Sam warns.

"Deal!" Courtney says. The two shake on it, and Sam groans. "To the zip line! The boys will go first and then will go back up to spot the girls."

"Works for me," Cole says, grinning widely.

Sam slugs him in the arm. "Some guys never grow up."

"So true. That's why you only dated me for a few months." Cole pulls her in for a bear hug, and Sam laughs.

"Exactly why," Sam agrees. "But now that we're just friends, I am free to school you. You and your boys are going down!"

I watch the boys unhook and run to the zip line course. Kyle winks at me as he runs by with a group of cute guys. "Is that your sister?" I hear one of them say. I don't hear Kyle's response because my heart is beating so loudly. I think I'm getting a migraine.

I grab Lina's arm as the panic squeezes me. "I didn't sign up for zip-lining! What camp thinks it's safe to send kids flying through the air on a rope?"

"It's easy. I swear!" Lina says. "I only choked up there once, and that was because my harness wasn't secured properly." My eyes widen. "But that won't happen to you!" she backpedals. "I'm sure you're going to love it once you're in the air. It's so freeing."

I think of what's at stake if I don't take the plunge. Fashion disaster the first week of school if I fail! No, I have to do it . . . but I don't want to. We reach the zip line, and I notice it's even taller than the rock wall. The course must be the length of a football field. The first half is an obstacle course with a rope wall and a log to walk across. One guy from another group—probably the CITs—is already on there, and he's attached to a safety rope that runs the length of the course. I hear people squealing as they step off a pillar and let themselves fly all the way to the next one. There are two pillars, which means we have to fly twice.

No. Way. They are not getting me up there.

Cole brings his group in for a huddle, and I hear more cheers during his pep talk. Kyle is right in there with them. How'd he get accepted by the Lifers so quickly? Why are girls so catty?

Kate's catty, too, a voice in my head says. *Just not toward you. Most of the time.*

"So, gang, are you ready for this?" Courtney asks. "All we have to do is beat their time. I know you girls can do it. You are zip line pros!" All the girls holler, including Lina.

Not all of us are zip-lining pros. Gulp.

I watch the boys get into harnesses and put on helmets as Cole heads to the first pillar to spot them. Watching him move across the course is mesmerizing. He looks like he could do it blindfolded. Another counselor, Thomas, who Lina says is the counselor for bunk 11B, heads up after him. I watch him stop at the first pillar, high-five Cole, and then zip across to the second one to be the spotter there. They must be standing thirty feet in the air! And all they have is a hook keeping them from falling to their death? Kyle and the other boys in the bunks cheer them on, which only gets me more worked up.

I cannot let Kyle win this. But I don't want to get up there. I can't let Kyle win. But I am not falling to my death. *AAAH!*

Before I know what's happening, Courtney has her stopwatch and is counting down to the boys' challenge. They've lined up and are now completely serious. Kyle jumps up onto the course first and speeds through it. I'm doomed.

"None of you better screw this up," Jeanie threatens. "I am not cleaning their plates. Boys are so sloppy." The rest of the girls murmur their agreement. I notice her glare at me. I attempt a smile, but I'm perspiring and don't want to open my mouth.

"The fastest girl should go first," Addison suggests. "That would be Lina."

"Yes!" she says, sounding pumped. "I am going to fly through the course!"

"That's the spirit!" Courtney marvels. "Addison, you're second..." Courtney goes down the line, ending with me. "You're last because I don't know your speed yet."

"Believe me, I'm not insulted," I say. *Relieved* is more like it.

"Time!" Sam yells loudly.

Cole runs back from the end of the course to hear the results. The boys are close behind him. "How'd we do?" he asks, and Thomas crowds in next to him, towering over Sam and Courtney. The guy is a muscular giant.

"Fifteen minutes and thirty-eight seconds." Sam shows him Courtney's watch.

Cole groans. "Guys! That blows."

"We can totally beat that time," Courtney says confidently. "Can't we, girls?"

That's our cue to cheer, but I'm too busy biting my nails.

Most of the guys hand over their harnesses, but I notice one keeps his and climbs right back onto the course. I guess he's going to be a spotter. I feel a helmet being placed on my head, and I jump.

"Don't worry, it won't bite," says a boy with shorn, light brown hair. "Although the spiders inside it might."

"What?" I scream, and some of the girls turn and give me a nasty look.

"There could be," the guy continues. "These helmets have been in storage all winter."

I start taking off my helmet, and Lina stops me. "Heath, stop scaring her! She's already freaked out about zip-lining as it is."

"Don't worry, I'll protect you, girls," he says with a smirk. He's flirting with us and he's kind of cute! I start to play with my hair and giggle.

"We don't need protecting," Lina says, bursting my bubble. I was all set to flirt back. "My dad is an exterminator," she tells me. "I have no issues with bugs." I blink.

He starts to laugh. It's laid-back and light, which is refreshing after the cackling I've been listening to all morning from the girls. "I love when your nose scrunches up and you get all mad, Lina," he says. "God, I've missed seeing you do that all winter."

Aww, that's kind of sweet.

"Well, now you can watch me do it for almost eight weeks," she says, missing his flirting entirely. She looks at me. "Heath thinks he's funny. He's not."

"Ouch!" Heath clutches his heart. He's standing so close I can smell Tic Tacs on his breath. "Lina, you hurt my feelings. I'm just trying to cheer the new girl up. She looks way too tense for someone about to go zip-lining. Are you really Kyle's twin sister?"

"Yep."

He adjusts the straps on my harness. "I don't see it."

"We're fraternal," I tell him as he tightens the strap around my waist and then reaches down and brings another strap through my legs and around. A few more clips and I'm in. "The sports gene skipped me."

Heath turns to Lina. "Most of the guys will never admit it,

but you're better than most of them at this. Why don't you give the new girl some advice?"

Lina shrugs. "Watch your balance and don't look down."

Shot down again. He sighs and hands me the strap that holds my tether. "You'll hook on once you start. Good luck, Camping Barbie." He winks. I can't believe he heard Kyle say that! "You too, Lina, not that you need it. I'll see you on the other side."

I hit Lina in the arm. "What's the matter with you? That guy totally walked out of an American Eagle ad *and* he was flirting with you. You totally blew him off!"

She blinks. "He wasn't flirting. Heath and I are just friends."

"Looked like he wanted to be more than friends to me," I say.

She snorts. "You are insane."

Kyle jogs over to me and hits me on the head. The sound vibrates through the helmet. "Nice look for you. If I had my phone, I'd take a picture to put up on Twitter."

"You don't even have a Twitter handle," I grumble.

He grins. "It would be worth getting one just to post this picture." He notices Lina, and his face changes. "Hey," he says smoothly. "We haven't been introduced yet. I'm Kyle, Harper's evil twin."

I wait to see what happens. Please don't like my brother. Don't like my brother!

"I'm on Team Harper," Lina tells him and walks over to the course. Ha! Lina is clueless when it comes to guys, but in this case, that's a good thing.

"Ready?" Courtney asks me, ruining Kyle's chance to go after Lina. "Get in line."

Sam is standing at the front of the group with a stopwatch, and I realize this is happening. Like now. "As soon as your first teammate makes it to the top of the obstacle course and the first pillar, your next teammate can start," she says. "Let's win this thing!" The group cheers. Lina gives me a thumbs-up. No one looks worried but me.

Don't look down. Keep your eyes closed the entire time. But if I do that how will I know where I'm going? This isn't good at all.

"Go!" Courtney screams, and Lina jumps onto the course. I see Kyle and Heath watching her. The rest of the girls cheer her on as I feel my heart pound harder inside my chest. We move up. Then we move up again. It keeps going until Camilla is just three ahead of me and on deck to go next.

"Go!" Courtney hits Camilla on the back, and she scurries up the wall like a spider. I watch in awe as she goes from one part of the course to the next without even a flinch. The boys on the ground boo her. "All right, all right! Girls, keep your eye on the ball!"

Maybe I'll be okay, maybe I'll just take it slow and . . .

"Oh!" I hear a collective gasp, and I look up. One of the girls has fallen off the log walk and banged into one of the wood pillars. That can actually happen? You can FALL? DOWN? She doesn't look hurt, just dazed, as Cole pulls her back up. Everyone cheers.

"That's going to really screw up our time," Jeanie grumbles. "You and I are going to have to book it."

Gulp.

Jeanie looks down. "Wait, you're not wearing sneakers?" she screeches.

Oh God. I forgot. "Um..."

"Someone give her your sneakers," Jeanie moans, and I watch Cole laugh as Courtney pulls off her Converse and throws them at me. "Quick! Tie them on," Jeanie barks. "I don't care if they're too big. Just wear something!"

"You've got sixty seconds," Cole sings. "If you don't get your last girl across in time, we win automatically. I say we move to the finish line to see how this thing plays out." Sam glares at him, and the two take off for the other end of the course.

Talk about the pressure! I reach down and with sweaty fingers tie as quickly as I can, not noticing Jeanie jump onto the course. Courtney leans down and ties my other shoe.

"You've got to go," she says, as she ties a double knot. "Now!"

There is no time to argue. I step onto the platform and start scurrying across the long rope wall. Okay. This part is not as hard to do as I thought. You just hang on and climb sideways.

"Hurry!" I hear Lina yell. The other girls are at the end of the zip line course waiting for me. "Fifty seconds!"

The second part is the log, and when I see it, I stare at it for a second before I hear the cries from the finish line. I take a deep breath and balance my first foot and then the other. Once I get the hang of it, I move faster and reach the end. Section two down! Then it's the jumping part—from one platform to the next, but they're close. I've had to jump from the boat to the dock before, so this is easy. The last jump takes me to the first pillar, where one of the guys is waiting. The next part is petrifying. Maybe

I'm better off staying exactly where I am—twenty feet in the air on a platform—than zipping through the air.

"FORTY SECONDS!" I hear Courtney yell, so I take a deep breath and jump to the cute guy standing there. He steadies me from falling over the other side.

"Steady there! You made it!" I notice he has a nice smile as I cling to him for dear life. "Kyle didn't think you'd make it this far. I'm Justin, by the way." He has a rope necklace and several bracelets on his arm.

"I can't do it." I stare at the next pillar, where a guy is waiting to spot me. It's only ten feet away, but from that pillar to the end is the long one. "I can't." I close my eyes and then open them again. You can see the whole camp from up here. It looks like a cute little miniature model I'd like to explore. If I live.

"You have to," Justin says. "If you don't, you're cleaning our trash for a week. Jeanie will not be happy. She'll eat you for supper after she roasts you first. In public."

"HARPER!" I hear the girls yell.

"I can't," I start to say and then realize he's holding my zip line rope, the one I swing from. He's starting to move it forward, and I cling to him tighter. "Don't!"

"I'm saving you!" he says. "Good luck!"

My feet leave the platform and are flying through the air, the grass and dirt below zipping by at a terrifying speed. I'm still screaming when I land. I grab the pillar and shut my eyes. "I'm out! Done! Not going again!"

"You don't have a choice. This isn't the end of the ride."

I recognize that voice. I open my eyes. "Ethan." I feel my

heart stop, which is funny because I thought it did already when I flew through the air a minute ago. "Hi."

"Hi." His brown eyes look vaguely suspicious. "What are you doing here?"

"Up here? Oh, you know," I say, holding the pillar tighter. "I thought it would be fun to train to be a trapeze artist this summer. This is circus camp, right?"

"Nope, that one is down the block." His mouth curls into a sort of smirk. "Kyle I get coming here, but you make zero sense. You are not the sleepaway camp type."

"THIRTY SECONDS!" I hear, but with Ethan, time seems to have stopped.

"What exactly would that type be?" I'm about to make a comment like Kate and say "lame," but I think of Lina and Courtney and some of the other people I've talked to so far. They don't seem lame. Instead, I reply, "I'm really sorry she tried to get you fired."

Ethan looks away. "You should really get going."

The end of the course seems so far away. I can't do it. I can't. "I think I'll just hang here for a while." I close my eyes again. The view is making me dizzy.

"FIFTEEN SECONDS!" Courtney yells.

"You can't just hang out on top of a zip line post," Ethan says incredulously.

"Yes, I can," I say defiantly. The screaming has intensified. The guys and the girls are all standing together at the end of the course counting down the time.

"You're going to lose," Ethan reminds me.

"I'm going to lose, anyway," I say. "I can't get across in ten seconds."

"You can if you go now," Ethan says. "Not that I want to clean *your* dishes."

Fair enough. I sort of cost him his job.

A slight breeze cools my face. I look at the ground, even though Lina told me not to. That settles it. "I'm not going." I've learned my lesson from my pillar time with Justin. I hold my tether tight and keep my arms around the pole so he can't push me off.

"TIME!" Cole shouts, and the guys erupt in cheers. My bunk is going to kill me.

"Are you planning to live up here?" Ethan asks, sounding agitated now.

"I lost, so there is no sense in going now." That gives me an idea. "Can you tell Hitch to bring me a helicopter? You guys have one of those here, don't you?" I hug the post, blocking out all thoughts of Jeanie roasting me like a pig. Justin was kidding. Right?

"As much as you might like to hang out here, I want to celebrate the guys' victory over lunch," Ethan says. He grabs my hands and pulls me off the pole.

"What are you doing?" I say angrily as he clips himself to my belt. I didn't even know he could do that. Won't we fall off? "I told you! I'm not leaving this post!"

"You might be used to getting your way back home, Harper McAllister, but that is not the way things work at Whispering Pines."

He throws his hands around my waist and then, before I

know what's happening, we're both flying through the air. I throw my arms around Ethan tight and scream the entire way like a little girl.

Harper McAllister @HarperMc
Didn't last two hours before someone tried to kill me by tossing me off a zip line. Can I come home now? Please @McDaddy? #sendhelp

6

New Digs

"CHIN UP, GUYS," COURTNEY SAYS. "We'll get them next round."

Seven girls shoot daggers in my direction. They're all sitting on their newly picked cabin bunks, which I'm told is supposed to be the best part of day one, but no one is happy.

"Why were you wasting time up there talking to Ethan when you were supposed to be zipping across?" Jeanie asks me for the hundredth time. "You were just standing there chatting!"

"No one gets to talk to Ethan but Jeanie," Addison says in a teasing manner, but Jeanie is *not* in a jokey mood, which makes me wonder: Are Jeanie and Ethan a couple?

"That's not it! We could have won," Jeanie insists from her bottom bunk. The bed is right under the ceiling fan that's supposed to cool down the room, but with her eyes on me, I feel nothing but heat. "Instead we have to clean their plates because you choked."

"I didn't choke." I am sitting on the floor near my trunk. "Ethan was helping me look for my contact lens." Jeanie eyes me skeptically. "Yep, on the first zip, it blew out of my eye. I thought it landed on the platform. Ethan was helping me look."

Note to self: Ask Mom to send vanity contact lenses, contact lens case, and contact solution. Otherwise people might get suspicious.

"*That's* why he had to bring you across?" Addison asks. "You were blind?"

"Exactly." I glance quickly at Lina and see she's buried her face in her pillow.

Stupid zip line. Who does Ethan think he is? He could have given me a heart attack! He didn't apologize when we landed, or at lunch afterward, either.

"Forget the boys!" Courtney says. "We'll retaliate soon enough. How are those beds, huh? Hitch sprang for new mattresses this year. Are they comfy?"

Everyone says yes, but I know they're lying. Would it have killed Hitch to get pillow-top mattresses? When I lie down on my top bunk bed, I can feel the springs. I also see cobwebs on the ceiling. There are probably bugs and spiders everywhere, too. I am never going to be able to sleep in here. *Never.* I might as well sleep on the porch. But then I'll get eaten by a bear and mauled by mosquitoes. Or is that the opposite?

These cabins Dad talked so fondly about on the ride up are in serious need of a makeover. I'll need to light a dozen candles to get the musty, damp smell out of here, and I haven't even approached the bathroom. Our bunk beds are made of black metal frames that look like hospital beds from the 1950s. The ceiling fan looks as old as my grandmother. And the walls of the cabin could use another coat of paint. You can still see signatures etched into the wood and notes from past campers. NAT, ERIN, MEL—BFFS 4EVA! PINES RULES, ASH DOESN'T—XO, COURT!

"Everything okay, Harper?" Courtney asks. "You look a little unnerved."

"Me? Nope!" I use a cheerleader voice. "I love bugs!"

Courtney looks at me strangely. She's standing in the doorway between our cabin and the hall that leads to 10B's cabin. Sam and Court have a room in between the bunks. The only plus I can find so far is that the bathroom is on our side, near Lina's and my bunk bed. I just hope it isn't as gross as the rest of this place.

Lina doesn't seem bothered by the one-star housing conditions. She's humming as she sets up her space. She has a black-and-white-print comforter spread neatly across her bottom bunk, and canvas sacks hang off the bottom of the bed, where she's stashed journals and colored pencils. A purple shag rug is on the floor, and a London Blue poster hangs behind her headboard. Her area looks homey. Most of the other girls have set up their spots the same way—adding fabric photo boards behind their pillows, posters of their favorite celebs, and lots of throw pillows. Two girls even have those Dream Lites stuffed animals. I only have my silk canopy for ambiance. At least it doubles as a mosquito net.

Sam pops around the bend. "Are you guys ready to go to the canteen yet?"

"What's the canteen?" I ask, and Jeanie snorts. Geez. I can't ask a question?

"You can buy snacks and supplies there," says Trisha, a girl with braces, who is wearing a boy band T-shirt. "Usually we go during free time."

There's a place here where we can *shop*? Why didn't anyone tell me sooner?

"I don't know if we can go right now," Court tells Sam to my disappointment. "They haven't finished unpacking."

Sam gapes. "You mean you haven't even played icebreakers yet? Or asked them what their best day all year was? You can't say today," she warns us.

"Philly, New Year's Eve," Jeanie, Camilla, and Addison say at the same time. Melody, Trisha, and Vickie—my other bunkmates who won't even say hi now that I've saddled them with kitchen duty—all start talking at once. The way the girls parrot one another reminds me of Margo, Kate, and me. Being on the receiving end is kind of grating, actually.

"Jeanie's mom invited us for a sleepover party," Camilla tells me.

"I throw the best parties," Jeanie brags. "We had one winter break, too."

"I was in Utah for winter break," I chime in, trying to get their attention. "The powder was so fresh! You guys know Park City, right? Home of the Sundance Film Festival? I ran into Emma Stone in the lodge bathroom, and she told me she loved my cardi. Such a sweetheart."

"Anyway," Jeanie says loudly. "New Year's was the best day of the year because my Pines roomies were there." The group cheers as if they were at a football game. I notice Lina is looking at her comforter. I guess she was the only one not invited. How rude!

I bet Kyle doesn't feel like an outcast in his bunk. Darn Kyle and his glorious three points already! I need to change the score ASAP.

"You know what else is fun?" I cut in. "Presents!" I open the Louis Vuitton trunk at the end of my bed and pull out a flat iron, a few cashmere sweaters, and a humidifier (I've heard the mountains can be quite dry) before I find what I'm looking for. "Here they are," I say, pulling bag after beautiful tulle-wrapped lavender bag out of the trunk. "Your housewarming gifts." I pass the gift bags around the room. The girls look at me with a mix of bewilderment and surprise as they open them. "They're aromatherapy sleep masks that double as neck roll massagers." I take Lina's and demonstrate. "They heat up in the microwave and massage your muscles. My masseuse swears by them." I smile widely, expecting to get a huge hug or thank-you. When I gave these to the teaching staff at school, they practically threw a lunch in my honor. But my bunkmates are staring at me blankly. "They'll go great with the lavender massaging slippers I got us," I add, hoping to sweeten the deal. "They're coming next week. They had to be express ordered."

"Um, we don't have a microwave," says Vickie with a sharp twang. Freckles dot her whole face. "You'd blow the fuse. You can't use a flat iron, either."

"Who brings a flat iron to camp? Right, Jeanie?" Melody

whispers loudly. I've already noticed she is always trying to kiss Jeanie's red head.

"Hey!" Courtney's shout startles Melody. "Harper gave you a present. You should say thank you. My bunkmates never even bought me a pack of Skittles at the canteen."

"Don't look at me," Sam says. "I had a tight budget back then and no job."

"Thank you," everyone says halfheartedly.

That's weird. I was sure gifts would win them over. They always make Kate happy. Well, maybe they'll like this next one. "There's more!"

Court consults her watch. I notice it is one of those cute rubber ones in a camo pattern. Why did I pack my fancy Marc Jacobs one? "Um, Harper, we have to go over camp rules before we head to free swim and the welcome back picnic on the beach."

"Beach?" I laugh. "We're nowhere near the beach."

Addison speaks slowly, "The lake has sand, so we call it a beach." Jeanie snickers.

"Oh, well, this will just take a second away from the beach." I pass out orange and tangerine aromatherapy candles. Melody opens hers and takes a whiff. "Doesn't that smell divine?" I don't hear the girls inhale sharply when I pull out a box of matches. "It smells even better lit. It will get that wet wood/bug spray smell right out of here!"

Courtney gently takes the matches from my hand. "I hate to burst your bubble, but candles are off-limits." She knocks on one of the walls. "This place is made of wood. We'd go up in seconds. No candles. Not even on moonlight walks with a guy."

"Didn't you once go on one with my brother, Hunter?" Addison asks Sam.

Sam's face colors. "Look at the time! We should really run. I'll meet you all at the canteen!"

Courtney hands her candle back to me. "Nice gesture, but they have to go back."

Bummer. Candles always cheer up a drab room. I stick them back in my trunk but decide I will keep one in case of emergency. No one has to know. "Can I keep these for makeover nights?" I ask, holding up some beauty must-haves. "A quick-dry hair dryer, two curler sets, and a Japanese home straightening kit that I'm told is totally legal in the US even though it isn't FDA approved." My bunk is staring at me like I'm deranged. "I also brought MAC and Bobbi Brown makeup kits and mud masks. I give the best makeovers. My friends call me the future CEO of Bobbi Brown!" I laugh, and the sound echoes through the quiet room.

"Harper, could I talk to you outside?" Courtney asks, and I nod. The minute I hear the screen door slam behind us, I can hear the girls whispering. "Before we decide what you're going to keep here, why don't we decide what you're going to send home?"

I stare at the six bags on the porch. They look a lot bigger now that they're out of the trunk of McDaddy's car. "I guess I overpacked a bit, huh?"

"I know how easily it can happen when you want to take your cutest outfits with you. I was boy obsessed, too," she says, understanding my logic. "I still am, but that doesn't mean we can cart a whole wardrobe to camp. Sort, choose, send back the rest. Got it?" I nod.

There is a squeal from inside the cabin followed by peals of laughter. For some reason, the sounds make me miss Margo and Kate even more.

Courtney's face softens. "Want some advice?"

"Sure." I unzip the first bag and spot my snorkel gear. Snorkeling? Why would I think I'd be snorkeling in a murky lake? This gear will definitely be going back.

"Squeeze your way into the bunk dynamic *slowly*," Court says. "This crew has done things the same way for years, so they'll need time to get used to sleep masks and makeover kits, but they will. Everyone can use an upgrade now and then. Even me." She pulls a strand of her dark brown hair. "How do you think I would look as a blonde?"

I smile. "I think you could pull it off." There's just one thing still bothering me. "Can I ask you something? Is it true we have to fork over our cell phones?"

Courtney's smile fades. "Yes." My stomach drops. "Harsh, but phones keep you plugged in to home rather than the here and now. At least that's what Hitch thinks."

"But I like knowing what's going on at home." I don't think Courtney wants to hear that. "Is there a computer lab?" I ask hopefully.

Courtney shakes her head. "No Wi-Fi for campers or Internet access. Counselors can use their phones, but we can't touch them during work hours. You can e-mail your parents through this service called Bunk One. They deliver notes to your parents."

I touch my phone in my dress pocket. "Sounds Big Brotherish."

"They don't read your e-mails." Court makes a face. "I think.

Listen, I've got to run over to 12A for a minute, but I'll be back in ten to check on your sorting progress." She pats me on the shoulder. "In a week, you'll be so busy here, you won't even remember you own a phone. I promise."

I doubt that. I have to ship back half my wardrobe? Give up my phone? Sleep next to a mildew-infested bathroom? Camp is a lot worse than I thought it would be. I need a snack to process this information. I head inside to grab the popchips I stashed in my shoulder bag, but as I grab the rusted door handle, I hear the girls talking.

"Makeovers at camp?" Vickie says. "Y'all, does she think this is beauty school?"

Melody snorts. "She must have gotten camping confused with glamping. I give her a week, tops. Did you see the way she melted down on the zip line? Ethan had to drag her across. The great outdoors is definitely not her thing."

"I give her three days till we break her," Jeanie says. "Once those cork wedges give her blisters, Camping Barbie will be crying for Mommy to pick her up." They laugh.

I listen for Lina's voice, but if she's in the cabin, I don't hear her.

"I give her two weeks," says Vickie, and everyone in the bunk objects.

"You're crazy," Addison says. "Camping Barbie will never hack it that long. One morning on kitchen duty, and she will be out of here."

"You're wrong," Vickie insists. "She's obviously here to prove something to someone. I give her two weeks. If I'm wrong, who cares? Either way, The Harper Show is going to be fun to watch." The girls roar.

I let the cabin door go quietly and blink back angry tears. *Camping Barbie will never hack it. The Harper Show is going to be fun to watch.* They're making fun of me after I gave them presents! This sort of thing has never happened to me before. I'm *not* Camping Barbie. Maybe I'm not a Lifer. And okay, so I don't want to be a camper, either, but if I'm here, then I'm not going down without a fight. I am going to prove to all of them—Ethan included—that I can survive at Whispering Pines.

I hear more laughter, but it's not coming from the cabin. I look over the porch railing and see a group of guys coming my way. Kyle is walking with Ethan, Cole, Justin, and a few other guys I don't know yet. Ethan looks like he's being nice to my brother, even though he's evil to me. What? Kyle being the popular one at camp is so wrong. He's upset the McAllister balance of order! I have to call Kate. She'll know what to do. I pull my phone out of my pocket and dial. Please pick up.

"Hi!" Margo answers Kate's phone with a screech. "We miss you!"

Just hearing Margo's voice makes me feel better. "I miss you, too! Why do you have Kate's phone?"

Margo hesitates. "Kate threw me her phone when she saw it was you. We just got mani-pedis, but I don't care if I smudge! I couldn't miss your call."

How could Kate not want to answer when I'm so far away? "Well, I'm glad you picked up." It sounds very noisy in the salon, and I try to imagine the smell of lavender and lemon sugar scrub, the paraffin wax treatments, and those awesome massaging chairs.

"Let me step outside." When Margo does, the noise level drops. "Are you okay?" She sounds worried. "Are they feeding you?"

I giggle. "They're feeding me, but I'd rather starve than give up my phone." Margo gasps. "I have to cough it up tonight. Can you believe?"

"Kate said that would happen," Margo says. "She just told me her cousin goes to camp and doesn't even have access to Wi-Fi."

Funny how Kate left that out when we spoke before I left.

"You can't even make one call a week?" Margo asks.

"Camp is tougher than prison." I hear laughter and look up. Ethan and Kyle are walking by. I duck down and watch as they make their way to the cabin just a few feet away from ours. Knowing Ethan is sleeping so close by is weird. "I'll try to hang on to my phone and text whenever I can," I whisper to Margo, "but it's going to be tough."

"Is there *anything* good about camp so far?" Margo asks.

"Well, there are a lot of cute guys." Ethan is not included on that list.

Even if he is cute.

"That's a bonus!" Margo says.

I hesitate. "Ethan Thompson—the busboy from Intermezzo—goes here."

"No way! Did he give you a major 'tude when you saw him?" Margo starts to ask but is interrupted.

"M?" I hear Kate whine. "Tell Harper you have to go! We're going to be late."

I hear mumbling and then Margo sighs. "We're going out on Cassie Anderson's boat tonight, and we have to get ready. I'm sorry."

Cassie's boat is like a cruise liner. "I should be going, too." For some reason, I want Margo to tell Kate I have plans. "There's a campfire tonight with a band, dance, buffet, circus acts, and fireworks." Hmm...I think I'm laying it on a little thick.

"Wow! That sounds really cool." Margo is genuinely excited. "Maybe camp won't be that bad after all."

"Maybe," I say softly.

But I doubt it.

Harper McAllister @HarperMc
Radio silent for 4 weeks w/o Internet or phone. How am I going to survive the summer w/o knowing what the Kardashians are up to? #signingoff

7

WAKE UP AND SMELL THE FRENCH TOAST

FOR THE FIRST TIME THAT I can remember, I wake up before the sun. On purpose.

There is no way I'm waiting for an eight a.m. bugle call that will leave me with only a half hour to get ready. I need to be the first one in the shower. Lina claims people "wash and go" to breakfast with a wet head, but "wash and go" has never been my style.

I need something to take my mind off the fact that I, Harper McAllister, am now officially off the grid. Court made me fork over my cell phone last night. Sam and Court tried to make the ritual fun by having each of us give a eulogy for our phones, but I still didn't take it well. (They had to practically pry the phone out of my hands.) I climb down my bunk ladder, careful not to wake any of the sleeping beauties, and shine my pink Hello Kitty flashlight at the floor to guide me to the bathroom. I close the creaky door behind me, turn on the light, and gasp.

The bathroom is even more disgusting in the morning! Battleship gray for a bathroom color? Shudder. Would it kill someone to install an air freshener that could knock out that musty, wet dog smell? And what is with the water everywhere? There are puddles on the floor, water clogging up one of the sinks, and little pools of water in the bottom of the showers. *Eww.* Note to self: Never enter the bathroom barefoot. Courtney is crazy if she thinks I am cleaning this room. She went over the chore wheel last night, and I've decided scrubbing toilets is worse than being put on kitchen duty. My pretty purple bathroom cubby is the only warm and inviting thing in here. There was no way I was parting with my straightening balms, so I crammed everything I could into these purple baskets. I pull out a bottle and several come tumbling down. I hold my breath and listen. My bunkmates are still snoring. Thank God.

I step into a shower stall. The water pressure might be the first thing I like about this bathroom. The hot water shoots out at such a high speed that it *almost* feels like the rain showerhead I have at home. I linger longer than I should to enjoy a few minutes of bliss. Last night's welcome-back barbecue luau was anything but welcoming. I wore my Hawaiian print dress with the cutest wedges anyone's ever seen, but no one else got into character. Jeanie was in jean shorts, and I think Ethan had on an old Color War tee. I didn't stand close enough to see for sure because every time I ran into one of the guys from his bunk they called me "zip line crasher" or "Camping Barbie" and then the girls from my bunk would chime in. Kyle barely acknowledged me (he had a hot dog eating contest with Justin that drew a huge crowd). Lina told me not to sweat it, but I couldn't shake the feeling that my first day had been a complete bust.

It's all I can think about as I plug in my flat iron and my blow-dryer. It's not going to bother anyone now. The sun is up, and I hear girls beginning to move around. That's what they get for not using their sleep masks. I see a light flicker on in the other room from under the bathroom door and someone turns on their iPod Shuffle (one of the few approved electronic devices we can have). The sounds of a boy band float through the door. McDaddy did their first video. As cute as they are, he said, the four of them are nothing short of overindulged brats. I clip part of my wavy blond hair back and prepare to dry the first section before it starts to frizz. As soon as I flip on the hair dryer switch, Courtney races into the bathroom—and slides in a puddle. I can barely hear what she's jabbering about over my dryer.

"What?" I yell as I weave a section of hair around the brush and pull. I have gotten so good at decurling my hair that I could do it blindfolded. "Is something wrong?"

Melody and Camilla show up seconds after Courtney. They all look pretty angry for eight a.m. By this point Courtney is at my side, and I can sort of hear her over the blower. "Turn it off!" she shouts. "Quick before it blows the—"

The lights go out and the room goes silent. I hear the angry voices of bunk 10B just a few feet away. Oh boy.

Jeanie marches into the bathroom wearing a tank top, boxers, and a smirk. "Of course it's you," she says. "Who else would blow the circuit the first morning here?"

Lina has appeared, biting a strand of her pink hair. I wonder how pink hair tastes compared to normal-colored hair. "Sorry," I apologize meekly. "I forgot that—"

"A blow-dryer and a flat iron plus lights and electronics could blow the power to an entire bunk?" Jeanie snaps. She rips the hair dryer out of the wall. "You have to ask before you turn on a power sucker like that, Camping Barbie."

"That's enough, everyone," Sam says, looking bleary-eyed and gripping her cell phone. When did she get here? "I'll call Hitch and tell him what happened." I eye her phone with envy.

"It won't happen again," I promise while Sam talks in hushed tones.

Jeanie looks at me stonily. "Why would you straighten your hair today, anyway? The first dance isn't until Friday. Your hair is going to get destroyed at today's Mud-a-Thon."

"*Mud*-a-Thon?" I am terrified even though I have no clue what that is.

"And if we don't beat the guys' bunk, someone is seriously going to pay." Addison looks directly at me. She's sort of scary. I think it's because she's such a tall girl with crazy muscles. Does she do shot put for track? I'm afraid to ask.

"Addison, it's eight a.m.," Lina says, coming to my rescue. "Could you save the threats till at least after noon?" She winks at me, and I mouth thank you.

There is now a huge crowd in the bathroom. They hover around Sam and Courtney, looking sleepy, frizzy, and unrefreshed (thanks to me), while they wait to hear the verdict. When Sam hangs up, her face is grim. "Hitch is already at the mess hall for breakfast." Groans. "He says this is a lesson for all of us on not abusing, um, electricity." Sam makes a face and looks at Courtney. "He won't turn the breaker back on till after breakfast." The girls groan loader. "Which we're going to be late to at this rate."

Courtney looks at her watch. "You guys get twenty minutes." Cries of injustice bounce off the tiles. "Just shower in the dark if you planned on showering!"

Everyone marches angrily past me. Lina comes to the sink to brush her teeth. "When Vickie said there was a lack of juice in the cabins, she really meant it, huh?"

Lina stops brushing. "It's pretty bad. I'm surprised they can handle an iPod. Are you okay?"

"I feel bad." Then I have an idea. "Does anyone need dry shampoo so they don't have to wash their hair?" Lina tries to wave me off. "Or hair balm? You won't have to—"

I hear an ear-piercing scream and flinch. "Who used up all the hot water?" Jeanie pops her head out of the shower, wearing a shower cap. She gives me a defiant look.

"You don't have to say it." I drop my beauty supplies in the cubby. I don't have to look in the mirror to know how strange my hair must look half straightened, half frizzed, but I'd rather look ridiculous than face this crowd. "I'll go wait on the porch."

The fun doesn't stop when we reach the mess hall almost fifteen minutes later than everyone else at camp. Everyone is already chowing down on pancakes and eggs. Hitch uses his megaphone to rub in our late arrival. "Bunks 10A and 10B have finally made it!"

I keep my head down as I walk, but I freeze when I hear Kyle's voice. His bunk is giving us an extra hard time as we approach. Our two bunks grind to a halt in front of the boys' table to whip up some comebacks. I catch Ethan's eye. He still seems stony, even though *he's* the one who humiliated *me*.

"Everyone knows what being late means," Justin gloats. "Kitchen duty!"

"Double kitchen duty," Heath reminds us. "You already have to clear our plates for losing the zip-line challenge."

Kyle mouths something to me, but I'm not sure what he's saying. Oh. "Three points." *Grr...*

"I cannot wait to see you in a hairnet, Jeanie," Ethan teases.

"I'm just glad you don't own a camera, Ethan," Jeanie says but actually laughs.

I watch them curiously and then stop when I realize my mutinous bunk is staring me down. I attempt a smile. 10B is hungry, so they walk away. My bunk stays put.

"Why were you guys late your first morning here?" Heath asks.

"Somebody used up the hot water and blew the circuit in the cabin." Jeanie glares at me.

"All right, already!" I snap, having had enough of the jabs. They all look at me. "Would it help if I volunteered to do kitchen duty after breakfast all by myself?"

Lina grabs my arm. "Uh, Harper, you might not want to..."

Camilla and Jeanie look at each other. "I guess it is the *least* you could do after this morning," Jeanie says. "As long as you know how to load a dishwasher." I notice Ethan's eyes on me. I look away.

I may be a princess, but that doesn't mean I don't know what Cascade is. "Of course I know how to load a dishwasher." It's been over a year, but still. "I'll take care of everything. It's the least I can do after this morning's ill-timed power outage."

"I'll help you," Lina volunteers. I smile at her gratefully.

"If Lina's on kitchen duty, then I am, too," says Heath, who slides next to Lina. I notice Kyle's frown. "We can suds up the dishes together," he says smoothly.

"Thanks, but I can wash dishes on my own," Lina says, missing his point.

"The whole bunk is on kitchen duty, anyway," says Parker, a stocky guy who looks like he could lift me with one hand. "We did it out of the goodness of our hearts."

"You guys don't have hearts," Trisha says, playing with her friendship bracelet. "If you did, you wouldn't have planted that family of frogs in our cabin last season."

"Hey, that was never proven," Ethan reminds her.

"It had your name all over it," Jeanie says, winding a curl around her finger.

"You talk a big game," Ethan says. "Let's see if you can bring it at Mud-a-Thon."

The guys turn back to their table with their egos inflated while my bunkmates head to our table with barely a thank-you to me for my kitchen duty offer.

"Kitchen duty takes a while," Courtney warns me on the way to the table. "You'll probably miss second period." She looks at Lina. "We're playing dodgeball."

"That's okay," Lina says with a shrug. "I'm zip-lining during free period and playing softball in the late afternoon. I can survive missing one dodgeball game."

That's really generous of Lina. When the infamous Bunsen burner episode happened at school last week, Kate was my lab partner and still refused to help me clean up. "Are you sure you don't mind?"

"Nope," she says. "That's what roomies are for." I grin.

"Perfect. We'll see you third period," Courtney says and walks off to meet Sam.

This is the first time I've been in the mess hall since yesterday's lunch. The room looks like the school cafeteria—*if* it were in a giant log cabin and had picnic tables with checkered tablecloths instead of tiny round tables. Everyone is eating family-style, which reminds me of the summer McDaddy took us to Lancaster, Pennsylvania, and made us eat at this restaurant called Good 'N Plenty. The volume inside the room is so high that I have to resist the urge to plug my ears. The bunk is already eating when we get to our table. Maybe we should have moved faster. Most of the platters are empty! There is a sad little piece of egg left on one and half a piece of bacon on another. The only cereal choice left is Cocoa Pebbles. Never a personal fave. Asking how I can get a half a melon or an egg sunny-side up will probably result in the bunk telling me I expect to be catered to. Sigh. Lina takes the Cocoa Pebbles while I pick at a piece of dry toast.

A high-pitched sound makes me jump. Hitch is at the front of the room with a microphone replacing his megaphone. "Morning, Whispering Pines!" Everyone claps as if they haven't heard that welcome a thousand times before. "How is day two treating you?" The cheers are so deafening, what's left of the orange juice in the pitcher on our table shakes. "I'd like to thank Beaver for those amazing pancakes he made today. Let's give it up for the big guy, shall we?" More applause. "Before I get to our regular morning announcements, I have something exciting to discuss. The Pines is entering a nationwide contest that could make all of us famous." A hush falls over the room. I grab the squirt jelly and try to shake some out on my dry toast. "How would you feel about a Grammy-winning musician shooting her next music video at our camp?"

The sound that comes next is so deafening I squeeze the jelly too hard and it squirts all over my Chloé shirt. I grab a napkin and begin dabbing it with water, but it's no use. I've just ruined a ninety-dollar T-shirt the first time I wore it.

"Settle down so I can explain," Hitch says. Pam hands him an index card, and he reads off of it. "This star has written a song about summer loves, and apparently she met hers at a sleepaway camp, so she's looking for one to use as a location for the shoot. She wants a camp with a woodsy feel, old-school cabins, a big lake, and large fields."

"That's the Pines, y'all!" Vickie whispers, and I notice a piece of cereal stuck in her braces.

Camilla grunts. "And probably every other sleepaway camp in America."

Hitch continues to talk. "Most important, she wants a camp with spirit because all the campers would be video extras." More squeals make my head throb.

"To enter, camps must submit an artistic piece—written,

painted, video, or otherwise—that highlights camp life and camp spirit." He makes a face. "The only problem is entries are due in three weeks. Do you think we can do it?" Kids start banging on the table with their forks, anything they can find. "Since time is of the essence, we will vote after breakfast on what type of entry to submit, and work will begin immediately. Those interested in participating can do so during their free periods and..."

"You still haven't said who the musician is!" Ethan interrupts.

"Oh, right!" Hitch looks at Pam in confusion, and she whispers something in his ear. "Er, it's London. London Blue? What kind of name is *that*?"

The last part is drowned out by the pandemonium. Our bunk is jumping up and down and screaming along with the rest of the mess hall. The plates on our table are jumping, and a few slide off the table, taking the remains of their breakfasts with them.

I'm going to have to clean that up.

"London Blue!" Lina's gray eyes widen. She is holding my arm so tight, it hurts. "Oh my God! We have to win."

"We will," I say confidently. I wish I could tell Lina the truth, but she's the first friend I've made here and I don't want that to change because of who I know. Out of the corner of my eye, I see Kyle. I know we're both thinking the same thing. Neither of us is going to use our connection to London against the other. I breathe a sigh of relief.

Another plate hits the floor. "I'm going to start kitchen duty," I say. I never thought I'd see the day where I'd choose cleanup over conversation. Another camp first.

"I'll go with you." Lina follows me out of the mess hall in a daze. It's so chaotic I can't breathe till we leave the London Blue zone.

"Wow, I think I'm going to be deaf for a week," I say.

Lina laughs. "Well, you might be deaf longer than that after kitchen duty. Beaver loves to play loud music during cleanup." She thinks for a moment. "And while he cooks. Basically all the time. His favorite is London. Wait till he hears what's going on."

We round the outside porch and stop in front of the kitchen doors. I can hear someone barking orders and boys talking over the sounds of pots clanging and table requests being shouted out. The music in the kitchen is blasting.

"Beaver?" I repeat.

"Yep," Lina says. "He's been the head cook here for years. He teaches all the cooking classes and loves to sing. He performed a U2 song in the talent show last year." I laugh, and she makes a face. "There's one thing you should know, though."

A huge guy wearing a Harley-Davidson tank and a red bandana throws open the door and scares me half to death. "Cleanup crew?" he barks. We nod. "This isn't social hour. Get in here!" He slams the door behind him, and a phone falls out of his pocket.

"He gets stressed out during cleanup before the next meal," Lina says a little late. "He never has enough help, I guess. Otherwise he's a total sweetheart. I swear!"

I pick up Beaver's phone and stare at his retreating backside. "I guess we should give his phone back." I begin to open the door and stop. "But first..."

Lina's eyes widen. "Harper—nooo! Back away from the phone. You can do it! Harper? Harper, are you listening to me?"

FROM: HarperMc15@gmail.com
TO: HomeBody@gmail.com
SUBJECT: Send care package ASAP

Mom, might have mispacked a teensy bit. Seems you were right—there is less of a need for Chloé shirts and more of a need for Old Navy tees (don't rub it in, okay?). Mailing some bags back. Can you send some tees ASAP? Also, may need a second pair of Converse.

Kyle is fine. He's ignoring me. Might you consider keeping him here all year?

Will e-mail when I can. My phone has been confiscated. (Tell McDaddy thanks for mentioning that camp rule.)

XO, H

Harper McAllister @HarperMc
I'm back, twerps! I've got limited phone access (shh!)
so stay tuned to find out how I'm surviving the summer.
#summersecrets

8

MUD BaTH, AnYONE?

"I CaN'T BELIEVE YOU USED Beaver's phone!" Lina is freaking out as we emerge from the kitchen an hour and a half later. "If he caught you, you would have been banned from overnight camping trips, sent to solitary confinement, not allowed to—"

"I get it," I interrupt. "Bad things would happen. Very bad things. Mwah-ha-ha!" Lina does not look amused. "I can't believe you're worried, Miss Extreme."

"I like watching extreme sports," Lina clarifies. "That doesn't mean I go to the extreme myself, especially when it comes to breaking camp rules the first week we're here. Someone is always watching at camp," she warns. "I do not want you getting in trouble. You're the only one I like in our bunk!"

"Same here," I say, and we both laugh.

We're on the way to the lake to meet Courtney and the others. By this point in the morning, camp is in full swing. A group of campers jog past us, singing a camp song as they go. On a nearby field, peeps are having a balloon fight and pez are playing a game of capture the flag. There's something going on every hour of the day here, which is pretty cool. I especially like the Pines's new policy this year that allows campers to switch activities every three days if they don't like something. That means that karate class Lina convinced me to take with her when we picked electives yesterday will soon be history. I look over at Lina. She still seems jittery.

"Beaver will never know," I reassure her. "I deleted his last few searches after I e-mailed my mom." I kind of feel guilty about using his phone after getting to know the guy a little better. Once the kitchen rush ended, Beaver seemed fun (even if he does sing off-key).

"Hi, ladies!"

Lina and I freeze, kicking up pebbles with our slowdown on the rocky path.

Courtney walks toward us, her dark brown hair tucked under a funky tie-dyed head kerchief. I immediately start chewing my nails. Did Courtney just hear me?

"I'm glad I found you two," Courtney says. "I'll bring you to Mud-a-Thon."

She silently leads the way down the path toward the lake. I notice there are lots of big rocks along the way, perfect for sitting on and staring out at the water. I'd prefer a view of the mall. Lina keeps looking at me out of the corner of her eye, and I try not to panic. Courtney would have said something by now if she heard me talking about Beaver's phone. I think. I look up and stop short.

"Welcome to Mud-a-Thon," Courtney says with a wave of her arm like she's introducing the elephants at the circus.

Someone has taken a giant dirt field the size of a baseball diamond and sprayed it with water, making it a mushy mess. The boys' bunks, 11A and B, are already there scoping out the setup. The smell of mud is overwhelming. No wonder Jeanie said there was no point in doing my hair.

I cover my mouth with my shirt. "What are we doing with that thing?"

"You're going to get *in it*." Courtney seems to enjoy my freaked-out reaction.

Lina jumps up and down excitedly. "Awesome! This is so much better than last year. We only got to dip our hands. It wasn't messy enough."

"Exactly," Courtney agrees, and I look at them both like they are insane.

This is not good. I don't want to embarrass myself two days in a row. "Do I *have* to participate? I'm a much better spectator when it comes to physical activities." I think fast. "Plus, I'm allergic to mud."

Courtney doesn't buy it. "Harper, you do not want to be called Camping Barbie for the next four weeks, do you?"

I look down. I wore my white Converse this morning, having learned the hard way wedges were not a good idea, and there is already a grass stain on them. I'm going to have to burn everything I own when I go home. "No," I admit. "I don't."

"Then show these guys you can handle a little mud!" Courtney nudges me hard.

"I thought mud was good for the skin," Lina says. "Consider this a spa treatment."

That's a thought. I take a deep breath and stare at the mud pit again. Nope! "I can't!" Courtney hangs her head. "I don't want to be called Camping Barbie, but maybe I am one. I don't do mud!" I freak out. "I sunbathe! I should be at a beach cabana right now ordering an iced tea from a cute waiter home from college. Not swimming in mud!" I look around the wilderness that is as foreign in nature to me as wearing a muumuu. "Instead I'm stuck here. And you're telling me that if I want to fit in, I need to take a mud bath. I can't do it!"

"You can do this," Lina says firmly. "Don't sell yourself short!"

"Show them you have what it takes to be a sleepaway girl!" Courtney agrees.

"A what?" I ask.

"A sleepaway girl," Courtney explains. "That's what Sam and I and our friends used to call ourselves when we were campers at the Pines. I know what it's like to feel like you're an outsider." She leans on one of the nearby rocks. "The girls in our bunk were always at war with one another, and it's exhausting! We needed to find a way to survive, and when we did, we grew to love this place more than we could have imagined. You don't have to be BFFs with these girls, but you can show them you can take whatever they throw your way. And you can start by doing the Mud-a-Thon."

Lina nods encouragingly. "I'll show you what to do."

I hear yelling. Ethan has grabbed the hose and added more water to the mud pool. The sight makes me want to vomit. "I don't know."

"If you do this, I might be willing to help you out with something, too," Court says.

I look at Lina, then back at Courtney. I'm curious. "Like what?" I take a seat on the rock next to her.

"I'll tell you a secret." Courtney leans forward. "If you stop by the counselors' room in the bunk, you might notice that neither Sam nor I keep our phone out. We don't want the campers to get it, of course. If a camper is caught with a staff member's phone, we could get into huge trouble."

My heart beats rapidly. Courtney knows I used Beaver's phone.

"I hate that rule." Courtney frowns. "I know how hard it can be detaching from what's going on with home. Sometimes you just need to check in, you know?"

I know! I know! I try to resist chewing on my nails.

"To keep from getting in trouble, I hide my phone under my bunk mattress," Courtney says. "Campers never think to look in a counselor's bed, and I keep my phone charged there all day. That way I don't lose it on a zip line or in a mud pit. Smart, huh?" Courtney looks at me steadily. Lina raises an eyebrow.

Courtney's saying it is okay to use her phone as long as neither of us acknowledges it! And I don't get caught. I'm so happy, I could hug her. But I don't. She doesn't seem very touchy-feely. "It's a good thing no one knows that," I say calmly.

"Yep." Courtney almost cracks a smile. "Well, now that we've done some sharing, I'd say it's time for Mud-a-Thon. If the girls don't win, I'm going to have to listen to Cole gloat for weeks. Will you win this for me?"

The breeze sends the stench of mud my way. I wrinkle my nose. "I'll try."

"Atta girl," Court says. "One more thing—you're on kitchen duty all week."

My head almost spins off. "Why?" I cry. "I already worked there this morning."

"Beaves said after he taught you how to wash a pot, you were a huge help. Being on duty is your punishment for stealing his phone and me not telling him about it." Courtney glares at me. I swallow hard, but I don't say anything. "Now go take a mud bath and stop blowing fuses and the Barbie comments will go away, I promise." She hits me on the back.

Lina guides me to the contest area where Kyle, Heath, Matt, Ethan, and several guys from their bunk are testing the mud. My bunk is already there, and the girls from Sam's bunk have arrived just in time to watch. Kyle sticks a toe in, and some of the girls squeal.

"That is disgusting!" Jeanie screams and laughs at the same time. I see she has her hair pulled up in a high ponytail and is wearing old clothes. So are some of my bunkmates. Smart. If only I'd known what I'd be getting myself into.

"We have three challenges for Mud-a-Thon," Sam tells us. "For each, you'll get three minutes to get the job done. The first team to complete the assignment wins." She grins. "Guys versus girls." Everyone cheers.

"Are you sure you guys want to lose again?" Cole taunts.

"It's you guys who are going to lose," Melody yells.

"You wish, Mel!" Justin hollers. The guys give a lot of smack talk.

Kyle pushes his way through the crowd to get to me. He's already got Whispering Pines spirit with his camp logo tee. "Bet you're looking forward to this, huh?" His laugh has always reminded me of a hyena. "Remember our bet? One point for every round won," he says. "You could so use the points—not that you're going to get them."

My blood boils. "I will get all of them," I say, getting in his face.

Lina claps. "Yes! Get pumped! It always helps me to stay in the zone before a game. Don't let anyone get in your head. Especially him." Lina stares him down. I'd told her all about Kyle and my bet. She's on Team Harper, obviously.

"Don't be like that," Kyle flirts in a smooth voice. "You don't even know me yet, but we can make that happen right now. Want to go to the canteen with me later?"

I know that goofy look on my brother's face. He gets it when Nina Dobrev is on TV. He likes Lina! I glance at my friend. Could she like him, too? They do have a lot in common.

"Sorry, I'm going with Harper," Lina says, and I bite my lip. Kyle deflates like a balloon.

"See ya," I say, pulling Lina away. "That was awesome," I whisper.

Lina looks at me blankly. "What was?"

"How you shot down Kyle!" I say. "I've been dying for a girl to turn him down."

Lina uses a long strand of pink hair to cover her face. "You mean he was asking me out?" Her voice is shrill. "I'm such an idiot. My friends at home always say this stuff goes over my head." She holds her head. "And your brother is really cute, too."

Now I feel bad. Lina's been so helpful. "You turning him down will only make him want you more," I say. "We'll see to that." She smiles with relief as we sit down on a log to take our socks and shoes off. The last thing I'm expecting is for Ethan to walk over.

"Hey," he says.

"Hey," I say stiffly.

"So you blew the fuse in the cabin this morning, huh?"

I feel my blood start to boil. Lina looks at me. "Did you come over here to throw salt in my wounds?" I snap at him. "It wasn't enough to humiliate me on the zip line?"

Ethan's face colors. "Actually, I was going to tell you I did the same thing last year." I look at him. "I snuck a DVD player in so we could watch *Top Gun*. Knocked the power out to three bunks, but no one remembered it was me after a few days."

I'm not sure what to say. "At least you picked a classic."

He grins. "I'm sorry about the zip line. I went a bit overboard. It's just, when I saw you here it made me think of Kate trying to get me fired. She treats everyone at school like they're servants," he says. "I guess I took it out on you. I'm sorry."

"Kate did not get him fired," I say to Lina. I feel the need to defend myself. "He'd already given notice."

"She still *wanted* to get me fired." He looks at me strangely. "What are you doing here, anyway? Kyle I get, but you I picture at Surf and Sand Beach Club or in Sea Cliff taking sailing lessons. Not at the Pines."

"I wanted to come, okay?" I lie, getting angry all the same. "You don't need to know why, and you don't need to humiliate me because you think I don't belong here."

"You're right." Ethan backs off immediately. "It is none of my business. I just wanted to say that was pretty cool of you to take kitchen duty this morning all on your own. Not many girls would do that." I realize he isn't trying to be cocky. If anything he seems to be looking at me with a newfound appreciation. We hear a whistle blow. "Time to play, I guess," he says. "See you out there." He walks to the edge of the playing field.

I'm too stunned to move.

"Wow, what was that about?" Lina asks.

"I don't know," I say. I'm not going to find out now, either. The two of us head to the playing area. I look at my stained Chloé top that is about to be completely destroyed. Kate is going to kill me.

"It's time to get in the mud pit!" Sam yells. Courtney is standing next to her with a tiny palm camera. Guess the "no technology" rule is just for campers.

I huddle up with my team. "The guys are going to dive right in and do whatever it takes to win," I hear Jeanie say. "We've got to do the same. I don't care how dirty we get! If they win two games in a row the first week, there'll be no dealing with them."

"I agree," says Camilla. "So what is our strategy? Do we fight dirty?"

Jeanie shakes her head. "We have to win this fair and square or we'll just have to play the game twice. Everyone better bring her A game." She eyes me skeptically. "Think you can manage that?" The girls look at me.

"Don't worry about me. I'm ready to win." Lina gives me a thumbs-up.

Addison surprisingly puts her arms around Lina and me. "Remember—never stop moving. Build, build, build, and beat them to the finish line!" We applaud, and I feel myself start to get pumped up.

I think I'm ready! Let my bunk call me Camping Barbie. The real Barbie has a camper, after all (I owned it). If I'm getting dirty, then I'm going to get dirtier than everyone here. I take a tentative step forward as everyone wades into the mud. I feel my foot sink into the ground and pull it back out. Maybe not....

Lina wades in quickly next to me. "You've got this," she encourages me.

The mud feels weird, but it is not that deep. I dip a toe in again. *Think of this as a mud body wrap at Red Door.* That seems to work. By the time I've reached the center, I'm in up to my shins and I can feel my heartbeat slow back down. I stand perfectly still and pray mud doesn't fly on me. Jeanie gathers our two bunks together for mud strategy. I don't go over. What more is there to say about mud? Instead, I get my game face on.

"Are you guys ready to get dirty?" Cole yells, and the four bunks cheer. The mud pit is packed now.

I scream, too, because I'm trying to be super sporty. Yes, that's me! Harper, super sporty girl. Maybe I have a whole new high school career ahead of me. I'll play rugby! They do have the cutest uniforms. I hop up and down trying to psych myself up.

"Mission number one," Cole says. "Build a giant turtle using whatever twigs, rocks, and mud you can get your hands on. You have two minutes."

"A turtle?" Lina and I say at the same time, but Ethan, Justin, Kyle, Dirk, Heath, and the other guys are already molding mud with their hands, the stuff oozing through their fingers and making me ill. Jeanie and my teammates are working speedily, too. At the sight of all that mud, super sporty Harper and her rugby dreams fly out the window. Lina is right in the middle helping them, but I am frozen with fear. It is one thing to wade in the mud. It's another to actually touch it with my hands.

"Harper, come on!" Lina calls to me. "Get in here!"

I know Courtney is watching me. I know the future of my phone access is at stake, but the mud...there is just so much of it! I watch in amazement as our team holds up one giant ball of mud and then another and sticks some twigs in it. It doesn't exactly look like a turtle, but they have to move because Ethan and Kyle are already running over to the judges with their version, slipping and sliding the entire way. Jeanie is right on his heels with a much bigger turtle, and she pushes past them. Ethan tumbles to the ground.

"Cheater!" Ethan grabs Jeanie's leg and pulls her down. She screams and almost face-plants in the mud. I start to laugh, but quickly find myself less amused when they begin flinging mud at each other.

"People, hold it together," Courtney tells them. "The girls win round one!"

Our team goes nuts. I flinch as pieces of mud hit me in the legs and land on my clothes. *Eww! Eww! Eww!* I try not to panic and jump out of the pit. I tap Kyle on the shoulder and hold up one finger. One point for me! Yahoo!

"Guys, we've got to get this next one!" I hear Ethan say as he wades over to my brother and the large group of guys, mud covering half his face and most of his body.

Addison nudges me. "Hey! What happened to you? You did nothing."

"I was gathering intel on the boys," I say as Jeanie glares at me. "I now know all their mud-building tricks."

Addison looks intrigued. "And they are?" Lina bites her lip.

"They use a lot of mud," I say, and Jeanie rolls her eyes.

"Your next assignment is a little tougher," Sam says. "Build a cabin. Go!"

"What?" I hear some of my bunkmates cry, but Ethan is already wading deeper in the pit, sloshing past me and shooting mud everywhere as he grabs sticks. Justin sees what he is doing and pitches in. One of the guys grabs a branch and starts breaking it in pieces while Kyle starts dripping mud over the sticks to hold them together. My team, on the other hand, seems at a loss. I watch as Melody, Trisha, and Camilla try to use the mud as glue for the logs, but the four walls keep falling down. Lina tries to construct a chimney out of rocks she's pulled off the ground, and I help her. I don't actually stick my hands in the mud, but I do attempt to hold the chimney together. It's no use. It falls apart. We watch Kyle slowly carry the boys' house over to the edge of the field. It looks wobbly.

"Move faster, everyone!" Jeanie cries. She gathers more twigs, but it's too late.

"Boys win round two!" Cole announces. "Round three is a tiebreaker."

Kyle holds up one finger. "One for me!" he says.

"The third assignment is the toughest," Sam says. "Build a snowman!"

"I am excellent at snowmen," Lina tells us. "I make one every time we go skiing."

"Good, then get in there," Jeanie pushes her. "Everyone listen to Lina!"

The group gets to work as Lina drops a vat of mud into my outstretched hands. The mud is cold and I feel like I might retch, but Vickie and Jeanie are watching me, so I inhale sharply instead. Some of the girls from the other bunk grab rocks and twigs.

"Make me the fattest bottom you can," Lina says.

Camping Barbie. Cell phone access. Beating Kyle. I can do this! I have to do this! Without giving myself time to panic, I stick my hands in the mud and mold a ball. I make it bigger and bigger.

"That's it," Lina says encouragingly. "Now give it to me." I hand the squishy mess over, Camilla sticks eyes in it, and Trisha puts arms in the second ball.

"We have to carry it in pieces," Jeanie yells, holding the head. I look at Ethan and Kyle. They've got their snowman together, too. Crud. "Otherwise it's going to topple."

"I'll take one, you take one, and Harper takes the third," Lina instructs us.

"Me?" My voice warbles.

"Yes," Lina says and passes my piece of the snowman back my way. "Now go!"

Ethan and Kyle run quickly past me, sending mud in all directions, and for some reason it clicks. Kyle is not getting two points for this game. Ethan is not going to beat me. I pick up speed—well, as much speed as I can, running through the muck—and when Kyle fumbles with a piece of their snowman, the girls blow past them. Both teams are screaming as we near the finish. And that's when it happens. Jeanie slips and drops the head into the mud.

"No!" She tries to find it, but it's no use. It already sank. Determined, I mold a ball quickly and slosh over to Lina as mud splashes up around me. She has the middle in her hands, and I hand her a head. Then I drop to my knees and start forming another ball using a rock I grab as the base. While Jeanie continues to search in vain, I hand the ball to Lina, stick eyes and a nose in it, and watch as it all comes together. It is a drippy, gross snowman, but definitely a snowman.

I give it to her just in time, too, because Ethan and Kyle are back in the race, and my brother is barreling toward me. I know that look in his eye. He's going to knock me down. Not this time. I kick mud up in their direction, and Kyle starts to flail around.

"What are you doing?" Ethan yells as he tries to hold the snowman steady. But it's no use. He falls trying to hold the snowman, and he takes me down with him.

I scream as I land sideways in the mud. Mud is in my hair, on my face, all over me. "Oh my God!"

"No!" Kyle yells as the snowman crashes into the mud. Lina, meanwhile, hands our team's snowman right over to the judges while Ethan and I continue to flail around.

"Winners of Mud-a-Thon are the girls of bunks 10A and B!" Sam crows. All the girls gather around and erupt in celebration. Everyone except for me.

"The mud is so cold!" I say, trying to stand up. I slip and fall down again, and Ethan starts to laugh. Then he drops a pile of mud on my head. "What are you doing?"

"Being a sore loser," he says to me with a laugh and tosses more mud my way.

"This is because I'm a sore loser about the zip line." I push mud in his face.

That shuts him up.

"All right, you two, that's enough," Courtney warns us, but she's smiling. "You did good, Harper." She lends me a hand.

I beam. "Thanks. So you mean...?"

"Yep," Courtney says cryptically. "What I said before still stands."

"Yes!" I cry, and Kyle comes over and glares at me. "Two points for me!"

"I still have four," he grumbles.

"Did I miss something?" Ethan asks. He still hasn't managed to get up yet.

"Yep," I say happily. "This." I pour more mud on him. Kyle

knocks me down. I grab him and pull him down, too. Everyone is watching us, but I don't care. Now that my outfit is completely ruined, anyway, playing in the mud is sort of fun.

"The girls pick a zumba class as their victory prize. Guys! Hello? Did you hear me?" Jeanie asks. She is staring at Ethan and me.

"I would have chosen doing laundry," I say. Jeanie makes a face. *Splat!* Ethan sends more mud my way. I send it back with a laugh.

"Ethan! Harper! Kyle! Smile!" Courtney has a camera pointed in our direction.

I decide to give Courtney a picture she won't forget. As she prepares to click, I grab Ethan and Kyle and push them down into the mud face-first.

Harper McAllister @HarperMc
Try a mud bath. They're smelly, but it does wonders for your pores. It's like a free facial. Beat that, Red Door Spa. #survivingthesummer

9

HOME NOT-SO-SWEET HOME

IT'S ALMOST MIDNIGHT. I'VE WAITED forty-five minutes, and there is still no sign of Courtney or Sam. Now is the perfect time to make a call, which is why I've jumped out of bed and quietly broken into Courtney and Sam's room. Courtney's phone is waiting for me exactly where she said it would be. My fingers tremble as I put in the familiar number.

"Hello?" A sleepy voice answers.

"Margo, it's me!" I whisper.

"Harper?" Margo instantly sounds more awake. "What number are you calling from?"

I need to be cryptic to protect the innocent. "A camp pay phone." I keep my eye on Courtney's bedroom door for movement.

"They still have those up there?" Margo says with a yawn.

"Um, yes! So how are you? Are you going to Hallie's Fourth of July party this weekend?" I try not to sound wistful.

"We were going to, but now Kate has a new plan," Margo says sarcastically. "She wanted to go to the Jersey Shore for the Fourth, but I said no. I am not leaving you out of that trip!"

"Thanks." Margo is so good to me. "I can't believe she wanted you to change it. We always said we'd go in August together when I got home."

"You know Kate—once she gets an idea in her head, it's all she can think about," Margo says. "She has us hanging out with this girl we met at the cabana last weekend. Her name is Amber and her mom is that supermodel Anastasia. She's getting her own reality show or something, and she gave Kate all these free clothes, so now Kate is obsessed with her. Get this: Kate asked if we could take Amber to NJ with us instead of you. Can you imagine? I told her—*BEEP*—and now I'm on her bad list, too. Oh, wait, that's her beeping in. What's with everyone calling at midnight? Hold on." *CLICK.*

It feels like I am on hold forever when it is probably only thirty seconds, but when you're not supposed to be using a phone in the first place, every second counts. I'm kind of regretting this phone call now. I feel worse than I did that time I tried a new spa for a facial and broke out in hives. How could Kate write me off so quickly? I've only been gone a couple of days. I'm about to hang up when I hear Margo again.

She groans. "Kate wants you to call her. I slipped and said I was on the phone with you." She yawns again. "And don't worry. You are not missing much. If anything, I wish I could get away. I need a break from Kate the Great." I giggle. "Miss you tons."

"Miss you, too," I say. I hang up and quickly dial Kate. I'm on borrowed time.

"Hey!" Kate sounds happy to hear from me. "I'm so glad I caught you!"

"Sorry I haven't been able to call. I have limited phone access, and I only called Margo because I had to ask her something." It's not entirely true, but I don't want Kate to think I'm playing favorites.

"I heard about losing your phone. Bummer," Kate says. "But you've got one now, so we can chat. I really want to hear about camp—another time—but right now I have a crucial favor. Can I pop over to your house and raid your closet? I figure you're not wearing Laundry dresses in the woods and someone should be seen in them!" She laughs. "We have so many parties coming up, and Margo and I met this awesome girl at the beach club—Amber—you will love her. I need some threads to keep up with her!"

I laugh weakly. So that's why she wanted to talk to me? To steal my clothes? "As long as you have everything back when I get home in three weeks," I say.

"Three weeks? Oh, I thought you were gone longer." Kate sounds sort of disappointed. "Okay. Oh, and if your dad gets any good concert tickets while you're gone, be sure to tell him to send them my way. Amber would love to go to a concert. I've got to get to bed. Love you! Thanks! I'll talk to you soon." *CLICK.*

I exhale. I will be home in three weeks. Everything will be

back to normal when I get home. I'm sure of it. I guess I should e-mail Mom though and warn her that Kate will be knocking on our door tomorrow morning.

FROM: HarperMc15@gmail.com
TO: HomeBody@gmail.com
SUBJECT: I'm still alive

Hi, Mom! Thanks for overnighting me some new tees!

    I've survived my first few days! Would you believe I'm a natural at paddleboarding? My new friend Lina is forcing me to do some sports electives with her (crazy, right?). I'm not thrilled, but she agreed to take a hip-hop dance class, so I had to compromise. What I won't compromise on is a good breakfast. I asked for an egg-white omelet with soy cheese the other morning and our cook, Beaver (yes, that is his real name!), harassed me about it. Their menu here needs some help. The best thing they serve is this stuff called bug juice (which is a camp drink staple, I'm told).

    I'm taking a videography class, too. McDaddy would be proud, I know, but do not tell him! I'm still mad. The counselor who teaches it says I have an eye for detail. Must be in the family!

    Miss you a ton. Write me back soon. How did your blog session with HGTV go?

P.S.—Kate is stopping by tomorrow, I think, to borrow some clothes from my closet.

XO, H

CREAK.

Uh-oh! Someone is up! I slip Courtney's phone back under her mattress, then hurry out of the room and into the bathroom so it looks like I was there the whole time. When no one appears after a few seconds, I slip back out and hurry into bed. When I look at the piggy alarm clock it says 1:00 a.m. Wow, I was on the phone awhile. Good thing everyone's plan has free minutes after nine p.m. Within a few minutes, I'm asleep.

BEEP, BEEP! TIME TO GET UP! TIME FOR MORNING EXERCISE!

Huh? I feel like I just fell asleep! I rip off my sleep mask to look at the time. It's actually six fifteen. I set my piggy alarm clock so I wouldn't be late for breakfast duty. I had so much fun working with Beaver on kitchen cleanup that I volunteered to help him out with the cooking this week as well.

Maybe I'm going insane.

BEEP, BEEP! TIME TO GET UP! TIME FOR MORNING EXERCISE!

Why did I set this darn alarm clock so loud?

I pull back the drapes on my sheer canopy and punch at the buttons in a half-slumber state, trying to find the one that shuts my piggy off.

"Harper!" Camilla yells. I've noticed she's the worst early morning riser.

"We talked about this!" Vickie chimes in. It's hard to understand her with her mouth guard. "Stop setting your alarm! That's what the bugle is for!"

"I need to get up before the bugle!" I say. My piggy alarm clock seemed like a good option for an earlier wake-up call, but the girls hate how loud it is. I can't find the button, and for some reason, the alarm only gets louder the longer you let it go on. At this point, I hear the door to Sam and Courtney's room open and girls in both bunks moving around. I've woken up the whole cabin.

Jeanie climbs up my ladder, scaring me half to death. Her hair looks like it's been in a windstorm. She grabs my piggy and I'm afraid she's going to throw it, but instead she finds the battery compartment and yanks out four AAs. Everyone applauds.

"I'm holding on to these until breakfast," she says in a gruff, sleepy voice. "And don't *ever* think of putting that pig on again."

We've had this same conversation every morning for the last few days. Somehow they keep missing my point: I don't have a phone that I can set on vibrate mode to the time I need to get up. I'll just have to make the volume on my piggy alarm lower.

"Sorry, everyone." I instinctively bite my nails. Must stop doing that. I see they're all yawning and stretching. Courtney is standing in the middle of our room, rubbing her eyes. "Go back to sleep! I had to get up early to help Beaver. I volunteered for breakfast duty this week." Courtney raises an eyebrow. "I know what you're all thinking: me! A girl who hates breakfast is making it, but that's what I'm doing and—"

"Jeanie, think you can find the batteries on Harper and take them out, too?" Camilla interrupts, and Jeanie and Addison giggle. Trisha snorts loudly.

I'm not fond of Trisha. Any girl who wears clogs can't be trusted.

"I'll be on my way now," I tell Courtney and Lina, who is still half-asleep when I climb down my ladder. They are the only ones who really care where I'm off to, anyway.

Snakes in the lake and mandatory rock climbs might be awful, but the worst part of being at the Pines is the fact that my bunkmates still won't give me an inch.

Can I help it if I like looking good? Or care about fashion? A person can look nice while hiking. If she couldn't, there wouldn't be countless outdoor clothing magazines dedicated to such a thing. I want to tell the rest of our bunk that it wouldn't kill them to wear a skirt once in a while.

"I'll go with you. I'm up." Lina stumbles out of bed to find something to wear.

"Just shut up already," Jeanie moans.

Hey, she's wearing her sleep mask! I don't say anything though as she's in a bad mood. Thanks to me. I hurry into the bathroom to wash up. I'm not showering. I learned that lesson the hard way yesterday. After two hours in the kitchen, I smelled like a combination of burned toast and pancake batter.

In ten minutes, we're on our way to the mess hall. The camp is quiet at this hour, and the two of us are still pretty tired, so we barely speak, which is okay. The sun is coming up over the trees, and it basks the lake in a warm orange glow. The birds

117

are chirping happily because no one is telling them to shut off their alarm clock, and the air feels cool rather than sticky. Since most of the camp is still asleep, no one is outside, and it feels like Lina and I have the place to ourselves.

I like it that way.

As we near the mess hall, things get louder. Lina and I look at each other when we hear music blaring from the kitchen. Beaver has been up for hours getting ready for breakfast, but he's still not the kind of guy I'd expect to have London Blue blasting at seven a.m. Lina practically races to the door when she hears who is playing. Then she stops short.

"What?" I ask. She points inside. I peek in and gasp. She throws her hand over my mouth.

Harper McAllister @HarperMc
Getting up early has its perks: Not only can you see the sun rise, you can also spy on the boys' pop-song sing-along! #campperks

10

REPORTING FOR DUTY

I CAN'T BELIEVE WHAT I'M seeing.

Apparently, the boys of bunks 11A and B are on kitchen duty this morning, too. They don't notice us as the huge crowd of them bounce around and sing along. I almost die when I realize Ethan and Heath know every word to London's song. Dirk, Kyle, and a bunch of other guys are banging on things while Justin uses a metal pot and two spoons as a drum. The best part is Beaver and Ethan singing with wooden spoons. They are belting out London's lyrics as if their lives depend on it. Ethan even gives a little air kick. He's in mid-riff when he sees Lina and me. We both start to laugh.

"You two do not get off that easily!" Ethan says and pulls us inside the bright silver kitchen with industrial appliances and long countertops. Everything gleams in the early morning light. Beaver is a stickler for a sparkling kitchen. "Kyle, grab Lina!" Lina is stiff as a board as Kyle takes her by the hand.

"We're testing out a little mood music. Your brother says it will inspire me. What do you want to rock out to next?" Beaver goes to his iPod dock. "Another London song?"

"Yes!" Lina manages to say, even though Kyle is holding her hand.

"I heard this one is her next single." He fires it up. "Have you heard it yet?"

Kyle and I exchange glances. McDaddy did the video already. "I think so," I say.

Beaver throws Lina and me each a wooden spoon. "Then let's hear it!"

Lina and I look at each other. "If I can survive a mud bath, you can sing in front of my brother," I whisper in her ear. "Make him want to ask you to the canteen again."

Her eyes widen. "Will he?" she squeaks.

"Come on, Adventure Barbie!" I say. That's what we call each other now as a joke—I'm Camping Barbie, she's Adventure Barbie. "You won't know if you don't try it." I lean into her and start to sing the song. Lina looks like a deer caught in headlights at first, but I start making all these goofy faces and she starts to laugh.

Justin uses his wooden spoon to make music on all the hanging pans. Two guys from the other bunk have pots on their heads and are dancing behind me. I sing louder, and Beaver joins me on the chorus. He knows every word of London's song! I notice Ethan standing near one of the counters watching us and I dance on over.

"You don't want to sing?" I yell over the commotion. All

this singing and dancing at seven a.m. has put me in a good mood. "I know you know the words."

"And you know that how?" Ethan asks, smiling.

"I saw you singing on the last one," I say. "Come on!" This time I grab his hand and pull him into the middle of the room with me. At first Ethan just stands there, but he can't ignore the beat and finally starts to sing into my spoon. I join him. Then he spins me around like a top. I'm sort of dizzy after that, and Ethan reaches out and steadies me. I'm disappointed when the song is over.

"That was great!" Beaver marvels. "I wish we had taped it to send to London." We all groan. "Why not?" He places his hands on his hips. "We were good!"

"Maybe we should take our act to the talent show," Justin suggests.

"I could juggle while you guys sing," says Dirk, who grabs a few strawberries and begins his routine. A few of the other guys try to join him.

Beaver holds up a hand to stop them. "We need those. Don't drop them."

Kyle moans. "Come on, Beaver. Let's try juggling kitchen utensils next. They do that all the time on *Daredevil*."

"You watch *Daredevil*, too?" Lina freaks out. "I live for that show!"

"*Xtreme Sport Television*, *Exotic Sports Locales*, and *Daredevil* are my faves," Kyle says.

I see Lina start to twitch. Now that she has realized Kyle is into her, she doesn't know how to act. As much as I do not want this pairing, I can't let her hang out there to dry. "Lina also loves *Armed and Dangerous*," I say, and notice Ethan watching me.

"That's the one with the guy with no legs, right?" Kyle is getting excited. "That dude is awesome! Did you see when he went skydiving?"

"Yes!" Lina's too into the topic to panic now. "That time the dude went—"

"You two—talk about skydiving while you set the tables," interrupts Beaver. Lina begins to blush, but I nudge her forward. "The rest of you guys tackle cleanup duty." The other bunk groans. I notice Heath, Dirk, and Justin hanging back to avoid being handed a mop, but Beaver is too smart for them. He walks right over with a bucket and Windex. "We got an early morning delivery and they tracked dirt in, so I need you guys to make it sparkle again." Justin and Dirk salute, then take the guys with them through the kitchen's swinging doors. Beaver points to Ethan and me. "You two prep the strawberries and the melons. I have to check on the bagel delivery."

Ethan and I move over to the prep table where the strawberries are waiting. The London CD is still playing in the background, and I can smell the pancake batter Beaver whipped up. A few days ago, this huge kitchen with its fancy appliances stressed me out, but since Beaver has shown me where things are, I feel more comfortable. The only thing making me feel weird right now is being alone with Ethan. He grabs a few melons and gets to work. I begin chopping strawberries. The two of us work quietly side by side, but it feels strange to not be talking.

"So," Ethan says suddenly as he dices melon. "How have you been?"

I try to concentrate on my strawberries, but my mouth starts to twitch. "You mean since I saw you yesterday when we had a group sailing lesson?"

I see him blush. "It's been twenty-four hours."

"You can admit it," I joke. "Twenty-four hours is too long to go without seeing me, I know."

He smirks. "Kyle's right. You *can* be funny." I bow. "When you're not shoving mud in my face."

"You deserved that." I take another few strawberries and place them on the cutting board. I stop when I realize Ethan is watching me. "What?"

"You dice pretty well," he says.

"I'm not completely helpless," I say with a laugh. "I cut a mean pineapple, too, but I can't stand cutting kiwi even if I do love to eat it. Too much work."

"So are potatoes," Ethan says. "I know they're not fruit, but I hate peeling them. Somehow I always get stuck with them on Thanksgiving and here when Beaver is on a homemade french fry kick." He grins. "Can't he just use the frozen ones?"

"No way! Put love in it, and it tastes better." I drop a few more strawberries into the bowl. I'm quiet for a second, and the only sound I hear are our knives. "Beaver taught me that in cooking class. I really like that elective. Karate, not so much."

Ethan turns to the prep sink and washes another melon. "So the Pines isn't killing you slowly, like you thought it would?"

I wash off another pint of strawberries. "I'm surviving, which is more than I thought I would last week. I still don't like bugs, mud pits, or canoeing, and I can't handle not having a phone! How can you stand not being able to check Facebook?"

Ethan shrugs. "The only updates I really care about are from people at the Pines with me already. I don't think I'm missing out on much at home."

"Well, I am missing out on a lot." I mince a strawberry. "My friends and I had a lot of plans."

"Slow down." Ethan puts his hand on top of mine. "We're not making preserves."

I feel funny with our hands touching.

Ethan must, too, because he slowly removes his hand. "Kate must have freaked that you were coming here. I picture her micromanaging every detail of your summer ahead of time."

I laugh. "That's Kate."

"She must really miss you," Ethan says. "Has she sent you care packages? Jeanie's always getting candy sent to her. Her best friend's dad owns a candy store."

I'm not sure which part of that question I want to tackle first. Kate hasn't sent me anything. She's just told me she wants to borrow all my clothes. I don't really want to tell Ethan that. I'm not sure I want to ask about Jeanie, either, though, but I'm curious. "I heard from Kate yesterday," I say, fudging things a bit. "She's really busy with...stuff." Ethan nods. "Does Jeanie give you some of that candy she gets?"

Ethan carves another slice of melon. "Yeah. She knows I love Skittles."

Deep breath, Harper. "So how long have you two been going out?"

124

"What?" I watch as his hand slips, nicking his finger. "OUCH!" Ethan grabs his finger and sucks on it. "Ouch," he mumbles again.

Oops. That might have been my fault.

"What are you? A vampire?" I look on the wall and spot the first-aid kit. I pull it down and grab Band-Aids and ointment. "Give me your finger," I say, and Ethan does as he's told. His cut doesn't look too bad. I put on the prep sink faucet and run Ethan's finger under the water, watching the blood disappear. Then I blot his finger with a clean towel and squirt ointment on it.

"Thanks," Ethan says quietly.

"You're welcome." I grab a Scooby-Doo Band-Aid and put it on him.

Ethan looks at me. "Jeanie and I are not going out, by the way." I can't help thinking his warm brown eyes remind me of my teddy bear stashed under my comforter. "We're just good friends. We have been for years."

"Oh." I try not to smile. "I just assumed from the way you two acted..."

"Just friends," he says firmly. "And you? Do you have a boyfriend?"

I shake my head. "Nope."

The sound of the faucet dripping slowly behind me suddenly sounds magnified, as does the London Blue CD on play. The two of us just stand there. Ethan opens his mouth to speak, but Beaver busts back through the kitchen doors.

"The bagel delivery won't be here in time!" His eyes are

wild. "I knew this day would come! What are we going to do without bagels? Our next cereal delivery isn't till tomorrow and I don't have enough pancake batter on hand."

"Good!" I say, and they both look at me strangely. "Aren't you tired of making the same thing every morning? There's got to be something else we can come up with."

"Don't say egg-white omelets with soy cheese," Beaver interrupts. "You're the only one who wants them. And we don't have enough eggs to cook regular omelets for the rest of the camp."

"You do not want the powdered ones, either," Ethan says to me. "They're nasty."

I walk over to the giant fridge in the back of the room and open it up. It's got a lot of labeled containers and premade food, but not a lot of supplies for breakfast. Then I spot the butter and the dozen or so loaves of bread calling my name. I grab one and show it to the others. "How about french toast?"

Beaver looks doubtful. "That's just like pancakes."

I'm insulted. "Not when I'm making it. I'll show you." I point to Ethan. "Fire up a griddle on the stove."

He salutes. "Aye-aye, captain!"

I take the large butter and a dozen eggs out of the fridge. The two of them watch as I add a little milk and an egg to a bowl and some cinnamon and then vanilla. I whisk it all together, then let it sit for a second as I add butter to the hot griddle and watch it sizzle.

"You actually know what you're doing over there," Ethan says, watching me.

I dunk a piece of toast in the mixture and then place it on the griddle. Then I add several more while Beaver goes to find more bread. "Before we moved, my dad and I used to cook breakfast every Sunday. I can make a mean batch of s'mores brownies, too."

"S'mores brownies?" Ethan asks. "That sounds like it has my chocolate chipper peanut butter cookies beat." I stop flipping with my spatula in midair. "Yes, I'm a boy who can bake." He smirks. "But don't tell anyone. I keep it on the down low."

"Your secret is safe with me," I say.

"Wow, that smells killer!" Kyle says as he walks back into the kitchen with the others. Even I have to admit the aroma is amazing. I love the smell of melted butter. He takes a piece from the pile and bites into it before Beaver can stop him. "Oh man, I forgot how good your french toast is. She can make awesome crepes, too," Kyle tells the others.

Curiosity gets the better of Ethan. He grabs a piece and splits it in half with Beaver. Lina takes a slice and splits it with Kyle, Dirk, Justin, and Heath. Everyone murmurs how good it is as I continue to flip, then add more french toast and butter to the pan.

"I'm glad you signed up for my cooking class," Beaver says. "You've got some skill. We can work with that."

"I think you might have found your camp calling," Justin says with his mouth full. Ethan winks at me.

I don't say anything, but I can't help but smile. Justin might be right.

Harper McAllister @HarperMc
Show the camp you can cook killer french toast and watch them beg for more! #survivingthesummer

11

GOTCHa!

I TOSS and TURN IN my bunk bed. It doesn't help that the mattress is springy and nothing like my memory foam one at home. Or that I'm sharing a room with seven other girls, some of whom snore and drool (like Jeanie). Even with a sleep mask, it takes forever for me to nod off, and when I finally do, I dream about the beach cabana. In the dream, I'm sipping a frozen smoothie and Margo is sitting next to me reading *Us Weekly*. A waiter walks by with a menu, and I notice he looks just like Ethan. Kate appears out of nowhere and whispers in his ear. Then she morphs into Jeanie, which is even stranger, but the worst part is when Ethan throws a slushy at me. I hear myself scream.

Wait, was that my scream?

There it is again!

I feel like I'm in a fog—half dream, half reality—and it takes me a second to realize I am not the one screaming. It's Addison.

"Eww! It's in my hair!" I think Camilla says. "They put it in my hair!"

"Mine too!" Trisha yells while Vickie cries. "Sam! SAM! We've been hit!"

That sounds like Trisha, but I don't care enough to find out. Maybe if I keep my eyes closed I'll fall back to sleep, but I keep hearing more voices.

"They put peanut butter on the floor!" Melody freaks. "Don't run or—" *BOOM!*

"Oh my God, are you okay? Melody, is that strawberry syrup in your hair?" Camilla's voice again. "Eww . . . what smells so funny?"

Part of me is annoyed about all this commotion. I want to get back to that dream and yell at Ethan about that slushy and . . . wait. Why do I feel wet?

My eyes shoot open. Where did my canopy go? Why am I sticky? I look down at my comforter and am amazed at the swirl of new colors decorating it. A river of what looks like honey, chocolate syrup, and whipped cream is oozing everywhere. It covers my sheets, and there is some in my hair. I look over the railing and sob when I see what has become of my Louis trunk. It's got peanut butter on the lid. Is that going to come off?

Without the canopy on my bed, I can see everyone's bunks perfectly. The view is not pretty. Someone has toilet papered the cabin, and streamers hang from every bed and rafter. Some have fallen to the ground and are sticking to the gooey mess on the floor. Camilla looks like a tree with leaves stuck in her hair and chocolate syrup oozing down her Whispering Pines Color

War tee that refers to the previous summer. Trisha is flipping out that someone put camouflage tape all over her pink lacrosse stick. Camilla is crying about her ruined Hello Kitty bed sheets, which look like a sundae gone wrong. Jeanie's red hair is sticking up as if she were the Bride of Frankenstein. Vickie's been moussed, and her face has some sort of white powder on it. Whoever did this is *good*. I wonder how they managed to do this without anyone hearing them.

I hear whimpering and look down. "Lina?" I call and don't get an answer. I pull myself out of my bed, trying not to freak out at the feeling of my legs touching the cold syrup. I throw my feet over the side and make my way halfway down the ladder before I burst out laughing. Lina's bed is a sea of feathers, and many are stuck to her face.

"They made me look like a chicken!" Lina sounds stunned as she peers in a mirror she has hanging from one of the bunk rails. Her eyes widen when she looks at me. "Did you try high-lighting your hair last night after I went to bed?"

I reach up to touch my head. "No, why?" I ask slowly.

Lina bites her lip. "Because your hair is sort of green. And if you didn't do it..."

I dart into the bathroom, but it takes a while to get near a mirror. The entire bunk is crowded in there. Someone has dumped what looks like marshmallow fluff all over the floor, and the room smells like Peeps, so everyone is moving slowly. Jeanie, Addison, Camilla, Vickie, Trisha, and Melody block my path, but I squeeze around them and gasp.

"My hair is Oscar the Grouch green!" I cry. Whoever

sprayed me did a horrible job. I have green streaks on my bangs, while other areas of my head are untouched.

Jeanie groans and tries to move her hair, which is sticking up on end. It barely sways. "I'm going to have to wash this four times to get all this out."

I look at her hair closely. "If we were closer to civilization, I would suggest going to a salon because they got you good." She whimpers as she looks in the mirror. "But since we're not, I've got some dry shampoo with me that you should start with so you don't strip all the shine out of your hair with so many washings."

"I don't need your help," she sniffs. I shrug.

"Look at me! They sprayed my hair pink!" Camilla cries before she notices Lina standing there. "No offense, but it is not my color. On you it looks somewhat normal."

"Thanks. I think." Lina plucks feathers out of her hair.

I look at Camilla's hair. "This is washable. You should be fine with a good shampoo, and I have plenty. You're all welcome to use my stuff," I tell them.

"Why didn't they do anything to your hair, Lina?" Trisha's rubbing hard at a Sharpie pen mustache on her face. It's not coming off.

Lina shrugs. "I guess they didn't see any need to touch it since it is already pink." She shows us her arms. There is black and red writing on it. "Instead they tattooed me." She reads something and laughs. " 'Daredevil in training' they wrote. That's me!"

"Kyle," I say before I can stop myself. Lina blushes. "I could see him doing that. He once drew Groucho Marx eyebrows on me the day before school pictures."

Addison takes a whiff of Vickie's shirt. "You smell like strawberries."

Vickie smells her shirt. "I do, don't I? Smells good."

"Guess whoever hit you likes you," Trisha grumbles. Her stick is next to the sink. I'm going to kill the guy who re-taped my lacrosse stick! Now I have to beg my mom to send new tape. She already thinks I tape the stick too much as it is."

I pick it up and look at the funky camouflage pattern. "I like it. Camo is all the rage again this season. I'd leave it like that."

Trisha takes it from my hand and looks at the stick again from all angles. "It is?" She looks at me strangely. "Thanks."

I'm taken aback by her politeness. "You're welcome."

"Ugh! What is that?" Jeanie sniffs loudly. "Does anyone else smell caramel? Between that, the strawberry syrup, and the fluff, I think I'm going to be sick."

"Me too." It's making me dizzy. I turn on the fan to get rid of the smell.

"No!" Camilla reaches her hand out to stop me, but it's too late.

The fan starts up, and in horror I see water balloons begin rolling off the fan blades. Girls shriek and jump out of the way as balloons drop to the ground in quick succession and burst, sending water everywhere, including all over Jeanie.

"Don't touch anything!" Jeanie is back to being cranky. Water drips from her pasty curls. "The cabin is probably booby-trapped—light switches, windows, doors—"

There is a scream from the hall and then the sound of more water balloons bursting. We push one another out of the way to get back into the cabin to see what is going on. I grimace. Sam and Courtney made the mistake of leaving their bedroom and got drenched. The other bunk comes out to see what happened. They look pretty bad, too.

"Cole and Thomas," Courtney growls as she brushes whipped cream off her polka-dot pajama pants. "They definitely put their bunks up to this!"

I imagine Ethan watching me sleep with my night guard in, and I shudder.

"Payback for winning the Mud-a-Thon," Sam says grimly and looks at her own bunk, which is standing in the doorway. It looks like they got hit worse than we did. At least no one glued packing popcorn to us. "I'm going to start helping my guys clean up." She shuffles slowly to her girls' bunk. Mine just stands there stunned.

Courtney wrings out her tank top, and water gushes all over the floor. "It's going to take hours for us to clean up this mess."

"We?" I look at the destruction around us. There is so much marshmallow fluff on the floor that it looks like a rug. All the windows have been whip creamed. Syrup oozes from the bunk beds and sticks to the feathers that are all over the floor and comforters. And that's all we've found so far. "Are you sure there isn't a camp raid–cleaning service that we could call? I'd be happy to pay for one if there is."

Actually, I think McDaddy took all my credit cards. He said it was a security measure. He feared I'd try to book a flight to London and hightail it out of here. I said he's watched that Lindsay Lohan version of *The Parent Trap* one too many times (he denies seeing it, but I've caught him watching it on the Disney Channel for "research").

Courtney shrugs. "Your cabin, your mess." Both bunks collectively groan, but I kind of smile. It feels good to be part of the action going on. I just wish the action didn't involve syrup in my slippers. "And it better not take all day to clean this up or you'll miss your chance to put the finishing touches on our London Blue spirit board."

Lina bites a strand of her hair. It's dipped in honey, so I push her hand away. "I can't miss the free period to work on my London drawing. It's not finished yet."

I nod. "It looked great yesterday. It's the best thing about that board."

I still think the camp could have done better than a spirit board, but that's the entry everyone wanted to work on. It's a giant board with pictures, camp memorabilia, and sayings. Beaver and I wanted a video. (The two of us are dying to sing a London number with the kitchen crew and post it to YouTube, but that sort of thing is not allowed.) London loves when fans do something original. The spirit board is *not* original. I don't want to bust Lina's bubble though, so I haven't said what I really think.

"Don't worry about the spirit board. I've—" *SPEW!* Sam gets a feather stuck in her mouth. She looks like she's going to gag as she pulls it out. "We'll get free time to work on it. I'll ask Hitch if he can do inspections on our cabin later today."

"Say a toilet overflowed," Courtney suggests.

Gross! I know this isn't why McDaddy sent me here, but I have a newfound appreciation for Marisol.

"See you all later," Sam says, sounding dejected as she heads back to her bunk with her girls. One girl drags a strand of toilet paper glued to her shirt behind her.

I stare at the wall behind Courtney. Chocolate syrup and caramel are oozing down it. The guys must have taken supplies yesterday morning when we were working in the kitchen. And here I thought Ethan and Kyle were trying to be nice to Lina and me. Kyle must be gloating right now. He'll want a point for hitting our bunk without us knowing, which means he has five points to my two. *Grr...*

Courtney looks at us and sighs. "They hit us much harder than they did last year."

"And so early, too," Jeanie whines. "It's only the second week of camp!"

"Didn't you guys strike the third night we were here last year?" Courtney asks, and Jeanie clams up. "Cole said it took them days to get the toothpaste and shaving cream smell out of that bunk. They had to sleep on the porch."

"Our strike was a masterpiece," Jeanie says with a far-off look in her eyes. "Remember the beard we drew on Justin?" she asks Camilla.

"Epic," Camilla recalls. "Like the sideburns we gave Ethan." They all laugh.

"Yep, it was fun till you guys used permanent marker," Courtney reminds them. "It took weeks for those Sharpie hair designs to rub off." She tries to smudge Melody's mustache. Melody's lip trembles. "It's payback time."

"Are you saying this is a regular occurrence?" I ask. Everyone nods.

"It's a raid." Melody continues to rub at the marks on her face. "All the bunks do this sort of thing on the down low. I should have known they were going to hit us," she grumbles. "They were so nice to you yesterday when you made that french toast."

"Well, it was good," I defend myself.

"It has nothing to do with french toast," Courtney tells us. "You guys have had this rivalry ever since that year we tried guys versus girls in Color War and the girls lost."

Camilla growls. "Well, we're going to make them pay for doing this to us. We have to strike back hard and soon."

"Before you plot the end of the boys' world as they know it, why don't you clean yourselves up." Courtney waves us off to the bathroom. "That's what I'm going to do."

No one argues. Jeanie, Addison, Melody, Vickie, Trisha, and Camilla take off at a run. There's only four shower stalls, so Lina and I don't bother moving fast.

"Feel free to use that stuff I told you to!" I yell to them as Lina and I wait by our bunk beds for our turn. Courtney trudges by us. "Do you have anything that will get this chocolate syrup stench off me?" she asks.

"Purple bottle that says Falling in Love Summer by Philosophy," I say immediately. "Fresh, floral, with a hint of romance. Second cubby down."

"Thanks," Courtney says.

"Harper!" I hear Camilla and Addison call me at the same time. I look at Lina, then run into the bathroom. The showers are already steamy. Jeanie is surprisingly waiting for her turn. She barely looks at me when I walk in.

"Harper, the pink isn't coming out!" Camilla cries from her stall.

"Try this!" I hand her my strongest shampoo, the one I bought when I tried dyeing my hair red once (it wasn't a good look for me).

"I can't find that dry shampoo stuff!" Addison complains as she raids my cubby.

I walk to my cubby and find Addison's product. "Do this twice, then wash your hair." I offer Jeanie a bottle. "This detangler works wonders on curls. Want to try it?"

"I'm fine on my own, thanks," she says stiffly.

"Let her help you," Addison says surprisingly. "I think Camping Barbie really knows what she's doing in this area." I curtsy, and Addison actually laughs!

"God, you'd think you girls had never been through a raid before," Jeanie sniffs. "You don't need Harper's help to clean up. Dove soap does the trick every time." She catches me wrinkling my nose. "What's wrong with Dove?"

"Nothing," I say quickly. "Except it's, well, Dove."

"Harper, do you have any nice-smelling shower gel?" Vickie asks from her stall. "I can still smell shave gel on my skin."

Trisha pokes her head out of her shower. "Anything that can rub off marker?"

As Jeanie glares at me, I hand Vickie a bottle of my Philosophy shower gel that I save for special occasions and give Trisha my Bliss body scrub. "Scrub, but don't scrub too hard. You'll just make your skin raw," I instruct.

"Wow, maybe you should thank the boys," Lina tells me as Jeanie huffily goes back to the bunk to wait for her turn to shower. "This raid has put you in high demand."

"Maybe I'm getting somewhere," I say as the girls all call out new requests. An hour later, we're all as clean as we're going to get. I still can't get that mustache off Melody, but I've promised to send a Bunk One e-mail to my girl at Nordstrom who does my makeup for McDaddy events and find out what to do. She seemed grateful. So did Camilla for that industrial shampoo. Her hair looks clean and luxurious now.

Now we're—*sigh*—cleaning. Lina and Addison have buckets and sponges while Jeanie is filling black garbage bags with whatever she can pick up. Camilla is stripping our sheets for Courtney to take to the laundry. Vickie is wiping down the furniture. Melody and Trisha agreed to help me scrub the walls. I close my eyes as I begin to wipe down syrup and toilet paper with my sponge, holding back the urge to get sick all over it.

"So," Addison says a few minutes after Courtney has left with our laundry, "Jeanie, how are we going to make them pay?"

"Oh, so now you want my help," she says. I know that look. It's the one Kate gives me anytime Margo asks my opinion over her own.

"Of course!" Camilla looks at her strangely. "You always plan the raids."

That pleases her. "I say we strike tonight while they're least expecting it."

"That will be when they are most expecting it," I disagree, and everyone looks at me. "Think about it. They'll probably have whipped cream cans aimed at anyone who comes through their bunk door."

"I'm with Camping Barbie on this one," Melody admits, and Jeanie frowns.

"Me too," says Lina. "Who else agrees?" Everyone but Camilla and Jeanie raises their hands.

"What does she know? She's been here a week!" Jeanie cries. "I'm a Lifer. I know this place better than anyone." Camilla clears her throat. "Well, as well as you guys do." She stares me down. "*You* got lost on your way back from the main office yesterday."

I shrug. "All the trails here look the same."

"The point is, you have no clue how the Pines works," Jeanie says. "Leave the raids to those of us who have done it before."

"Are you saying Harper can't offer suggestions?" Lina looks menacing right now. The other girls look at her. "She's trying to help here."

"That's not what I said!" Jeanie sighs. "I need time to think. The smell in here is still making me nauseated."

"I could light a candle," I suggest. "I still held on to one."

"No," they all say at the same time, and I shrug.

"We don't have time to debate this," Camilla tells Jeanie. "The decision is up to you—do we strike tonight or do you think we should go with Harper and strike in a few days? Before or after the first overnight camping trip? That's three days away."

I can't keep quiet any longer. "What if we got them back this Saturday after the All-Camp Night? We go to bed late, so everyone will be tired and they'll never see us coming."

"I like it," Addison says. "Sneak attack!" The others murmur their agreement. Lina looks worriedly at Jeanie. She does *not* look pleased, but I don't care. Now that I have their attention, I can't stop talking.

"I don't know what you guys usually use for raids, but I would do something completely different." I pick up a whipped cream can and throw it in the garbage. "Forget syrups. Let's put glue on plastic wrap and hang it over the doorways so they get stuck in it when they try to go to the bathroom." Vickie applauds. "And let's put something super sticky on the floor like Fruit Roll-Ups, so they can't walk." Trisha and Melody cheer.

"Fruit Roll-Ups?" Jeanie looks disgusted, and I'm not sure if it's because of my suggestion or because she's holding a whipped-cream-covered lamp.

"I like it! That will be easy to get our hands on," Addison says.

"I saw it in a movie once," I say. "I've got loads of ideas like that one. I helped the seniors at our school plan the Halloween fun house last year, so I know how to make really disgusting things. I just wear rubber gloves while I work." Everyone laughs.

"Well, I guess Harper is running our raid then," Jeanie says, and I do a double take at her abrupt change in attitude. "I know when I'm beat," she tells the others. "I can't wait to see what you come up with. You said Saturday night, right?"

"Saturday night," I repeat, practically beaming. Jeanie is agreeing with me for the first time ever! "I'll have everything ready."

Jeanie offers me a thin smile. "I'm sure you will."

Harper McAllister @HarperMc
Camp tip: Only a security camera could stop
nighttime raids, but that's okay. We'll get them back.
#revengewillbesweet

12

GET PACKING

LINA EYES MY OVERNIGHT BAGS warily. "I think you may have overpacked."

I look at my two Louis Vuitton duffel bags and frown. One has swimsuits and pajamas; the other is clothes and hair accessories for any type of weather (torrential rain: headbands; wind storm: hair ties). The hipster slung across my waist holds my makeup, bug spray, and a heinous reality-TV-star fragrance Kyle gave me for Christmas that I am sure will ward off bears and mountain lions. I've never been "real" camping before— as opposed to "fake" camping—which is what everyone says Whispering Pines is. *Not* camping would have suited me just fine, too, but Courtney didn't buy my whole "Beaver needs me in the kitchen" excuse. So here we are.

"Haven't you ever seen *Doomsday Preppers*? I'm in survival mode," I tell Lina. "What if we get into the woods and we forgot our toothbrushes? Or toilet paper?" I pat one of my duffels. "I'm prepared for any situation."

"Prepared would have been taking that survival elective I am in," Lina says. "The obstacle course was insane! Kyle and I had the same time for the course yesterday."

"Glad you're having fun with it. I am perfectly happy in pottery," I say. I hate not taking all my electives with Lina—Margo, Kate, and I do everything together at Friends Prep—but I cannot survive boxing, Tai Chi, softball, or whatever else she has planned next. "I pulled a calf muscle while paddleboarding, even though I never moved my legs."

"You did not pull a calf muscle!" Lina says, and we both laugh.

The cabin door springing open startles us. The two of us go quiet as our bunkmates file out behind Jeanie. We're both still upset that they left us out of the raid on the boys' bunk. The wannabe Merida doesn't make eye contact with me, but I think she can feel my anger. I'm channeling Darth Vader at the moment.

"We're heading to the canteen before the hike. Do you need anything?" Addison asks us tentatively. They're all wearing hiking boots. I've only got my bedazzled Chucks.

"Already went," Lina says curtly. "Thanks."

Addison nods. I notice her guiltily glance my way and then quickly look at the lake again. Vickie and Trisha stare at the tattered porch floor. "Okay then. See you in a bit." She starts to leave, but Jeanie puts out a hand to stop her.

"Those bags are kind of large for an overnight trip," Jeanie says, pointing to the duffels at my feet. My bunkmates' bags are lined up on the porch. Everyone has hiking backpacks, which are much smaller than my duffels. Lina included. "Any chance you're moving out?" Jeanie asks boldly, and Camilla stifles a giggle. That's the last time I give her my good shampoo.

The hairs on my arm stand up. I take a step toward Jeanie, and she takes a step back. "You'd like that, wouldn't you?" I say quietly, and the rest of the girls watch us. Lina grabs my arm, but she needn't worry. "It's not happening."

Jeanie shrugs. "Your loss. Just like the raid all over again." She smiles sweetly. "I can't believe I forgot to tell you about the change in plans, especially when you gave us such good ideas for getting back at the boys. The sticky plastic wrap trick was a real winner. Ethan and the guys still don't know how we came up with it." She and Camilla laugh and hurry down the porch steps after Addison and Vickie. I notice Melody and Trisha look back at me before following her.

When they're out of sight, I drop to the porch floor with a thud. "Maybe I should pack it in," I say to Lina. "I can't plan a raid without it being stolen out from under me, and I've failed Camping Trip Packing 101 before we've even left. Who knows what will happen if I actually hike into the woods?" I sit on one of my bags. "I bet today isn't even the overnight trip. Jeanie just wants you and me to *think* it is." I glare at our cabin, which is the place where Jeanie's deception started. "She'll also probably give me directions to the wrong campsite, and you'll have to send out a search party."

Lina sits down on the floor next to me. "That's not going

to happen. We all travel together." I look at her. "But I know what you mean. What Jeanie did with the raid was rotten. I can't believe the rest of the bunk let her get away with that."

I place my elbows on my knees and bite my nail. Lina swats my hands away. "I'm smart!" I say. "I should have realized Jeanie was never going to let the bunk go with my suggestion. Instead she took all my ideas—and the Fruit Roll-Ups Mom FedExed—and used them herself."

"Did you see Addison's and the other girls' faces just now?" Lina asks me. "You can tell they feel bad about leaving us out, but no one goes against Jeanie."

I wonder if Ethan realizes Lina and I weren't there that night. Even though Jeanie and Ethan are not going out, it bothers me that she got to play a trick on him and I didn't. He saw me drool in my sleep! I should have been able to see what kind of pj's he wears to bed. Does he snore or does he sleep like a baby? Jeanie knows and I don't. But why do I care? To Ethan, I'm just Camping Barbie.

"She had me fooled, too," Lina reminds me. "I should have known something was off the way she kept complimenting my London Blue drawing."

"Your London Blue drawing *is* good," I tell her. "Why do you think Hitch wants it to anchor the board? It's brilliant, just like my ideas for the raid were brilliant. The only way raiding last night would have been better is if the girls hit the boys' bunk so hard they weren't able to clean up in time to go on the overnight camping trip. Then we would have had to cancel it." I stare dreamily at the lake. "I would have loved that."

"I have something that will cheer you up." Lina gets up and goes to her backpack and pulls out a piece of loose-leaf paper. "I was going to give it to you tonight after you survived your first hike, but I think you need it now." She hands me the paper. "Presenting *Super* Camping Barbie!"

It's a drawing of me in a shiny red cape and high white boots. My hair is whipping around as I fly over the Pines in the cutest dress I've ever seen. On the top Lina's written: "She's braver than she looks! She's stronger than they realize! She's going to take the whole camp by storm! She's Super Camping Barbie!"

"I love it." I feel teary. I can't remember the last time a friend did something for me. Kate and Margo may buy me jeans, but that's nothing like this. "Thank you."

"You're welcome." Lina grins. "I wanted you to see that you're better at camp stuff than you think." She plays with one of her pink braids. "I'm glad you're here."

I hear an animal calling in the distance, and I jump. "That came from the woods, didn't it?" I ask. "The woods we're going to now. For twenty-four hours! Outside! With real animals! *Big* animals!" Suddenly I feel very sweaty and am ready to hyperventilate. "I love you, Lina, but I've got to find Courtney and get out of this trip. When she mentioned overnighters, I thought she meant to places like Boston, Rhode Island, or Six Flags, where we would stay in a hotel. Not sleeping in the woods. Is it hotter all of a sudden?" I clutch my chest.

"You're going to be fine," Lina says, and breathes in and out hoping I'll copy her. "I'm going to be there with you. Hiking is a piece of cake. I'm just bummed they canceled the regular first camping trip—white-water rafting. It's too bad the river overflowed."

My eyes nearly pop out of my head. "Yeah, too bad."

"Rafting is so much more of an adrenaline rush," Lina says. "Hiking is meditative. And then once we get there and set up camp, it's fun. We have sing-alongs, make s'mores, and tell ghost stories."

"Do any of them involve a city girl getting eaten by a mountain lion?" I ask.

"You've seen one too many horror movies." Lina reties her hiking boots. She's got all the hiking must-haves—compass, binoculars, birdcall whistle.

The screen door to the cabin slams again. Courtney is wearing jean shorts and an official camp tee with a sweatshirt. She has a *small* backpack on. Yep, I overpacked.

I am also overdressed in a chiffon halter top. I still refuse to dumb down my fashion for camp. I even bedazzled my Converse sneakers with pink and silver rhinestones to give them a little bling. When I get home, I'm thinking of suggesting to McDaddy that we create a camp fashion line for fashion-forward campers like myself.

"You ladies ready to go?" Courtney asks. "Where is everyone else?"

"They ran to the canteen for snacks," Lina says.

I stand up and feel my legs almost buckle. "I'm not sure I'm ready for this," I tell Courtney. "I think my breakfast is ready to come back up, and I only had a grapefruit."

Courtney looks skeptically at my bags. She lifts one. "You're not going to make it a quarter of a mile up the trail with this load, and we've got quite a walk to the campsite. Hitch already dropped off all our camping equipment. The most you need is a change or two of clothes, your swimsuit, and bug spray. What do you have in this thing? Bricks?"

"She's ready for the end of the world," Lina tells her.

"We'll be back tomorrow by noon, so you do not need to bring your whole trunk," Courtney says. I start to protest. "You can shower right away when you get back, so you don't need any toiletries, either. Camping is about roughing it. Start repacking."

I drop to my knees again. "Fine." I look at the duffels sadly. Sorry, old friends. I guess this is one trip you're too good for. Wish the same could be said for me.

Harper McAllister @HarperMc
Overnight camping trip starts now. If you don't hear from me in 24 hours, alert Good Morning America and send a search party! #ihatecamping

13

INTO THE WILD

WHEN COURTNEY SAID "HIT THE road," I didn't know she meant literally, but a half hour later, the marshmallows are hiking down the road like hitchhikers. Lina says this is a back road out of camp that the food vendors use, so there is little chance of us being run over, but I'm more worried about passing out. Cole, Thomas, Courtney, and Sam keep yelling out camp songs for us to sing and are forcing us to play I Spy. I'm so winded from walking, I can barely speak, let alone think of where Sam is looking when she says, "I spy a sign that says 'No firearms in this area.'"

"Five points," Kyle sings as he passes by me. Ethan is walking with him. I don't comment on his green hair. "Ready to make it six to two?" Kyle asks. "That's going to be the score when you ditch the hike." I'm trying not to laugh in his face. He has a green goatee drawn on his chin.

"Ignore him," Lina says to me.

"Or I'll tell you what." Kyle keeps going. "If you make it through the campout, you can have three whole points to make us even again. *If.* I know there is no way you're trekking two miles to the site," he adds. "Maybe if you were an alicorn like Twilight Sparkle and could just fly there."

Lina's head practically spins off. "You're a brony?" Kyle nods. "Did you like the episode where—"

The two of them pick up their pace as they get into a deep My Little Pony discussion. I can't keep up with them. Nor do I want to discuss Ponyville politics. Kyle and Lina are so fast, soon they've caught up with the rest of the pack. Jeanie, Camilla, and Addison are in the lead with Cole and Thomas, followed closely by Sam, Courtney, and all the campers, including Sam's bunk and the rest of mine. Justin, Heath, and Dirk have partnered up with Vickie, Melody, and Trisha. Ethan and I are now bringing up the rear.

"Not a brony?" Ethan asks me. His hair has a green hue, but he's dressed appropriately for camping in a fitted navy tee with a slogan I don't recognize and lacrosse shorts. Suddenly I feel foolish for wearing chiffon. It may be pretty, but I am sweating. I wish I could change, but I don't think there is a changing room where I'm going. Just tents. I shudder.

"The only club I belong to is 'fashionistas,'" I joke.

"Hence the Camping Barbie title," he says. His expression changes. "Does the nickname bother you at all?"

I shrug. "A little, but I'm trying not to let it get to me. The truth is, I'm a girly girl who prefers facials to camping. Might as well embrace the title."

Ethan looks impressed. He hikes his backpack higher. "I'd say 'good for you,' but I'm still a little bitter about my green hair." He gives me a hard look. "And the fact that I've been cleaning up smushed Fruit Roll-Ups all morning. Thanks for that. And this." He holds up his left hand, and I see there is Sharpie written on his arm. "HIT ME. I DESERVE IT!" it reads. He gives me a smile that could melt a Popsicle in seconds. "Although I must admit, whoever's idea it was to put glue on plastic wrap and hang it in a doorway is a genius. Dirk walked right into it when he was racing to the bathroom to get shaving cream out of his hair."

"That was my idea," I say proudly. I just wasn't there to put the plan in action.

"Smooth," Ethan says admiringly. "Did you also come up with the idea to put Fruit Roll-Ups on the floor?"

"Yes, but I'm sure Jeanie will say that was all her idea." I try not to sound bitter, but Ethan still looks at me strangely. "Lina and I weren't part of the raid," I admit. "We wanted to do it after All-Camp Night. Jeanie agreed, but then I guess she decided to do it last night instead without us. Maybe she didn't want me to miss my beauty sleep."

Ethan grimaces. "Red can be tough to deal with sometimes."

Red. He even has a cute nickname for her. Gag. I wipe my mouth with my hand before I realize what I'm doing is completely unlady-like. I can't help it. I am sweating in this grueling heat! I swear, camp is ripping away at my proper-girl image bit by bit. I lean too far back for a second and nearly fall backward.

"Whoa, are you okay?" Ethan asks. "Let me carry that for you for a bit." I don't argue when he slips my backpack off my shoulders and slings it over his arm. "Geez, what do you have in here?"

"Essentials." I may have left my survival gear, but I was not heading into the woods without a good humidity-busting hairspray.

"Don't sweat Jeanie," he tells me. "She's been fiery ever since we started at the Pines together. Once you get to know her, she'll back off. She's just protective of this place."

"And who am I? A logger bent on destroying the Pines to make paper out of the cabins?" I ask angrily. "Of course you'd take her side. You're both Lifers." I try to speed up to get away from him. Sadly, I am not that fast.

"Harper, wait," Ethan says. "I'm sorry, okay? That was stupid of me to say. Jeanie and I have been friends for a long time, but you're my friend, too."

We're friends now? I stop, but I won't look at him. The others are barely a dot in a distance. Any minute they're going to go over that next hill, and who knows which way they will go next. I kind of need Ethan's help here, but I'm too mad to even look at him.

He hesitates. "Being popular has always come easily for you, but camp is different. Most of us have grown up together. They've seen me make a fool of myself in a blueberry pie–eating contest and when I'm full of myself for winning Color War and need a bucket of water dumped on my head. The people who go here are as real as they get, so they're a little more guarded about who they let into their fold."

Real. I don't think I've ever seen Kate without eyeliner. Margo maybe (she loves listening to Bruno Mars while she wears slices of cucumbers on her eyelids). "Everyone here seems like family," I admit as we trudge uphill. Why can't hikes be on flat roads?

"They are," Ethan agrees. "Which is why they don't open up overnight."

Kate let me in the first day I met her. We've been shopping together ever since. I've always considered us the three amigos, but when I think of Lina's gift this morning, I have to wonder what defines a real friend. Is it someone with a lot of rules to the friendship or someone who likes you without conditions? I'm not saying any of this to Ethan. I'm still annoyed that he is such a Lifer like the rest of them. "They have two weeks to let me in. After that I'm out of— OUCH!" I stumble a bit. "Foot stings! I need a pedicurist STAT!"

"Let me look." Ethan drops to his knees to examine my right leg. "Nice Chucks."

"I bedazzled them myself," I say through the pain. "I just wish I hadn't washed them the other night. They're so tight now I can't wear socks with them." He massages my calf, and I flinch.

"I don't think it's your leg that bothers you—you have a blister on your heel," Ethan says. "You're not going to make it around the next bend if we don't get you a Band-Aid. Sit."

I don't argue, even if I feel weird having him help me after I just bit his head off. I take a seat on a large rock on the side of the road as he rummages around his backpack. Ethan's really organized. All his clothes are rolled tight, and he has Ziploc bags with a first-aid kit, bug spray, and other mini products. He hands me two Band-Aids and a pair of bright pink socks. "Put these on. And don't tell me you are anti-socks."

I look at the rolled-up pink socks. "Nope. These are actually cool."

"They should be. They're my lucky basketball socks." He blushes. "I wear them every game. I play on the same team as Kyle, you know."

"I know." *I've just never taken the time to talk to you,* I think guiltily. I pull off my shoes, stick Band-Aids on my blisters, and then gently pull the socks on. They go up to my knees. "These look good on me! Can't you just see me racing down a basketball court?"

Ethan makes an indistinguishable noise. "Running down a basketball court is exactly how I picture a girl who gets out of PE half the year on account of her asthma."

My jaw drops. "How do you know about my asthma fake out?"

"I was in the main office one time when Coach Biggins came in complaining your excuse was a scam," Ethan says with a smirk. "There was nothing they could do about it because you had a doctor's note. How'd you sweet-talk yourself into getting one of those?"

I swing my feet happily. "I have a non-athletic cousin who just became a pediatrician. She feels my pain."

He laughs. "You are something else, Harper McAllister." He stands up and offers me his hand. I can feel the heat of his hand against my palm, and it makes my stomach do a somersault.

Oh, man. I officially have a crush on a boy who is friends with a girl I loathe. How did this happen?

I stand up and let go of his hand. "This is much better. Thanks," I say awkwardly.

Ethan puts his backpack on again. "Don't mention it."

I wave my hand, hoping to make a breeze. "Has it gotten hotter?"

"No." Ethan stares at my outfit. "It's because you're wearing jeans."

"I know." I stare down at my chiffon top and capris. "This outfit is all wrong for a camping trip. Now I'm stuck wearing it till tomorrow."

"Why till tomorrow?" Ethan asks. "Didn't you bring a change of clothes?"

I look at him like he's insane. "Yes, but I'm not actually changing in the woods."

He grins. "Um, we do have these things called tents, you know."

"I'm not sleeping in those or catching my own dinner or bathing in the lake, either."

Ethan scratches his head. "This is a *campout*, not a survival training course. Beaver sent hamburgers, hot dogs, and lemonade. You can go fishing, but you're not catching your own dinner. And the tents are huge and have bottoms."

"Oh." I didn't realize any of that.

"Before you say anything else, let me just add that I've never seen a bear here," Ethan adds. "Justin and I think we saw a yeti once, but that's never been documented."

A yeti? My face goes from hot to cold. Those things are real? "We should get a move on."

Beads of sweat roll down Ethan's forehead. "Think you can do a jog to catch up?"

"How about we walk fast, but not so fast that we get there in time for tent setup?"

He shakes his head. "Funny. You're definitely not the girl I thought you were."

I push my long layers away from my face. "Is that a bad thing?" My face feels even warmer, if that's possible. I have an urge to bite my nails when he stares at me like he is doing right now.

"No." Ethan gives me a half smile. "You're just different. I thought a girl like you would be out of here day one, but you're sticking with it. That's pretty cool in my book."

Ethan effortlessly hikes uphill, even with the two bags on his back. It's easier to keep up now that my feet aren't crying. In fact, now that we have a good pace going, I kind of like it. We're both quiet for a bit, and that's okay because I'm just enjoying the view. The path ropes lazily around giant pine trees and flowering bushes. Wildflowers grow here and there along the way and make me wonder how no one has stepped on them before. Other than the birds chirping, it's so quiet I can hear our feet pounding the dirt path. He turns right, and we follow everyone's footprints just a little farther. I can see smoke coming from what I pray is a grill (not a forest fire about to consume half an acre and me in minutes like in the nightmare I had last night). I'm bummed when I realize we've reached the campsite. I liked having Ethan to myself.

Ethan turns to me. "Not scary, right?" Campers are raising tents and unrolling sleeping bags. A few guys and girls from the other marshmallows bunks are playing a game of touch football in the clearing. Hitch is at the grill making hot dogs. There is even music playing on someone's iPod shuffle. Dirk, Heath, and Justin are moving some logs around what looks like a campfire.

"It doesn't have horror movie written all over it, at least," I say. "But I still don't think I can put my head on the ground. Spiders. Worms." I shudder. "What if they start crawling on me in my sleep? But if I sleep outside the tent, they could still climb on me and then I could be eaten by a bear, too." I grab Ethan by his T-shirt and pull him toward me. He looks alarmed. "Maybe I could swim to safety and go back to the Pines. Although that lake over there looks big. A canoe, maybe? Did you bring a raft in that handy backpack of yours?"

Kyle jogs toward us. "Is she having a panic attack about the bugs again?" Lina, Heath, and Justin walk over behind him.

Ethan nods as I continue to grip his shirt. "I think so. I'm afraid to move."

"Hey, H?" Kyle waves a hand in between my face and Ethan's. "You in there?"

I let go of Ethan. I'm hyperventilating like I really do have asthma. I look at Lina. "I should go back to camp. Tell Courtney to radio the chopper to come pick me up."

"Chopper?" Lina questions. "Harper, there's no—"

I twitch as I hear an owl hoot in the distance. "Or a van? Maybe a nice Jeep? I like Jeeps even if they are open in the back half the time and I could get mauled by a yeti."

"Dude!" Justin hits Ethan in the arm. "You told her about our yeti sighting?"

"It was not a yeti!" Lina jumps in. "It was an overgrown bush."

"Oh yeah?" Justin asks. "Then why did it have teeth?"

I can barely hear what they're saying. My eyes are on those tents. I have an aversion to spiders. Did I mention that to Courtney before? Why wasn't that a question in the "getting to know you at the Pines" pamphlet Hitch handed out?

"I think Harper needs to sit down," Ethan says. He puts a hand on my back. I cringe when I think of how sweaty I must be.

"Ethan!" Jeanie yells to him from the field where she's hanging out with Addison, Camilla, and my bunkmates. Her hair looks even prettier pulled off her face in a ponytail. She's wearing a green football jersey and cutoff shorts. The look is adorable. I dislike her even more than I did this morning. "We're playing capture the flag. You in?"

"Ethan! Ethan!" My bunkmates chant. Behind them, Dirk and a few guys from the other boys' bunk are tossing a football.

Ethan's eyes meet mine. "Want to play?"

I shake my head. "As much as it kills me, I think I'll sit this one out," I quip.

"You're going to play though, right?" Kyle asks Lina.

"Of course!" She looks at me and hesitates. "If that's okay with you."

"Go!" I tell her. "I'm going to get a drink and look for marshmallows. Roasting one sounds just my speed about now."

"Save me one," Ethan says, and then he and Lina jog over to meet the others.

The afternoon goes quicker than I would imagine an afternoon in the middle of nowhere with no technology would be. I manage to calm down a bit about the bug situation, and Cole stirs up the boy-versus-girl bunk rivalry again with a nasty game of dodgeball that ends with Melody getting a fat lip. That keeps her from joining us on the lake for a jump on one of those giant inflatable trampolines. I shock everyone by staying on longer than anyone (I don't reveal that Kyle and I have done this before in Cabo San Lucas). I don't even notice dusk approaching because I'm enjoying my hamburger so much. They really do taste better on a charcoal grill! Then Thomas lights the campfire, and Hitch tells a story in the form of Mad Libs, where we each contribute a word. Dirk does one completely on his own, and the result is so hilarious I almost spit out my lemonade all over Kyle and Lina. We play for so long that it takes me a minute to realize what is happening when people get up from the campfire and start to turn in. That's when my heart starts to pound again.

"Ready for bed?" Lina asks through a half yawn.

I put another marshmallow on my stick and place the end in the dwindling fire. "Um...I'll be there in a minute. I'm still hungry."

She nods and heads to our tent, which looks perfectly nice, if you like tents.

I sit quietly and watch the campers disperse around me. Courtney is still sitting on the other edge of the fire with Sam, their heads close as they talk softly. Cole is helping someone find a lantern so they can head out to the "bathroom" in the dark while Thomas and Hitch secure the camp for the night. I can hear Jeanie, Camilla, Melody, and Addison, who squeezed into a tent made for two, giggling across the way. Vickie and Trisha are in the tent next to theirs, which is next to the guys from Thomas's bunk. I stare at the crackling fire and lose myself in the amber colors, which are making me sleepy. I feel a tap on my shoulder.

"Ethan!" I jump. "Hey."

"Hey." He crouches down next to me, looking like he's about to make a break for it. If he is, he's taking me with him. "What do you think of your first campout?"

"It hasn't been as bad as I thought it would be," I admit.

"Are you turning in?" Ethan asks.

I resist the urge to bite my nails in front of him. "I'm going to wait it out a bit. I still have some s'mores left to eat."

He half grins. "Haven't you eaten like a dozen?"

"Maybe." I act indignant. "Who's counting?"

He shakes his head. "Again, not what I'd expect from someone who sits with girls who eat salad with fat-free dressing at lunch."

"You're the one who said the beauty of camp is being yourself," I tease. "I'm being true to me, and I have decided I really like s'mores."

He offers me his hand. "I think I've found something you'll like even better. Come with me."

I wonder if he's letting me sleep in his tent so he can protect me against spiders. My cheeks flush at the thought.

"Just taking a bathroom run," Ethan says to Thomas and Hitch when we walk past them. They're too involved to even reply. Most of the campers have already gone to their tents. I can see their lanterns glowing and the shadows of people inside talking. Ethan moves in the opposite direction of our campsite and heads into the darkness. I tug on his arm.

"Are you sure you know where we're going?" I try to keep the panic out of my voice. I'm not sure it's working.

"Yep, just a few feet farther." He waves the lantern in front of him to light the way. "There it is." He shines the light on a tree, and I see a ladder. "Start climbing."

"Where are we?" I ask, but Ethan is already on the way up. I have no choice but to follow or be swallowed up by the darkness around us. The sounds of the forest seem louder than they were at the campfire. I hear an owl hoot in the distance, and the hair on my arms stands up. I can still see the glow of the tents, so we're not that far away, but it's pitch-black out here. I've only climbed a few feet when I feel Ethan grab my hand again.

"You've reached the top. Just pull yourself up."

"The top?" I pull myself onto a platform and look around in awe. "It's a tree house!"

"It's been here for years," Ethan says. He places his lantern on the floor, and the light fills up the tiny space. The cabin is entirely made of wood and has a low roof and a few windows from which I can see the campfire perfectly. "They used to use it as a lookout when they did camping trips out here more often. We used it last year when we were doing a Color War game, so I remembered it when you were freaking out."

Freaking out is kind of a harsh term . . . but true.

"I needed a few minutes to find it, but when I did and saw it was fine, I thought I'd bring you here." Ethan's smile has an amber glow to it in the lantern light. "Beats sleeping on the hard ground with spiders, doesn't it?"

Ethan went looking for this place just for me. I'm incredibly touched and not sure what to say. Maybe he doesn't think I'm

Camping Barbie after all. Could he actually like me back? "Am I allowed to stay up here?"

He shrugs. "I don't see why not. I was thinking of going back down and telling Lina where you are though. She can bring back your sleeping bags, but you can hold on to my lantern. I brought a flashlight with me to get back. Just get to your tent before breakfast, which, I warn you, will be early. People rise with the sun on these trips."

"Don't use my sleep mask. Got it." The space is cozy and feels secure from a bear attack. Or a yeti. If you believe in those sorts of things. I realize Ethan is staring at me, waiting for me to say something. "Thanks for finding this for me, Ethan," I say shyly. "If you hadn't, I probably would have eaten myself sick on s'mores all night."

"And thrown up the whole hike back," Ethan says. "I'm really saving myself." He heads over to the ladder and pulls out his flashlight. I watch him throw his legs over the side. "So you'll be okay up here?" His eyes are searching. "Until I send Lina back?"

I smile. "I think I'll be just fine."

And for the first time since I came to the Pines, I really mean it.

Harper McAllister @HarperMc
Seeing my first sunrise from a tree house.
#survivingthesummer

14

IF YOU'RE HAPPY AND YOU KNOW IT

"NICE SHIRT," KYLE SAYS WHEN I run into him.

I look down at my new-and-improved Whispering Pines tee as campers in boring identical red shirts file into the Pines Theater around us. We're on our way to All-Camp Night. Lanterns cast a cool glow on my shirt in the evening light. "Thanks! It gives it a little something extra, don't you think?"

I got bored when it rained all day yesterday, so I bedazzled the camp logo on my tee with silver rhinestones, fringed the bottom, and added sparkly beads. Lina wanted hers done just like mine, and it came out so awesome that Trisha, Vickie, and Addison asked me to fix up theirs, too. This started a war with Jeanie and Camilla, who couldn't help stating—loudly—that the shirt looked ridiculous and we were going to get in trouble for tampering with the tee. Then Addison went to the camp rule book and snippily said there was nothing in it about tee tampering, and we all started arguing about camp wear, which turned into a fight about Color War.

It was a long day.

I wouldn't admit this to Mom in my e-mail last night, but my time here has gone quicker than I imagined. I can't believe that in two Saturdays, McDaddy'll be here to pick me up.

"Are you going to wear that shirt at home?" Kyle teases. "If so, I should write our camp challenge score on the back: Kyle: eight, Harper: two."

"Ha-ha," I say, and the crickets singing in the night seem to laugh along with me. "I have *five* points now, by the way. You said if I survived the campout, I got three points, so that gives me five to your eight. I still don't think *you* deserved three points for making it through the campout, though. You weren't afraid of being attacked by a yeti."

"Yeah, but you cheated when your boyfriend found you a tree house to sleep in," Kyle says.

"He's not my boyfriend," I say quickly, looking around to make sure neither Ethan nor my bunkmates heard my brother say that. "We're just friends."

Kyle shrugs. "You seem pretty tight for friends."

"So do you and Lina," I point out as a group of campers race by us to get into the theater. "Be good to her," I warn him. "I don't want my friend to get hurt."

Kyle is taken aback. "Look at you being all protective. The most you say about Kate and Margo is 'stop calling them users!'" he mimics my voice. "Which they are."

"They're not," I say. "Margo sent me that great Kiehl's gift basket just yesterday."

"What's Kate sent you?" Kyle asks. "Photos of things she wants you to buy for her when you get home?"

"Ouch!" I say. He really does have her pegged. The only time I heard from Kate was when she wanted to borrow my clothes. Meanwhile, Margo has written twice, sent the Kiehl's basket, and says she's counting down the days till I get home. "Just be nice to Lina, okay?" I tell Kyle. "Or I'll have her unhook your harness from the zip line the next time you two are racing each other across it."

Kyle clutches his heart. "Nice to know how much you care about me." I smirk. "So are you really out in two weeks?" Today is the first day of my third week here.

I falter. "Yeah. I mean, I told McDaddy I'm only staying four weeks, so..." I trail off when I hear laughter coming from the theater. The doors are open, and the volume inside is only getting louder. "Besides, I already have plans at home for the rest of the summer. McDaddy is going to take us to Cancun. I hope. And I haven't been to the cabana yet so..."

Kyle is giving me the same look he gets when I won't let him cannonball into our pool (I hate getting wet when I'm reading *Us Weekly* on a float). "You really think you'll be happier spending the rest of the summer at home than you would here?"

Since when can he read my thoughts? I hesitate. "Yeah." I play with the fringe on my shirt, letting the beads knock together.

"You won't miss canoeing with Ethan on the lake, cooking with Beaver, or eating four bowls of caramel ice cream at the

I Scream for Ice Cream event with Lina?" he prods. I don't say anything. "You just seem to be having a good time lately. The other day I even noticed you were wearing a tee that said Old Navy on it. You've downsized," he jokes. "You sure you want to race home to work for Kate?"

"I don't work for Kate." I notice the edge to my voice.

"You're different here," Kyle says. "This is why Dad wanted you to come—to see how you could hack it without facials and nail salons. Here, you're the old Harper, and I like that one better. Stay for the summer," he insists. "Lina wants you to, too."

The old Harper? He's talking to Lina about me? Now I'm mad. "Well, I didn't ask what you thought, did I?" He looks startled. "You just don't want to lose our bet or look bad in front of Lina," I snap.

Kyle's expression darkens. Our lovey-dovey twin moment is over. "If you really think those things, then maybe you should go home."

"Kyle!" Cole pops his head out of the theater doors. "Get a move on, dude!"

"Coming!" Kyle leaves me standing there, my thoughts stretching and shrinking like a rubber band. *Is there really an old and new Harper? Who's the real one?*

"Hey." Courtney walks up behind me carrying a box overflowing with what looks like wigs and clothes. "Shouldn't you be inside already?"

"Yeah." I can't even fake the enthusiasm. And I had been so looking forward to this. "Sorry. I was talking to my brother, and he was being a jerk."

Courtney nods. "He looks like a real pain in the butt." I laugh.

"Ignore him." The bell rings, meaning we should be in there already. "Hitch is about to announce this week's All-Camp theme, and it has everything to do with this box I'm carrying." She half smiles. "I'll give you a leg up to beat the guys—bunk karaoke."

"Bunk karaoke?" My voice warbles. I don't feel like I have an edge at all in this category. "Are you saying we *all* have to sing? Even if we have a terrible voice?"

Courtney grins. "The worse the voice, the better the performance. Trust me."

As Courtney and I make our way inside the theater, the room is buzzing with its usual Saturday night giddiness. The theater has a real stage, but the auditorium side doubles as an indoor basketball court and dance room so whenever we're here for an event, we have to sit on the floor. No one seems to mind. I've decided it's my favorite night of the week at camp because everyone is so casual. Actually, it turns out every night here is casual—even camp dances—and I didn't even need half the stuff I brought with me on this trip. I'm secretly starting to like that.

Every Saturday is an All-Camp Night, and it's the one night of the week the entire camp gets together to do the same activity with their counselors and the staff. Last Saturday we broke into teams to play charades. This week it is karaoke. I hear the last week of camp they have a talent show. The best part about the evening—other than just hanging out together—is that the winning team gets to pick a cool prize, like making your counselor clean your bunk.

As I make my way to where my bunk is sitting, I sidestep over guys still wearing dirty T-shirts from an earlier baseball game and peeps who have their faces painted like Spider-Man or princesses. People are wearing sweats and pajamas and zero makeup. Even I'm only wearing lip gloss and mascara. I can't think of a single place I could go at home where it would be this acceptable to just let it all hang out. My bunkmates are sitting with Thomas's bunk in a cluster a little ways away, but I head straight for Lina, who is sitting alone.

Lina is sketching a London Blue drawing in her notebook, which is balanced on her knees. "I thought you handed in your favorite drawing for the spirit board already."

"I did, but..." She frowns. "I'm not sure I like London's nose in that one. I think the nose ring I gave her is a little large, don't you think? And the blue streak in her hair should be more near her bangs, not the back of her head." She sketches a deeper pencil shade along London's hairline. "I think I can do better."

I place my hand on top of the paper. "Your first drawing is perfect, and they're lucky to have it. It's the best thing about the spirit board. Even Jeanie said so the other day, and she doesn't compliment anyone."

Lina grins. "She did, didn't she? I think we have a real shot at winning." She bites her lip. "I just wish you were going to be around to find out what happens."

Why is everyone talking about me leaving today? "We'll write, and you'll tell me what happens."

"I wish you could be here to find out the good news with me." Lina traces a finger over her drawing. "Kyle and I both want you to change your mind."

Ever since the overnight camping trip a few days ago, Kyle and Lina have been hanging out 24-7. They've gone rock climbing or zip-lining together daily and even canoeing. Courtney told me things move quickly at camp, but I had no idea how quick. My only consolation is that she'll have him when I leave in less than two weeks. Wait. Did I really just consider having Kyle around a good thing?

"Leen," I say with a sigh because I don't know what else to say. I hate leaving her, too, but I have a whole other life to get back to. So why do I feel so torn?

"Good evening, Whispering Pines!" Hitch's megaphone-amplified voice drowns out our conversation immediately.

I've never been so happy to see him use that thing.

All eyes turn to the front of the room, where Hitch and Pam, along with most of the senior counselors, are lined up like they are about to be part of a flash mob.

"Welcome to All-Camp Night!" Hitch says and is met with the usual cheering.

(We do an awful lot of cheering and clapping in this place. Some nights my hands are actually sore from all the clapping. I need a good manicure and paraffin treatment when I get home for sure.)

"We hope you had a good second week at the Pines and are enjoying the start of week three," Hitch says. "The peeps had their dance contest and wowed us with their Will.i.Am routine, and the marshmallows got to go on their first overnight camping trip, which was a lot of fun. Most important for all of you, this week is the last week you can work on our submission for the London Blue contest. I think it's incredible so far. Want to see how it looks?" The crowd applauds.

Sam, Courtney, Cole, Thomas, and a few other counselors carry the giant spirit board onto the stage. I can't believe how big that thing has gotten since I last saw it. It has to be the size and length of a door. It's hard to see everything on it from where I'm sitting, but it's covered with pictures, camp patches, a piece of a camp T-shirt, slogans, camp bracelets, and, in the center of it all, Lina's beautiful sketch of London Blue, which I have a feeling London is going to flip for. She loves pictures of her hair looking really wild. The board is so packed, I can't see them fitting anything else on it, but there is still a week left to do so.

I squeeze Lina's shoulder. "Yay, Lina!" I shout out, and she hits me.

Hitch puts his hand on an edge of the board. "Pam thinks we should deliver this monster to London's people in New York by hand a few days early so that it doesn't get damaged in transit. For that reason, we'll end any work on the board in four days. Until then, keep tacking stuff on there! We'll have the board on display on the theater porch all night for you to look at your handiwork up close. Go Pines!"

Cheer! Cheer! Clap. Clap. Clap.

The counselors carry the board offstage again. "And now for the real reason we're here: All-Camp Night! Tonight's theme: bunk karaoke!" Clap. Cheer. Cheer. "For those of you who have never played, I'll give you the rules—there are none! You can team up with another bunk or work with your own, but the trick is to be a group when we throw songs at you. You don't pick the karaoke song, we do! And no lyrics. That's the fun part, folks."

Clap. Cheer. Groan. (That last part is me.)

"Feel free to use this basket of props we have up on stage and have fun!" Hitch says. "Your counselors and I will be judging you. Top score gets a prize that has never been offered before." A hush falls over the room. "A day of pampering that starts with breakfast in bed, free periods all day, and dinner cooked for you by Pam and me at our house. You'll finish the day with a private pool party at our place in early August."

Mega claps! Mega cheers! Utter pandemonium.

"Wow, that sounds fun," I admit to Lina.

"Stick around and you can be here if we win," Lina baits me. "I've heard he has a great house. Sam is always raving about it."

"Pam and I are going to start you off," Hitch adds. "Make it a bit less scary."

Pam looks like this is news to her. I see her try to get off the stage, but Hitch pulls her toward him. Seconds later, Hitch and Pam are handed mics and the sounds of Kenny Rogers fill the air. Hitch's singing is terrible, but he seems to be enjoying himself. He knows every word. Pam not so much. But at the end, everyone goes crazy for them.

Courtney was right. It doesn't matter how horribly you sing. This crowd is going to love you, anyway. It gives me hope that I can get up there.

"Do you guys want to work with us, or are you doing your own thing?" asks Addison gruffly. A few feet away, Jeanie and Camilla are whispering heatedly while Vickie, Trisha, and Melody stand nearby looking miserable.

"You want to work with us?" I ask incredulously.

Addison is uncomfortable. She pulls at the camp tee I just

bedazzled yesterday. "Jeanie would rather it just be the three of us, but I think karaoke is better with a crowd, so I told her I was asking the rest of the bunk, too." Her mouth twists awkwardly. "I'm hoping more voices will drown me out. I'm practically a baritone. What do you say?"

I look at Lina, who shrugs. The thought of doing a Hitch-and-Pam-style duet is less than appealing. "Okay, we're in," I say and follow Addison over to the others.

Jeanie frowns when she sees me. "So you're actually joining us? You better be able to carry a tune."

She acts so much like Kate sometimes that it is scary. I'm not having it tonight. "Same goes for you, you know. I really don't want to lose out on that pool party."

The girls look at each other and then at Jeanie. "I thought you were going to be home by then," Jeanie stammers, playing with one of her curls.

I shrug. "I'm supposed to be, but cost Lina that pool party and I might have to stick around for a karaoke rematch."

Jeanie grimaces. "Fine. Let's get to it. Our strategy is always the same," she reminds the others. "No props. No gimmicks. Zany may draw a crowd, but it won't give us the points we need to win. We keep it simple and just sing."

"That's boring!" I protest, and the others look at me. "I don't care if you've won that way in the past. With a prize this good at stake, it's time to kick things up a notch. We should use wigs or boas, or anything wacky that is in that prop box."

"I'll stop you there. *Some* of us may have wanted a bigger team for karaoke," Jeanie says, looking at Addison, "but we don't need one." She looks smug. "Camilla is recording a demo this fall."

"A *real* demo," Camilla brags.

I bite my tongue to keep from going all music industry pro on her and saying, "Do you know how many non-talented people record demos?"

"And I'm on All-County Choir at home," adds Jeanie like I should be impressed. "I got to the semifinals in New York once, and Bruno Mars was a judge, so I think I know how to do a sing-off." Her eyes narrow. "Let me handle this."

Who cares if she's met Bruno Mars? When it comes to a production, McDaddy has taught me how to get things done. Problem is, they don't know that.

"You girls want to team up?" Justin appears out of nowhere and pushes into the center of our circle, followed closely by Heath and a few other guys from Cole's bunk. "A boy-girl group could take home the big prize. Think of how much fun that pool party would be." His eyebrows go up and down. "Bikini time."

"Eww!" Melody pushes him. "No, thanks. Right, Jeanie?"

She sighs. "How many people am I supposed to share the stage with?"

"Don't be like that," Ethan tells her as he approaches. "You have a great voice, but even Beyoncé has backup singers."

"True," Jeanie says as she winds a curl around her finger. "But I'm already stuck with seven of them now. Why do I need more?"

"Because we're switching things up for a change," I try again.

"You can play the diva role all you want, but if we want to win, I still say we need to do something different from everyone else."

"I agree," Lina seconds.

"I like the way Harper's thinking, too," Ethan agrees, and Jeanie looks horrified. Dirk and some of the others nod. Kyle still won't look at me. "I think a guy/girl truce should be in order—for tonight only, of course. You guys need us."

"And why is that?" Camilla asks. "I've heard you guys sing. You stink."

"Ouch!" Justin pretends to be hurt. "That's not true. I'm told I sound like Usher in the shower."

"You don't," Kyle says and pretends to sock him in the stomach. "Dirk is a good performer though. Our ace in the hole. You do not want this guy on a rival team."

"I might trip you on your way up to the stage, too," Justin confesses.

Ethan winks at me. "And I've been known to cause a scene during performances I'm not in." I give him a look. "What do you guys say? Can we team up for a one-night-only performance?" Jeanie hesitates, and Ethan dances goofily in place. Heath and Justin play air guitar for backup. "Our bunk has got the moves and the talent. We are a boy band waiting to happen."

I giggle. "If they're this funny standing here, imagine what they'd do with a Kanye song playing," I say to the others. "I say we let them in."

"I'll give them a shot," says Vickie.

"They could make the audience laugh," says Trisha, and Addison nods.

Jeanie sighs. "Fine! What's a few more at this point? You're on," she tells Ethan. "Just don't hog the whole stage!" The two shake on it.

We watch two acts go before it is our turn. The first group we watch—a girl bunk of peeps—perform with their counselor, which is pretty cute, especially considering they get a Katy Perry song to do. All the girls know the words, but none of them move unless their counselor runs over and moves them herself. The second group is a bunch of pez guys who get a rap song. It's comical that they botch every word. They can move though, and I wonder if they've been secretly practicing in their cabin.

"They stole our routine," Justin says in horror.

He's joking. I think.

The whole theater is in hysterics by the time that act is done. Entertaining, but they still only scored a five out of ten.

"Wow, some harsh critics up there," I say to Ethan, Lina, and Justin, who I'm standing with. Jeanie, Kyle, and the others are talking strategy, but how much strategy can you have when you don't know the music? What we have agreed on is that the girls will grab boas and boys will take wigs. Everyone must have some sort of costume. Jeanie is not thrilled, but she still gets the mic so that makes her happy.

"Haven't you heard?" Ethan asks as we head to the side of the stage to wait for our turn. "Summer camp critics are even more brutal than the popular clique at school."

"Funny," I say. "Maybe we should have asked to do stand-up instead."

Jeanie is hopping up and down a few feet away from us. "J, you okay over there?" Ethan asks. She walks over to us.

"I'm fine. Just getting psyched. I think this might work," she says more to Ethan than to me. "Everyone knows their part except *you*," she says to me. Ethan coughs. "You're new here, and I doubt you've done anything like this before. Do me a favor: Stay out of my way up there." I bite my lip to keep from screaming. "Watch me and Ethan for cues. *We* will lead the way, whatever the song is. And when in doubt, just mouth the words and move in place. No standing like a frozen robot. Got it?"

"Yes, my queen," I joke. Ethan bites his lip, and Jeanie stomps off to talk to Camilla, who is doing vocal practice.

"She's just nervous," Ethan tells me, squeezing my hand. I immediately feel tingly. "I can already tell you're going to be great up there."

I hear Hitch make the announcement, and I know it's time to go on. "And now we have the bunks of 10A and 11A teaming up for a boy-girl combo!"

We run up the stairs and take our places on stage as the crowd cheers. They settle down when the lights dim in the audience. I find it hard to see anything offstage.

"Follow my lead," Jeanie reminds me again. She pulls Ethan to the front, and the two look like lead singers when they get handed wireless mics. The rest of us huddle around a few microphones on stands. I glance over at Sam, Thomas, Courtney, Cole, and the other counselors. They are debating what song to use.

Then I hear a familiar Pink tune that seems to be the anthem of the summer only a few weeks into it.

"Aw, yeah! This one is easy," Dirk whispers to me. "Pool party, here we come!"

"It's too easy," I say and eye the control booth. The group is still whispering heatedly even though the music is playing.

Jeanie doesn't notice. She sways to the music and sings along with Ethan. The two are belting it out, and the crowd is loving it. The rest of us do our background thing.

It's boring, to be honest. McDaddy would be ashamed at what copycats we are. Everyone knows the moves to Pink's video. It's got a zillion hits on YouTube.

Then the song screeches to a halt, and we all stop moving.

"Now what?" Ethan hisses.

"I don't know," Jeanie whispers. "Just keep smiling and moving. We've got this."

"Do they usually change the song?" I ask Justin and Lina.

"Never," Lina says, "but look at Cole. He seems pretty pleased with himself. So does Courtney." The two are smiling as wide as that cat in *Alice in Wonderland*. A new song starts, and Jeanie and Ethan freeze. They've never heard this one.

"I don't know this song," Lina says.

"No one knows it." Justin continues to sway, but that's all anyone can do. Even the crowd is quiet. "We are going to lose this thing."

I recognize that instrumental! It's that new band McDaddy played on the way up to the Pines!

I look at Kyle. He nods. I know he knows it, too. We can save this thing.

Jeanie is frantic. "Do something! Anything! Cartwheels!"

"That pool party really did sound like fun," Dirk says dejectedly.

I grab Justin's wig and put it on my head. Kyle steals Jeanie's mic before she knows what's happening. I take Ethan's mic. "It's not over yet. Follow our lead," I say. The two of us break away from the group and move to the front.

"What are you doing?" Jeanie hisses.

"Saving you," Kyle says. He winks at me. "Let's show them how it's done, sis."

"With pleasure," I say and take his hand. I turn to the crowd. "This is a kick-butt new song by a group called Hudson Street that you're going to love! Here it goes!"

I look over at Cole and see his jaw drop. He was not expecting us to know this group. Too bad.

I'm not nervous in the slightest as Kyle and I run around the stage together, whipping the crowd into a frenzy. When we get to the chorus, which is a rap, I let Kyle take the honors. Ethan hollers his support and salutes me. My voice isn't fabulous, but no one seems to care because I'm selling it for all it's worth, and I'm having a ball. This camp that never seems to want to give me a chance is loving me. *Me!* And I'm soaking it all in.

"Let's hear you clap! Clap! Clap!" I yell. "I know you know how to do that!"

"You heard my sister! Let's hear ya!" Kyle seconds.

I wave my boa in the air, and Ethan grabs it, swinging it

around. Justin runs over and grabs the other end, and they pretend to have a tug-of-war to the beat. Dirk, Lina, Trisha, and Vickie join them. The rest of my bunk sees what's happening and grabs opposite sides. The group moves to the beat as Kyle and I dance across the stage. A bewildered Jeanie just stands there. Finally I grab her arm and swing her around with me. And then the song is over. The crowd goes nuts.

Ethan picks me up for a victory lap around the stage before I even realize what he's doing. "You were amazing!" he says in awe as he puts me down. I notice he doesn't let go of my hand. "You should audition for *The Voice*."

My checks flush, and I look down at our joined hands. "Thanks."

I notice Jeanie grimacing. Then she starts whispering to Camilla. She does not look thrilled, but Addison high-fives me.

"Didn't know you had it in you, Barbie! Nice one!" she says.

"If that doesn't win, I don't know what will," Melody adds, sounding giddy. "Thank God you took over!" I see Jeanie look at her. "We were drowning out there."

"We were doing fine," Jeanie insists, but everyone is too busy talking to Kyle and me about our performance to listen to her. "I had it under control!"

"How did you two know that song?" Dirk asks.

Kyle and I look at each other. "Our dad listens to this new-music station on Pandora. I guess we heard it on there."

"Cool dad," Heath says.

We all stop talking at once when we hear the counselors

begin to give their scores. They hold up their cards, and we get nines and tens across the board! The crowd goes wild. So does my own team. Ethan hugs me again. I could get used to that.

"Victory party!" Justin yells.

"We haven't even won yet," Camilla reminds them.

"Oh, we will," Ethan says. "The Barbie twins rocked this joint! I think a party at the lake is in order." He looks at me. "What do you say?" I'm so surprised, I can't speak.

There's an unsaid agreement between counselors and campers that we can go down to the lake at night as long as we keep things low-key. Lina and I haven't been invited down there—till now. And by Ethan! Lina pinches me, and I know she's thinking the same.

"I'm in for the party, but do not call me a Barbie twin," Kyle says. He grabs me and swings me around, and Melody and Addison move out of the way. "I would give us each five points for that display."

"Ten!" I joke. "Infinity!"

Jeanie walks over with Camilla. "Are you guys going to come to the lake tonight?" she asks. "It's really fun. You should."

Lina and I look at each other. Jeanie wants us to come, too? I guess I did help us win (well, we haven't won yet, but I am pretty sure we will!). "I think we are."

"We can't go like this though," Camilla says to Jeanie. She points to her own frizzy hair. "We're sweaty messes." She looks at me hesitantly. "Do you think you'd be up for going to the bunk first to do a quick makeover before we head down there?"

"That's a good idea," Jeanie agrees, and I almost swallow

my tongue. "What do you say, Harper? I have been dying to try out that flat iron of yours." She blushes. "I've just felt too funny to ask."

I'm gobsmacked, and I know Lina is, too. Jeanie is finally giving me a chance to be one of them, and I know I have to take it. "I'll head back to the bunk early to get everything heated up and ready," I say excitedly.

"That's perfect! We'll meet you back there as soon as the show is over." Jeanie whispers in my ear. "It would look too obvious if we all ducked out of here early."

"Understood," I agree.

"We'll see you soon," Jeanie says, and the two head into the crowd.

Lina and I don't know what to say, but Kyle does. "That moment deserves a point all on its own, which means we are eight to six now," he says. His eyes have a mischievous twinkle to them that I know well. "Could be fun if you stuck around longer to see how high our scores could go, don't you think?"

Lina looks at me hopefully.

I push my hair out of my eyes and try to catch my breath. "You two are not going to let this rest, are you?"

"Never!" they say at the same time.

The truth is, part of me hopes they don't.

Harper McAllister @HarperMc
Do something you've never done before—like
hijack a karaoke session and bring down the house.
#rulesofsummer

15

FLAMING THE FIRE

IF THERE ARE ANY RACCOONS or possums lurking nearby on our walk back to our cabin, Lina and I have managed to scare them all away. The two of us can't stop laughing as we let our flashlights guide us back to the bunk.

"I cannot believe Jeanie was groveling to *you* tonight." Lina is still amazed. "She actually asked you to straighten her hair!"

"I know!" I can't believe it myself. "She finally wants a makeover just when I've gotten over giving them! I haven't looked at that flat iron in over a week."

Lina's face sparkles in the glow of the lanterns lighting our way. "She keeps pushing you down, but you keep getting back up. Maybe she's finally realized there's no fighting it. Is there anything you can't do?" she asks. "Maybe you should take that boxing elective with me next week!"

"No, thanks!" I say quickly. "Ask Kyle to do that with you."

Lina gets quiet, like she does whenever I bring him up. "Not that I want you to date my brother—there'll be no living with him if you do—but I can't believe I won't be here to see what happens," I realize. "Of course it would happen that I finally start liking the Pines when it's almost time to go home. I've had so much fun that I haven't e-mailed my mom to complain about camp in days. She must wonder if I'm still alive."

Lina stops short. "Are you saying you might want to stay?"

I hesitate. I'm not ready to say that, but I am all of a sudden thinking about it. "All I know is I don't want to miss that pool party at Hitch's house. I have to be there to see Jeanie's face when someone says Kyle and I saved the day."

Lina does a little happy dance, and I join her. We must look like idiots, but no one is around to see us. Then my flashlight gives out.

"Oh man," I groan. "That was my last set of batteries."

"Same here," says Lina. "We'll have to get more at the canteen tomorrow. At least we're at the cabin."

We hurry up the porch steps to get ready. I flick on only one light in the cabin when we enter. I'll need the rest of the power for my hair tools (I've learned my lesson on that one). I kneel down by my trunk and unlock it.

Lina whistles. "Wow, you really do have a whole hair salon in there. My trunk just has art supplies, hiking boots, and extra sunscreen."

We stare at the assortment of hair dryers, flat irons, light-up makeup mirrors, and curling wands I felt was absolutely necessary to keep with me at camp. Looking at it all now I feel kind of foolish. In two weeks, I've only used a handful of them, and that was all on the night we had the camp dance. I've become a wash-and-go girl myself. Turns out my curls dry in a half hour in this heat, which means I can sleep in a few minutes longer. ME! The girl who gets up two hours before school to get ready. I do, however, make time for eyeliner and mascara (I haven't become a full mountain girl yet).

It doesn't take us long to have the room completely set up. My makeup is on one table with the mirror and the other holds all sorts of face creams and perfumes. I put out my best hair products in the bathroom in case someone wants to wash her hair before I blow it out. My half a dozen brushes and combs are lying near one of the hair dryers. And for the final touch, I attach Lina's iPod shuffle to my portable speaker so that Bruno Mars fills the room. When I'm finished, I'm pretty pleased with myself. Then I look at my watch and frown. "It's after ten."

Lina plays with her hair in front of my makeup mirror. "They should be here any minute then. Want to do my hair first before they get here?"

I grab the crimper that is heated up. "I thought you'd never ask."

When I'm done, Lina looks in the mirror. I've braided the top and made funky curls out of the pink strands in the back. The look is sort of punk meets princess. "I think you've found your calling," she says as she plays with the curls. "The girls are going to fight over who you do first."

I look at my watch again. It's now ten forty-five! "What time did you say All-Camp usually ends?"

Lina shrugs. "Ten at the latest. Why? What time is it?"

"Ten forty-five!" I say, and she pales. "They should be here by now, right?" She nods. "It's almost eleven, and our curfew is twelve," I realize slowly, "that could only mean one thing..." We both rush to the cabin door and go out on the porch. Lights are on in the other cabins nearby, and we can hear distant voices and laughter. Not only is everyone back, they've already turned in. Lina and I lean over the railing to get a view of the lake. Just as I suspected, I can see a bonfire roaring. The marshmallows party is going on all right; Jeanie just didn't want us to be a part of it. "She tricked me!" I say angrily. "I should have known she was never going to let me give her a makeover!"

"Technically Camilla tricked you," Lina says. "That's probably why we didn't realize what Jeanie was up to."

The happiness I was feeling earlier vanishes like a puff of smoke. It all makes sense now. Jeanie was bent out of shape that I helped with the karaoke number. She hated everyone congratulating me and Kyle, so she decided to get rid of me for the after party. It's like the bunk raid all over again. "The guys must notice we're not there." I freak. "Why haven't they come looking for us? If they cared, they would have come up here by now. They're all jerks!"

"Harper, calm down," Lina says. "Maybe they are looking for us. We don't know what's going on down there."

My face flushes angrily. "You're right. Let's go down there then and see for ourselves," I declare, grabbing my sweatshirt from the hook by the cabin door and throwing it on. "When I get my hands on Jeanie, I am going to crush her." I think of what Kate would do in this situation. She would show no mercy. She'd make the girl cry. "I will publicly humiliate her the way she humiliated us and tell everyone what a frizzy-haired, big-nosed, psycho camper she really is."

"Yikes." Lina looks annoyed with me. "That has nothing to do with why we're mad. You're just being obnoxious now."

"But she ruined our night," I say. "Again!"

Lina shakes her head, her curls bouncing vigorously. "Don't you see? If we march down there and cause a scene, we're as bad as she is."

"So what?" I channel Kate, whose mantra has always been "the meaner, the better." "Sometimes people deserve to be taken down a peg, and there's no better place to do that than in public."

"Believe it or not, not everyone is a fan of public humiliation, including me," Lina says incredulously. "When people find out what they pulled on us tonight, they're going to be on our side. You'll blow that by going down there and going ballistic. Trust me." We just stare at each other as the porch door slams open and closes on its own. The wind has picked up. "I'm tired," she says, sounding suddenly beat down. I can't help but think how our night went from such a high to such a low so quickly. "I think I'll just go to bed and deal with Jeanie tomorrow. Do the same," she begs. "We can tell the guys what happened when we see them then."

But I don't want to wait till tomorrow. "I need air," I say and let the porch door slam shut behind me. Part of me is mad at Jeanie and another part is mad at Lina for being such a pushover.

We have a right to put Jeanie in her place! I take deep breaths and listen to the crickets and sounds of the other cabins turning in around us. Lights are going out all around me, which should be calming, but it's not. I can't let this go. The sounds of the lake travel all the way to the bunks. I can hear them down there having a good time. Jeanie is probably bragging about the trick she played on us. Does Ethan hear her? Meanwhile Lina and I are on the outside looking in again. It's not a feeling I'm used to, and I hate it. I pace back and forth on the porch, weighing my options. Lina may be the bigger person, but I'm not. I'm going down there.

I grab my flashlight, which is still lying on a porch chair. Then I remember my flashlight died and so did Lina's. What am I going to use to get to the lake in the pitch dark? I pause and spin around, looking back toward the bunk. One of my candles! Lina's already turned in and our cabin lights are out, so I quietly sneak back into the cabin. I hear music playing softly and realize Lina must have put her headphones on to fall asleep. Tiptoeing over to my trunk, I pull out the one candle I kept for safekeeping. It's a big, fat pillar that will last for days if I let it. I grab the box of matches I hid inside a pair of socks and exit the cabin, waiting until I'm at the bottom of the porch stairs to light it. Then I duck into the woods rather than going on the path. It's the best way to sneak up on those creeps without getting caught.

Walking by candlelight is tougher than I thought, though. If I trip, I might fall into the candle and set my hair on fire, so I walk slowly and look down for rocks and snakes. Concentrating on that keeps me from freaking out that I'm off the path, in the woods, alone, in the middle of the night. When I hear people talking, I stop short. Cole and Sam are whispering quietly on a rock a few feet away. Quickly, I walk in the other direction, silently praying neither of them sees the flame from my candle. It's so dark, I'm not sure where I am headed now. When I finally see lights ahead of me, I turn toward them.

I reach the clearing and realize I've somehow turned myself around. I'm by the theater now. The weather is written on a board on the path, and I see it's supposed to be rainy and windy tomorrow. Great. I'll be locked in my bunk with Jeanie all day, hearing about her and Ethan's amazing time together at the lake. I walk up the porch steps and sit down. It's dark, so I know everyone has gone home. I can see all the way down to the lake from here, and it doesn't take me more than a second to see the bonfire. Even in the darkness, I can see the outlines of people moving around the fire. They're probably all laughing about Lina and me being stupid enough to fall for their charade again. And Ethan and Kyle are doing nothing to stop them. I stare at the flames of the bonfire in a sort of trancelike state and feel my anger rise. I want to hit something hard! I put the candle down and begin to pace.

I can see it plain and clear now. No matter how hard I try to connect with these Lifers through camp sing-alongs, make-overs, cooking sessions, or overnight camping trips, they are never going to let me feel like one of them. I've been kidding myself. This is how *McDaddy* wanted me to spend my summer. Not me. I gave it a shot and it didn't work. A girl in dirty sneakers and official camp tees is not me. I want to go home.

I back away from the railing and bang into something hard. I turn around and see it is the spirit board. I can't believe they haven't brought it in yet, but the theater does have a large over-hang on the porch. I shoot invisible daggers at the contest entry. That board and everything it stands for is exactly what I can't stand about the Pines. How can everyone here preach about togetherness and friendships that last a lifetime when Lifers like Jeanie try to keep newbies like me at arm's length? "I hope the Pines loses the London Blue contest," I whisper, surprised to hear my thoughts out loud. "You hear that? I hope you lose!" I say loudly as if I'm placing a curse on it. "You don't deserve to win." There is nothing around to punch, so instead I kick at the theater doors nearby. "You! Deserve! To! Lose!" I kick even harder, and the doors vibrate so hard that I fear I'm going to bang one of them in, but I can't stop myself. When I've had enough, I stomp down the porch steps, failing to notice the person walking toward me.

"Harper!"

It's Ethan. I'm so mad I don't even know if I can look at him. "Hey!" I say with fake enthusiasm. "Did I catch you on your way back from the big victory celebration at the lake? I bet it was loads of fun." He looks baffled, but I don't care. I head the other way, stumbling a bit since it's dark. In my hurry, I leave my candle behind. I am not going back for it now. Ethan runs in front of me.

"What's going on with you?" he asks. "I've been trying to find you."

"Find me, huh?" My voice is venomous. "You looked real hard." I check my watch. "You've been there over an hour and *now* you go searching?" He opens his mouth to protest. "Lina and I have been waiting at our cabin. My sweet bunkmates suggested meeting us there to get ready to go to the lake together, but they never showed up." He doesn't say anything. "Jeanie made sure we weren't there for the victory party."

Ethan looks upset. "Jeanie? That makes no sense. She's the one who asked me where you were. She thought maybe you were mad at her for how she reacted after the karaoke number."

"And you believed her?" I'm incredulous. "She lied to you!"

"Jeanie wouldn't...," he starts to say, and I put my hand up.

"I'm sorry, of course you would believe her over me. She's a Lifer, just like you, and Lifers stick together. You guys think you're better than everyone else here."

Ethan's face hardens. "Being new has nothing to do with why you're not popular here, Harper. Is that all it's about for you? Collecting friends? Some of us want real relationships. You've got to know by now, when you choose to be different, people are going to treat you differently."

"Why should I pretend to be someone I'm not?" I push my hair away from my face even as the wind keeps bringing it forward. "I like me, and if you guys can't look beyond the clothes and the hair and the comments to see who I really am, then I don't want to keep trying with any of you." I find myself getting choked up. "I'd rather go someplace I'm already wanted. Home."

"Harper, I—" Ethan stops. "Do you smell something burning?"

We both turn around and see the small fire on the theater

steps. I know immediately what happened. "My candle!" I cry. "It fell over!"

"You had a candle burning out here?" Ethan asks. "Are you crazy?"

I don't answer him. Instead I run toward the theater porch and look for something to put the flames out with. Ethan's right behind me, but neither of us knows what to do. The flames have shot higher thanks to the wind and have already reached the railing. The heat is intense, and I watch in horror as the flame shoots all the way down the porch, making a half circle around the front of the building. The fire is moving too fast to stop it on our own. It's going to destroy the whole theater if we don't do something.

"There's a hose!" Ethan grabs it from a hook near the water fountain a few yards away. He turns it on, and a gush of water shoots out. "I'll hold it off. Go get help! Now!"

I don't argue. I run as fast as my legs will take me to the counselor lounge up the hill. I burst through the doors and find Courtney and Thomas there with some other counselors. Sam and Cole run in behind me.

Sam touches my arm. "What's going on? We saw you running."

"The theater," I manage to get out with deep breaths. "It's on fire."

"What?" Courtney cries and pushes past me onto the porch. Everyone follows. "Oh my God. Look!"

The flames are visible even from here. Within seconds, everyone runs toward the growing blaze. I hear Thomas yell to the others that they're going to make sure some of the nearby cabins with campers don't have to be evacuated. What have I done?

Courtney pulls me along as Sam runs alongside us. She pulls her cell phone out of her pocket and dials Hitch. "You've got to get to campus now. The theater is on fire."

A crowd has arrived by the time we get back.

"What happened?" Jeanie cries as she and my bunkmates reach the theater at the same time we do. A group of marshmallows from the other bunks are behind her. Even a few pez are out of bed now. Counselors hold them at bay.

"Stay back," Ethan yells as he tries to hold the hose steady. Cole takes it from him. All I can do is stand by and watch the monster I've created take over the porch.

I hear a camp whistle, which is our emergency alert system, and lights start springing on all over campus. It isn't long before Lina is running toward me in her pajamas. The scene is pandemonium with campers running up from the lake, counselors trying to hold them back, and Cole still trying to put the fire out. But the flames are too big. I see Hitch appear out of nowhere holding a fire extinguisher. "Move back!" Within seconds the three of them have got the fire under control. Even so, I can still hear fire trucks roaring toward our camp in the distance. The flames are gone. So is the porch.

"Did anyone see what happened?" Courtney asks.

"Thank God it didn't torch the whole theater," Sam says.

Lina grabs my hand. I stare at the pink and red friendship bracelet on her wrist. The one she just made today to match the one she made me. "Are you okay? When I heard the alarm and you weren't in bed, I got so worried."

I wish I could jam all my fingers in my mouth at once. I bite my pinkie nail instead.

"It's all right," Hitch says. He looks bleary-eyed and pained, and I feel the same way as I stare at the destruction one tiny candle just did. "The fire is out. Counselors, please get your campers back to their bunks before the fire department gets here. If anyone has any information about what caused this fire, please alert your counselors."

I see Ethan looking at me. I don't hesitate. "I do, sir. It was a candle."

"Oh, Harper," Courtney whispers in a disappointed voice, but I continue, anyway.

I let go of Lina's hand and take a step forward, feeling the heat of all those eyes on me. "My candle," I say shakily. "I placed it on the porch steps and then—"

Jeanie gasps, interrupting my confession. I see her point toward the porch. "The spirit board! It was up there!"

I feel a pang in my stomach. Oh my God, I've ruined the spirit board.

Jeanie whirls toward me. "You destroyed it on purpose!" Others start murmuring their agreement.

"Come on, Jeanie," Ethan starts to say. "She didn't mean for this to happen."

"I didn't!" I agree, but no one will listen. I turn and look for Lina. When I see her face, I know it doesn't matter whether I ruined the board on purpose. Her eyes say it all.

192

"You couldn't listen to me, just once," she says in a hoarse voice. I reach for her hand, but she takes off into the darkness.

I've lost Lina's friendship, and that was the only thing I had left.

Harper McAllister @HarperMc
I've never been a quitter, but sometimes that's the only option you have left. #walkingdisaster

16

FACING THE FIRING SQUAD

I'VE NEVER HEARD THE MESS hall so quiet before.

It's as if I'm the only one in here, but I'm not. Right now over two hundred pairs of eyes are on me, and I can hear them whispering, too.

"That's the girl who set fire to the theater porch."

"I heard she torched the theater because she hates London Blue and didn't want us to win the contest."

"I heard she had a breakdown because she has no friends here."

"She should be expelled. Can you be expelled from camp?"

I give my Cheerios a milk bath and watch them get soggier. I can't eat. I don't want any of Beaver's chocolate chip pancakes, which he made the camp special this morning as a pick-me-up. I tried sneaking into the kitchen through the back—Court said I'm not allowed on kitchen duty right now. I only saw Beaver for a second. He didn't directly come out and say it when I stopped

194

by the kitchen this morning, but I know he's disappointed in me. I put my spoon down. Who could eat when she's responsible for destroying a camp's dream in minutes?

I sit at the edge of our bunk's dining table while the rest of my bunkmates huddle at the other end like I have the plague. Even Lina has joined them. I don't blame her. I tried talking to her when I got back to the bunk last night (I didn't want to leave the scene till the fire was completely out), but she pretended to be asleep. Courtney told me to try to get some myself since today would be a long day. The two of us are supposed to go right from breakfast to Hitch's office to hear my punishment. I have a suspicion my parents are on their way to pick me up right now. I discreetly glance around the room, hoping to catch Ethan's eye, but he's nowhere to be seen. I don't see Kyle, either. I wonder what he thinks about what I did.

It was an accident. But accident or not, I've ruined everything this camp has worked for this summer.

Feedback from the microphone stand draws my attention. The campers around me groan and wince. "Sorry about that." Hitch's voice is mellower than usual. Pam is standing beside him, looking mournful as well. "Good morning, Pines."

I hear a few halfhearted good mornings.

"By this point, most of you know what happened at the theater after All-Camp Night," Hitch says. "For those of you who don't, an accidental fire caused our theater porch to go up in flames, along with our entry for the London Blue video contest."

Hitch doesn't mention my name, but the word *accident* doesn't seem to make people any less upset.

"Unfortunately, the entries are due a week from today, and there is just no way to put such an elaborate project together again in time."

A pez starts to cry. Complaints rise up around the room, making my cheeks burn.

"We know who's to blame for that, don't we?" Camilla glares at me, and Jeanie tries not to grin. I spin my Cheerios around some more. Lina looks at me and away again.

"But I don't want you guys to be upset because we have a lot of great things coming up this summer," Hitch says optimistically. "Our first session of Color War is less than a week away. There is another overnight trip tomorrow for the marshmallows and a campers versus basketball players game with the famous Harlem Wizards later on in the week." Pam tries to get the usual applause started. A few halfheartedly join in. "We don't need London Blue to have fun!" he adds, getting caught up in the moment.

"It still would have been nice to be in a music video," Melody mutters.

Addison leans in so the entire table can hear her. "Did you hear Hitch was going to let the first session campers come back the day London shot the video if we won? And we so would have. Our spirit board was ah-mazing!"

It was beautiful. It was a great collage. But *ah-mazing* is taking it a bit too far. There were probably hundreds of camp entries for this contest, and that board was not going to stand out from the pack. It was too vanilla to do that. The only spark was Lina's drawing. I don't have the nerve to say any of that now.

196

I should have said it when it mattered, but I didn't do that, either.

"So please eat up because Beaver made those chocolate chip pancakes special for today," Hitch says. "He was really upset about our contest entry being destroyed, so he's been cooking for hours. Wait till you see what he's cooking up for dinner!" He lowers his megaphone and immediately his smile vanishes. He looks as beat up as I probably do.

"Harper?" Courtney comes up behind me. "Hitch would like to see you in his office in fifteen minutes. I have a few things to deal with beforehand, so I'll meet you there."

"Okay." A feeling of dread washes over me as Courtney walks away. That's when I see Kyle. He's wearing a baseball cap, but that doesn't hide the grim look on his face. He calls me over to the side of the mess hall.

"How are you holding up?" he asks. I can see my bunk-mates watching us.

"Not good," I whisper.

"I'm sure." He nods. I can't read his expression. "What were you thinking carrying a candle?"

"I wasn't thinking!" I say. "All I was thinking about was how you guys were celebrating at the lake while Lina and I were miserable in our bunk."

He looks down. "I should have realized why you two weren't there. I feel awful. Lina won't even speak to me now." He looks up, his eyes a mirror image of my own. "But you can fix this, you know. Call Dad. Tell him what happened. You can get him to extend the contest deadline."

I shake my head. "You know we can't do that. Everyone will find out what McDaddy does and how we know London."

Kyle gives me a look. "So? Ethan knows Dad works with London. He goes to school with us, and he doesn't treat us any differently. What are you afraid of?"

I am startled. Ethan *does* know our connection to London, and he's never even mentioned it to me. The only one who ever really talks about it is Kate. My best friend Kate who couldn't even text me back last night. She had nothing to gain from our conversation. Margo, on the other hand, immediately called Courtney's phone when she got my text, because that's what real friends do. Like Lina, who tried to stop me from making this stupid mistake in the first place.

"No." I shake my head. *All I've done since we moved to Brookville is spend McDaddy's money and use his name. I am not going to let that happen here, too.* "That's cheating. I am not calling in favors."

"Why not?" Kyle clearly thinks I am nuts. "It would fix everything!"

"No." I am resolute. "I either fix this on my own, or I don't fix it at all."

"Fine." Kyle pulls his baseball cap lower. "Have a good trip home."

"Don't be like that. Kyle!" It's no use. He's already walking away, and now I'm standing here by myself while my bunk-mates continue to glare. I have to get out of here.

I leave the mess hall and take the long path to the office so I can think. But fifteen minutes comes quickly, and I soon find myself at Hitch's office. It's the first time I've been there. When I walk inside, the cold air blasts me in the face.

Ah, air-conditioning. How I've missed you, old friend.

The hum of the air conditioner has a soothing sound, making me feel at ease as I walk up to the secretary to ask if I can see Hitch. Her phone is ringing off the hook.

"Whispering Pines. Hold, please. Whispering Pines. No, no one is in danger. The fire was put out immediately and no campers were inside the building. Please hold. Whispering Pines. Alan Hitchens is in a meeting right now and will have to call you back. Yes, we did have a fire, but everything is fine. Please hold."

I clear my throat, and the older woman looks up.

"Harper McAllister, I presume?" She is less than thrilled to see me, but I can't blame her. I've made her morning more hectic than usual. "He's already in there with the others. Go on in."

Others?

When I push open Hitch's door, I see Courtney and Sam, but I'm surprised to find Ethan and Lina sitting there as well.

"What are they doing here?" I ask.

"I thought it would be best if I asked everyone involved to be here," Hitch says wearily. I see the red lights on his phone blinking wildly. "Please have a seat, Harper."

I pull out the available chair next to Ethan. I am too hurt to look at him.

"I've called all of you here to find out exactly what happened last night." Hitch runs a hand through his bright white hair. "Needless to say, I am not happy. The fire made the local news. My phone board has been lit up like a Christmas tree all morning by concerned parents." His cool blue eyes look from one person to the next. "What I need right now is answers. All I know is that we have a burned porch, no shot at getting London Blue, and only one person to blame for this mess." He looks directly at me. "This is not what I thought would happen when I agreed to let you come here this summer, Harper."

"I know." I am barely audible. It's embarrassing to hear someone talk about the mess you've made.

"What were you doing with a candle?" Hitch complains. "You know they're forbidden. Your counselor should have confiscated that on day one." He gives Courtney a look.

"I did," she jumps in. "At least I thought I got them all. She brought aromatherapy candles as gifts for everyone, but I wouldn't let her give them out. Even though they smelled amazing," she adds under her breath.

"I hid one," I admit. Courtney looks even more disappointed. "I never planned on using it. I just liked how the lavender made my trunk smell." Hitch's eyebrows go up. "But then the last of my flashlight batteries died, and I needed a light to get down to the lake to see where everyone was last night, so I lit up the candle." I look down at my lap. "I only put it down on the porch for a second, but I guess the wind knocked it over."

"It was really windy," Sam says on my behalf. She looks at me curiously. "Be honest: You weren't trying to destroy the camp's chances at getting London Blue, were you?"

"No!" I protest. "Why would I do that?" I glance sheepishly at Lina. "That contest meant a lot to people close to me. I know how hard they worked on that board. I wanted them to win. I was mad last night," I tell everyone, "but I did not try to destroy the spirit board."

"What were you doing up at the theater then?" Hitch wants to know.

"I was on my way to the bonfire at the lake, but then I stopped myself." I blush. "I knew I wasn't wanted there."

"That's not true," Ethan says, but I ignore him.

"There was a bonfire going on at the lake?" Hitch asks. "I didn't approve that."

"They go every week after All-Camp Night," Sam tells him. "The counselors know about the get-togethers. The campers are back in their bunk by curfew. Well, except for last night."

"We'll talk about that part later," he tells Sam sternly and then looks at me again. "First I want to hear how that candle accidentally tipped over."

"I put it down to think for a moment," I say, getting upset just thinking about it again. "I didn't know what to do. Go back to the cabin? Head to the lake? A wise person told me to just let it go and not give anyone there the satisfaction." I look at Lina, but she doesn't make eye contact. "I was so mad that I started kicking a door, and someone heard me."

"You were kicking the theater door? Now I need to add property destruction to your list." Hitch sighs. "Ethan, you were the one she ran into?"

He nods. "Yeah. But she wasn't starting a fire or anything. She was just standing there." He clears his throat. "Arguing with me." I begin biting my nails.

"Did you notice the candle?" Hitch asks.

"No," Ethan says. "We were fighting, and then I smelled something burning and we saw the fire. That's when she mentioned the candle." He plays with a duct-tape bracelet on his right wrist. "Sir, I really don't think Harper meant for this to happen. It was an accident."

"Is that what you think, too, Lina?" Hitch asks. "I know you two are close."

"I don't think Harper meant to start that fire, either. I just wish she would have listened to me when I warned her not to go down to the lake." Lina looks at me. "Friends trust each other."

"You're right." My voice warbles. "I was wrong. I've screwed up everything I've done since I got here. It's obvious to everyone, myself included, that I don't belong at camp. I don't fit in no matter how hard I try. If it's okay with you, I just want to go home. Call my dad and have me picked up," I beg Hitch. "I'll be out of your hair by dinner."

"Harper," Lina whispers. "I'm upset, but I don't hate you. Stay." I shake my head.

Hitch sighs heavily. "I wanted to make sure this wasn't done deliberately because I must tell you, the campers are very disappointed. I'm very disappointed. Pam is devastated. She thought having London here would put Whispering Pines on the map."

I twist the friendship bracelet Lina gave me around and around my wrist. "I understand that, sir."

"But I haven't called your father." I look up, surprised. "You still have almost two weeks left and you're going to finish them, like you promised. I usually say the punishment should fit the crime." He scratches the goatee he's started to grow. "So in this case, you'll have to help rebuild the porch."

I'm stunned. "Okay." I've never wielded a hammer before, but I'm not about to argue with someone who is not going to press charges against me.

"You're sure there's no way we can get an entry in on time?" Courtney asks.

"No." Hitch sounds disappointed. "That board took weeks to finish, not hours. We've got the Harlem Wizards coming this weekend and the overnighter in Boston. We'd never get another spirit board together in time."

My wheels start spinning. *We* may not be able to do another board, but maybe *I* can. I need to fix the damage I caused.

"I'm afraid, in addition to rebuilding the porch, your punishment will also include skipping the overnighter tomorrow," Hitch says. "It wouldn't seem fair to send you after what happened."

"I understand," I say. Secretly I'm relieved. After what I've done, the other campers would probably try to find a way to leave me in Boston. And if I'm here and no one is speaking to me, that gives me time to put a plan in motion.

"Well, that's it," Hitch says and stands. "I'll see the rest of you on the bus early tomorrow morning for the away trip."

I bolt from the room before anyone can stop me. I have a lot of work to do.

"Harper!" Courtney rushes to catch up with me. "Where's the fire?" I groan. "Okay, that was a bad choice of words."

I give her a half smile. "You're forgiven."

Courtney puts an arm around my shoulders as we walk out of a patch of trees and into the bright sunlight. "If it makes you feel better, you're not the first person to screw up at the Pines." She grins. "One year Sam caused a campwide food fight in the mess hall and got banished to a cabin with Hitch's daughter for several days."

My eyes widen. "Are you serious?"

Courtney nods. "Yep. Not only did they manage to not kill each other, they created this cool video for our talent show that was a peace treaty of sorts for our whole bunk." She pats my back. "You'll figure out a way to win them back, too. You've got more spirit in you than most of the girls in this place."

"You think?" I stare at my sneakers, which were once so shiny and now, after weeks of trudging though the dirt at camp, have lost some of their shine. Just like me. "I was just so angry last night at everyone." My voice cracks. "I fought off liking this place for so long and now that I like it here, I get knocked on my butt again and cause a fire." I gulp. "It's not the way I thought this week would go."

If you had asked me what would have happened last night at the lake, I could have pictured Ethan and me taking a long walk in the moonlight or talking on the dock. Not me yelling awful things at him and accusing him of siding with Jeanie.

The truth is, I don't think he knew what Jeanie was up to, but I'm still mad he wasn't smart enough to sniff out her plan.

Just then, I see Ethan cut across the lawn in front of us. He doesn't look my way.

"What's the story there?" Courtney asks, nodding in his direction.

"Ethan?" I stammer. "I thought we were friends. Now I'm not sure what we are."

"Boys are great at saying one thing and doing another," says Courtney with a sigh. "If I know Ethan—and I've known a lot of Ethans—he knows he let you down last night. My advice: Give him a chance to explain himself. Same goes for Lina. Talk to her. That's what real friends do."

"Thanks," I say without much enthusiasm. I feel so beat down. "I'll try."

Courtney looks at me hard. "You found something you like about the Pines. Don't give up on it now just because you hit a rough patch. I wouldn't have believed it two weeks ago, but I really think you belong here."

You belong here. I hesitate. "When you were a camper here, did you act a lot different at camp than you did at home?"

Courtney laughs. "Of course! It's easier to be yourself when you're not pigeonholed into what everybody thinks you are. When you're out of your comfort zone, you act more like the person you *want* to be. Being that person all the time takes work."

Focusing on me has never been the problem. What I need to do is figure out who the real me is. Am I the girl I was before McDaddy struck it big or after? Is it okay to be a little of both?

"Are you still friends with people from home?" I'm afraid to hear her answer.

"Some," Courtney says. "My closest friends are the girls from my bunk." She smiles. "Sam, you know. My friend Grace is on a traveling college soccer team so she couldn't be a counselor this year, and my friend Emily Kate is a real brain so she's in Europe this summer taking some college classes, but we're all still close. We try to see each other a few times a year. Usually we get together to do something fun, like do a road trip or karaoke, like you guys did last night. We still like to shoot videos of us together. The videos remind us of what our lives were when we were at the Pines." She grins. "They were some of the best times of my life."

The videos remind us of what our lives were when we were at the Pines.

That is what my video needs to show—the best of the Pines. Not photos or scraps of T-shirts. Snippets of our lives that show real people—like Beaver, who slaves over his recipes to make the meals more fun. Friendships like the one I have with Lina—someone who listens to me, tells me when I'm being an idiot, and knows how to cheer me up with a drawing when I'm down. Something that shows how everyone comes together during activities like karaoke night and how this camp breeds fierce loyalty. Jeanie may not be my favorite person, but I admire how much she cares about the Pines. I need to be McDaddy for a day and shoot a video that shows London a camp she'll never forget.

"Listen, I have an idea that just might save the London Blue contest and prove to everyone once and for all that I'm more than just Camping Barbie," I tell Courtney excitedly. "But to do it, I'll need full access to your cell phone."

Courtney looks at me strangely, but I can tell her interest is piqued. "Go on."

I outline my plan. Courtney doesn't interrupt me—which is

very un-Courtney-like. By the time I'm talking about my ideas for the video finale, she looks as pumped as I feel. "You really think you can do this on your own? And in just a few days?"

I don't hesitate. "Yes. I might need to get on a laptop to do some editing, but it can be done. I've seen my dad do videos in a day when he has to."

"I have a laptop back at the cabin," Courtney says. "The bigger issue is explaining why a camper on probation for setting a fire is running around campus with an iPhone, shooting a video." She grimaces. "I'll have to come up with something to tell Hitch. Maybe I'll say part of your punishment with me is to shoot a video that shows how great the Pines is. To make you see what you've been missing."

"That could work!" I exclaim excitedly.

"I'll have to give the same speech to all the counselors and staff so you have access to them," she adds. "I'll say you're using the footage for the camp video yearbook." She gives me a stern look. "No one can know we still have a chance at the London video. What if you don't get this done? It will kill some of these kids if we break their hearts a second time. Shoot as much as you can today and tomorrow when the rest of the marshmallows are on the overnighter. If they see you with an iPhone, they'll be suspicious."

"Gotcha." I grin. "But, Court? I know I can do this."

Courtney grins. "If you're anything like me, Harper, which I think you are, then I believe you." She surprisingly hugs me, and I feel her slip something into my pocket. "Here's my phone," she whispers. "Do not let anyone see you doing anything other than

207

videoing or we're both busted. I'll tell the bunk you're punished and not coming with us. Good luck, Camping Barbie."

"Thanks!" I head to the bathroom by the mess hall since we're in between dining periods and it will probably be empty. I check that the coast is clear and then make a call.

"McDaddy Productions," a voice says.

"Sydney? It's Harper McAllister," I say to my father's personal assistant. I crouch down on a toilet seat so no one can see my feet in the bottom of the stall.

"Harper! Hey, honey. How is camp? Why are you calling my line?" she asks. "Do you want me to get your dad?"

"No!" I say quickly. "Don't tell him I called." I am doing this without McDaddy's help. There's only one thing I need from Sydney. "I was wondering if you could find out where I can e-mail an entry for the London Blue Camp Video contest." I cross my fingers. "There is an entry coming in that will blow the rest away."

Harper McAllister @HarperMc
Summer may be short, but the memories you make will
last forever. #nevergiveup #neverquit

17

Smile for the Camera!

London Blue Video Must-Haves:

1. Needed: a perky narrator to guide London through the ins and outs of Whispering Pines and why it's the perfect place for her next video.

2. Load up the video with London facts and details that show what big fans Pines campers really are. Research London's favorite foods (Beaver can make her fave dish on camera!), her loves, her hates, and work them into camp segments. London needs to know the Pines has her back!

3. Important Pines places to highlight: lake dock (great view from a canoe), zip line (if she's not afraid of heights like I am). What if we have the narrator taped as she zips across the zip line? (Obviously this will not be me.) Should also include the cleanest bunk, the mess hall, and possibly the rock wall. (Could someone climb up to the top and sing a London song? Again, can't be me.)

4. Must find enthusiastic campers to talk about London! Problem:
    Campers can't know I'm making a video, so how do I do this?

I throw down my pen in disgust. Looking over my list of must-haves for the London video, I have a sinking feeling I will not be able to get all this done in the next twenty-four hours, and certainly not on my own. How can I get people to talk about London when no one knows I'm doing a London video? I can't narrate it myself. Seeing me and hearing my last name on video might make the judges not pick us on purpose, or sway London's decision. I want to win this because we have the best camp for the job.

Even with Courtney's laptop and permission from Hitch and the counselors to talk to campers and tape them, I think I've bitten off more than I can chew. One day. Today. That's all I have to make a kick-butt London video, edit it, and e-mail it in to London's label in the morning. Sure, I can take a few extra days, but Courtney's warning rings in my ears: I can't let the other marshmallows see what I'm up to. It must get finished today. The only thing I've done right so far is get the correct e-mail address to send the entry to from McDaddy's assistant, Sydney.

I throw myself back on my pillow and stare up at the sheer pink canopy above my bed. I had to wash it after the cabin raid, but it's clean now and as good as new. The raid feels so long ago, and the cabin feels empty now that everyone has left on the overnighter. They were supposed to leave in the morning, but the weather is supposed to be bad so they left today instead.

Good for me and the video. Bad because now I have no marsh-mallows to get on tape. I can't just have peeps and pez in this thing. What am I going to do?

What's that buzzing sound? I look around for a bumblebee or a horse fly, but there are none. I can hear the slow *drip, drip, drip* of a leaky faucet in the bathroom and the creak of the ceiling fan on low above my head, but this sound is neither of those things. It's a constant vibration. It's Courtney's cell phone! Oh my God! Not having access to a phone for a few weeks has com-pletely made me forget what vibrate mode sounds like. I recog-nize Margo's number and pick up immediately.

"Hey!" I'm elated. "You called me back!"

"Harper?" Margo says. It feels good to hear her voice. "When I saw the area code, I figured it had to be you calling. Is everything okay? How are you able to call me in the middle of the day?"

"Long story," I say, "but I don't have a lot of time. I need your help with something."

"Anything!" she says.

"You're a huge London Blue fan. Tell me everything there is to know about her," I say, "and don't stop till I tell you to."

"Okay," she says cheerily. "Here it goes."

Ten minutes later, I have more than enough London stuff to go on, and I feel a little less stressed about this video. *A little.*

"Thanks, Margo. I have to run, but I will explain everything later."

"Wait!" Margo yells. "Tell me one thing—are you okay? Your Tweets have me worried. Kate didn't seem that concerned, but I am. Is everything all right up there?"

I smile. Margo is a true friend. No matter what happens, she and I will be okay. I could tell Margo how Ethan is here, how I thought we were friends, how I want to be more than friends but that's not going to happen, plus who Jeanie is, and what Lina is like. I could mention how into cooking I've gotten, how I conquered my fear of sleeping outdoors and how I rocked it at karaoke, but I don't say any of that, either. Nor do I mention the fact that I am now considered a pyro.

Maybe some things are better left unsaid.

"I'm fine," I say. "I miss you."

"I miss you, too!" Margo wails. "Get home already so we can enjoy the rest of the summer. I have your beach chair waiting for you, and we can go shopping and veg out. You'll de-stress in no time. Just two more weeks, right?"

"Something like that," I say, trying not to feel guilty for being so unsure.

I hear the screen door open. "I've got to go!" I whisper, and shove the phone under my pillow. When I realize who is there, I do a double take. "Shouldn't you be on a bus to Boston right now?"

Lina walks toward me. She's wearing her Whispering Pines tee and navy shorts—the official "I'm leaving camp" outfit for trips of any kind. "I decided not to go. Courtney told me what you were up to, and she thought you might need some help."

I climb down from my bunk bed. "You're the last person who should have to help me with this. I'm the reason we're in this mess in the first place." I head to my trunk to see what props I might have in there. Maybe if I can disguise myself, no one will recognize me as the narrator of this video.

No, that won't work. Mom made me leave my Halloween costume wigs at home (I had thought they'd come in handy for camp theme nights).

"Maybe you did screw up, but you made a mistake. I shouldn't have bailed on you because of that." Lina leans on one of the bunk beds. "Having you as my friend is way more important than meeting London Blue."

I blink rapidly to keep from getting misty-eyed. "You think so?"

"Absolutely." The two of us hug. "I should have gone to the lake with you instead of making you go alone." Lina sniffles.

"I shouldn't have tried to go down to the lake," I cry.

She looks at me. "Yes, you should have! You were sticking up for us. Maybe you did sound a little vindictive, but you're right—everyone should have her say." Lina's big eyes seem fiery. "Jeanie can't keep getting away with being so evil. I've watched her do this stuff and just shrugged it off because I threw myself into other things, but it shouldn't have to be that way. The Pines is as much ours as it is theirs. Let me help you."

"But you were so looking forward to Boston."

Lina shrugs. "Once you've seen the Old North Church and ridden the duck boats, what more is there? I'd rather win over London." She smiles shyly. "I already know what your title screen should look like." She pulls something out of her back pocket. It's another London Blue drawing. This one has been done in color. It's even more eye-popping than the last one.

"When did you do this?" I carefully take it from her.

Lina plays with one of her pink braids. "After our meeting with Hitch, when we decided we were stupid for being mad at you."

"We?" I question.

The screen door opens again, and Ethan waves a white T-shirt as if he's surrendering. It makes me smile despite myself. He's dressed in the same outfit as Lina, which should look cheesy on a boy, but Ethan somehow manages to make all clothes look good. "Permission to enter?" he asks.

I'm not softening toward him. Will not soften! Cute or not. "No."

Lina and Ethan look at each other. "Okay, but will you hear me out before I'm banished?" he asks, his cheeks reddening.

I turn away. How could Lina take his side? He left her hanging, too. "I don't have anything to say to you."

"Well, I have something to say to you," Ethan says with a half smile. "I even have a guard outside who will forbid you from leaving if you try to bolt before I get my time." I try not to smile. I'm sort of impressed he isn't backing down.

The door creaks open again, and Kyle ducks inside. "Hey, sis."

"Did anyone get on that bus?" I say incredulously.

"After I groveled to Lina for forgiveness for being a moron last night, Lina told me what was going on," Kyle says. "There was no way I was letting you hang out to dry. So a video, huh? Very McDaddy of you."

"I didn't get his help, if that's what you're asking," I tell him moodily. My guard is still up.

"I know." Kyle looks at me. "You don't need any of our help, but we'd still like to pitch in. I feel bad about giving you a hard time about everything."

"I'm listening." Kyle is not getting off easy, either.

"I should have come looking for you and Lina last night instead of enjoying myself and letting you roast." Kyle flashes the smirk that makes girls swoon. "No pun intended."

"I yelled at him, too," Lina tells me. "For both of us."

I can't believe Lina has gone from being afraid to talk to a cute boy to telling him off. I'm so proud! I look at Kyle skeptically. "Well, if you yelled at him, I guess I don't have to."

"I'm ready to work." Kyle salutes me. "Even if it means you'll win our bet by pulling this off."

"You've got that right." The two of us hug. Then I remember Ethan is still standing there waiting for his turn to grovel. "I'm not going to go as easy on you as I did on him," I say to Ethan. "He's family."

"I know." The floorboards in the cabin creak as Ethan inches toward me. Kyle and Lina move out of the line of fire. "I'm sorry Jeanie lied to you. I'm even sorrier that I believed her. We've been friends for a long time, so I generally believe whatever she says. But I should have realized by how upset you were that Jeanie wasn't telling me the truth. She and I are going to have a long talk when she gets back." He runs a hand through his thick hair. "I guess I kind of knew something was off because I was on my way to your bunk when I ran into you." His eyes are glued to mine. "Hanging out at the lake was no fun without you there."

"Really?" I can't help but be a little happy about that.

"Really." Ethan moves closer. "I didn't think the Pines could get any better. Then you showed up." I feel myself inhale sharply. "You may have hated camp at first"—he raises an eyebrow—"but then you surprised us all by dominating this place." He takes my hand. "You're fearless, Harper, and I love that. Here I was telling you to break out of your comfort zone when it was really *me* who needed to do that." He looks at me searchingly. "There's so much more to you than I realized when we went to school together."

My face feels flushed, and I know it's partly because my whole body is tingling at Ethan's words. The other part of me is horrified that he is saying these things in front of other people. But I don't want him to stop, either. "You only got one thing wrong in that speech," I say, and he looks at me oddly. "There is one camp activity I will never enjoy—sleeping outdoors. I don't want to come face-to-face with a yeti."

Ethan shakes his head. "No, you do not." The two of us stare at each other and grin. The only sound in the room is the ceiling fan whirring above our heads.

"Well, as much as I want you two lovebirds to work this out, I think we have a video to create," Kyle says.

The video! That has to come before my boy problems. "Right! I've been thinking about this video a lot." I grab the notes from my bunk. "The only way we're going to win this thing is if we're as flashy as possible. London needs to see the glamour of Whispering Pines and how much we love her."

"Works for me," Kyle agrees.

"The first thing we need is a narrator to act as a tour guide for London on the video," I explain. "The guide needs to be bubbly, welcoming, and funny." I look at Kyle. "And it can't be you. We don't want London to realize the connection between our family and this contest till after we've won." Kyle nods.

"Connection?" Lina asks. Ethan doesn't say anything. I realize now that's just another reason to like him—he hasn't brought it up to me once this summer.

Kyle nods encouragingly. "Our dad shoots music videos for a living, and he's done a bunch of London's," I say, and Lina's jaw drops. "I didn't tell anyone because I didn't want that to be the reason you hung out with me." I look at the cobwebs on the ceiling. I have to remember to dust those.

"Harper, that's incredibly cool, but it wouldn't have made me like you any more or less," Lina says. "I like you because you're you."

I feel an overwhelming urge to hug her, so I do. Kyle follows my lead and squeezes us both, and then Ethan creates a sandwich with the four of us. We're all cracking up.

Finally I break up the moment. "That's enough! We have a video to shoot."

"I'll narrate," Ethan volunteers. "I'm cute." True. "Some people say I'm funny." He is. "I know this camp inside and out." Also true. "And I can lay it on thick and leave London drooling over the Pines. I'm a natural."

"Sold!" I look at the three of them excitedly. We have a narrator! This is going to work! "What are we waiting for?" I reach up to my bed and grab Courtney's phone. I have my video notes in my other hand. The gang watches as I walk to the cabin door and hold it open for them. "Let's get out there and make London beg to see more."

McDaddy would pull his hair out if he knew I was trying to shoot a video in eight hours. He'd cry if he knew we tried to finish it in six. We got enough footage for an hour-long video, but ours has to be five minutes max. When Kyle, Ethan, Lina, and I start to sort through the footage we've shot, I know our video has to include a few key scenes:

1. Making dessert for London.

"I'm nervous!" Beaver says when I point the iPhone at him to start shooting. He's the only other person at the Pines I told the truth to about the video. I knew he'd keep a secret, and he'd want to make his part extra special for London. After a quick shower, a fresh apron, and hair styling (by me!), Beaver has all the supplies he needs to make London's favorite dessert: bananas Foster. I didn't even have to tell Beaver what it was. He knew!

"Don't be nervous," I say calmly. "Just pretend we're in Baking with Beaver and you're teaching me how to make bananas Foster instead."

Kyle chuckles as he holds up an extra light to make the kitchen brighter. "Baking with Beaver." Lina and Ethan make warning motions to him, but it's too late.

"Have a problem with a guy baking?" says Beaver. "Haven't you heard of Bobby Flay or Guy Fieri? They'd flatten you if you laughed at them." Kyle gulps.

I steal Lina's line. "He's a teddy bear when you get to know him." I look at Beaver. "Pretend I'm London." I do a giant toss of my hair and sing a few notes from our favorite song. "You can even sing if you want to."

Beaver's eyes light up. "Not a bad idea." He fires up the stove. "Start taping before I change my mind."

I turn on the iPhone video and press record. "Rolling!"

"Hi there, London!" he says. "This is Beaver, the head cook at the Pines. When you come here, you can forget the craft services truck. Who needs one? I'll make your every culinary desire on command. My specialty is bananas Foster," he adds. "I'm going to make it for you now to get your mouth watering..."

2. The Peeps London Sing-Along

How do you get thirty six-year-olds to sing a London song

when they don't know they're making a video for London? You let them think it is karaoke.

After All-Camp Night, I've grown fond of karaoke. It makes even the unlikeliest of people come together for a song.

"Why are we singing?" asks a cute six-year-old with pigtails. "Is it Saturday already?"

Ethan crouches down. "We always sing at the Pines. Don't you like to sing?"

She looks at her friend, a redhead with short hair. "Yeah. I still don't want to sing for you, though," she says, and Lina and I try not to laugh.

"Will you sing for me?" Kyle does a hip-hop move called a donkey kick in front of them, and a few kids laugh. "If you sing, I'll dance as goofy as you want."

The kids say no. I can't blame them. Kyle's moves are not great.

"We have fifteen minutes till next period," their counselor warns us.

I look desperately at Ethan. "If you sing, we'll give you a reward, just like they do on All-Camp Night," he pipes up.

This gets them fired up. "Like what?" a boy calls out from the back.

"Free ice cream for everyone at the canteen this afternoon," Ethan says.

They all cheer.

Ice cream is a dollar a bar. And people say *I* like to buy friends with presents. I shake my head at Ethan, but the funny thing is, his bribe works.

Lina starts off the song, and the redhead is the first to join in. Then they all do. By the time they reach the chorus, they're so loud I wish I could drop the iPhone and plug my ears. They're dancing around at this point, too. If London doesn't like it, I don't think she'll like anything she sees on our video. Pint-sized singers are video gold.

3. Canoeing at Sunset with the Perfect Date

"We have to hurry with this last shot or we'll lose the light!" I say as Kyle rows me out to the center of the lake. Ethan rows his own canoe alongside us with Lina tucked inside. It was his idea to show London how romantic the lake could be at this time of day. Since I don't think I should be on camera, I tapped Lina to play Ethan's date for the ride.

Kyle tries to stop in the center of the lake, a few feet from Ethan's canoe. The amber glow from the setting sun makes the water look like glass. The lake is quiet (everyone else is at the mess hall for dinner), and the crickets offer a perfect sound-track. Ethan adjusts the new shirt he put on: a turquoise polo that looks really good on him (he got a little muddy after climbing the rock wall and doing the zip line as part of London's tour).

"Are you ready?" he asks me as I continue to zone out.

"Oh! Yep!" I hold up the iPhone to start shooting. "Whenever you are."

"Hey, London," Ethan says in a smooth voice. I can see the reflection of Ethan and Lina in the water. "We hope you enjoyed your day at Whispering Pines with us. We've saved the best moment of the day for last." He motions to the darkening sky. "The sunset. If you shoot your video here, you'll definitely want to spend time on our lake and maybe even shoot at this exact time of day." He looks at me when he is supposed to be looking at Lina. "With the right person, this lake can be pure magic." I feel goose bumps. He starts to row away. "Until then, have a great summer and enjoy the sunsets."

"Cut!" I cry, and he stops rowing. "That was perfect!"

Kyle frowns. "I don't know. Enjoy the sunsets? Sounds a little cheesy to me."

"That's just because you've never had anyone to share a sunset with," I say.

"You do now," Lina says quietly, and we all look at her in surprise. Her face is flushed. "If you want to, I mean, you could watch it with me. We could swap canoes."

"I was thinking the same thing," Ethan says. He rows closer until our canoes knock together. Kyle carefully helps Lina while Ethan helps me and we cross the canoes at the same time for balance. After a rocky few seconds, we are settled where we should be.

"See you back at the shore," Kyle says as he rows away with Lina. She looks nervous but isn't freaking out.

For a moment I feel strange, too. I look at Ethan. "I—"

"Shh..." Ethan puts a finger to my lips, and I go numb. "You've done all you can for this video today. Now it's time to enjoy the moment." He takes my hand, and we watch the

222

sun beginning to slip below the trees. I'm not sure I could have come up with a better moment if I tried.

Harper McAllister @HarperMc
Sunsets are even better than sunrises … when you have someone to share them with. #whoknew?

18

LONDON CALLING

Harper McAllister @HarperMc
Time moves much slower without TV and Internet. That
wouldn't be such a bad thing—if I wasn't waiting on huge
news!

Harper McAllister @HarperMc
Sat for a drawing by a friend then got misty when I found
out it was a going-away present. Had ice cream at the
canteen to cheer up. #sad

Margo Is Divine @MargoDivine
@HarperMc What is the canteen? This camp sounds fun.
I'm so over the cabana. It's the same people vying for best
lounge, bikini, & bod.

Harper McAllister @HarperMc
Confession: The one thing I didn't see coming at camp this
summer: me being sad it was over. #revelation

Margo Is Divine @MargoDivine
@HarperMc Don't be sad! Are you coming home tomorrow?
Miss you! Dying here . . .

FROM: McDaddy@McDaddyProductions.com
TO: WhisperingPinesBUNKONENOTES@gmail.com
SUBJECT: For Harper McAllister

Hi, sweetie! Thought you'd want to know that I am
shooting London's next video, the one being shot at a
summer camp. Did the Pines ever enter the contest?
I know Hitch's wife said you guys were thinking about
it, but you haven't said anything to me. If the Pines
did and they win, you can come with me and watch
me film—that is, if you can tolerate being back there
so soon.

Hope you're trying to have fun. Mom says you haven't
e-mailed her all week and you usually e-mail her daily. She
called the main office to make sure you weren't sick, and
they said you were fine. All okay?

We'll see you this Saturday around 11:00 a.m. We
promised Kyle we'd stay through lunch. Hope you can

handle the mess hall one more time. I got sick of hamburgers and sloppy joes when I was there myself.

Love, McDaddy

"You forgot this." Lina hands me the crimper I hid from
Courtney (who banned all my hair tools after the fire). Who
knew oversized makeup cases were such a great place to hide
things?

No, I didn't." I gently push her hand away. "I left it there for
you. It's a gift."

"Seriously?" Lina holds the crimper tight, and I see her smile
for the first time all morning—and it's been a long morning. We
walked down to the lake together so I could see the sunrise (the
view there is my favorite spot at the Pines). "Are you sure you
don't need it for Cancun or one of those beach party nights at
your cabana?"

Hearing Lina talk about my other life is weird, like I'm
cheating on her. For weeks all I could talk about was home, and
now I just want to talk about here. Cancun isn't happening, but
I haven't told anyone that yet. Not even McDaddy, who I haven't
talked to all week because I haven't checked my Bunk One notes.
I had a low-technology-dependent week. I only tweeted occa-
sionally, and I was afraid to read any e-mails from Kate or Margo
about the second half of the summer and our plans. I have a
feeling I'm going to change all of them, anyway. McDaddy was

226

right—I shouldn't have to buy people's affections—not at the Pines, not at home, not anywhere.

"I will not be wearing my hair like that to the cabana, if I even go to the cabana. You're the only one who could pull off that rock star look, anyway," I tell Lina. "Whenever I used it, I looked like I was trying to bring back the eighties."

"It did come in handy for eighties night," Lina points out.

True. "That is why you should hold on to it," I say. "For next summer."

We're both silent. I've said the "S" word. Summer. Next summer, meaning this summer is over. At least it is for me. In two hours, McDaddy and Mom will be picking me up. Then, after a quick lunch with Kyle, I'll be on my way home.

Which is what I've wanted and yet...

I pack up my last item—my piggy alarm clock—and then my little corner of the cabin is empty. It's been stripped of sheets, my canopy, my trunk, and that lavender pillow that Addison always complained made her feel ill. My space looks depressing. "I guess that's it." I zipper my last duffel closed, then Lina and I carry the three bags to the door. Strange to think Courtney was right about me not needing all the other things I sent home weeks before. I can't even remember what I had in there.

"We should get down to breakfast," Lina says. "Beaver is going to run out of french toast if we don't, and he made this version especially for your last day."

Aww...Beaver. I miss him already. He made banana-walnut french toast just for me because he knows it's my favorite. I sliced the bananas for him myself this morning, and we both got a little choked up. It was sweet seeing a guy that manly be all vulnerable.

Yes, I hit the mess hall kitchen after seeing the sunrise. Who is this girl who rises with the sun? I'm not sure. But when you have just a few hours left...

"He should have enough for several batches." I step off the porch. Then I take a look back at the cabin with its rickety porch. It wasn't such a bad place to sleep after all.

I'm not telling McDaddy that though. Better to let him suffer a bit for holding me hostage here.

"I wonder what Beaver's going to make in his next cooking class," I say out of nowhere, and Lina looks at me oddly because we were just talking about breakfast. "I thought he should do Mexican food since you're having a fiesta party next session."

"If you stay on, you can help him prepare," Lina hints again.

"Leen..." I sigh. "You know I can't."

"Why not?" Lina asks loudly, and a bird on a nearby tree actually flies away. "Camping Barbie and Adventure Barbie aren't done having fun yet." She grins. "I haven't gotten you back on the zip line."

"You wouldn't even if I did stay." I laugh. "My feet are staying on the ground."

Lina looks determined. "Stay on with Kyle. Call your parents and tell them to turn the car back toward Long Island. You know you want to."

"They're already on their way." I dig the toe of my now beat-up crystal-covered Chucks into the dirt path. "Besides, can you imagine how Jeanie and Camilla would react if they knew I changed my mind about leaving?"

"Who cares? We don't hang out with them, anyway," Lina says. "I bet Melody and Addison would be okay with it. Vickie and Trisha, too. They've warmed up to you just like this guy." Ethan walks over. He looks like he's come straight from the showers, and he smells like green soap. I like green soap. I also like brown eyes. He has a lot of pluses in his column. But no. I said I was leaving after four weeks, and it's been four weeks. It's time to go home!

The two of them stand side by side like they are going to block my path to the parking lot. Behind them I can see bunks filing out of their cabins to head to the mess hall for breakfast. The normal sounds of nature suddenly get drowned out by laughter and talking. Most of the campers don't even make a comment about the fire when they see me. That could be because Hitch made an announcement that no one was allowed to talk about the fire anymore or who started it. I still don't think they've gotten over losing their London Blue spirit board though.

Ethan looks directly at me. "Say you haven't had fun this week, and we won't say the 'S' word again."

I give him a puzzled look. "Summer?"

He reminds me again that he has an excellent smile. "No. The 'S' word is 'stay.'"

Oh! "Guys, this week *has* been great, but I have people waiting for me at home."

"Like Kate?" Ethan hates even saying her name, so it sounds strange on his lips. "You know she'll be waiting for you with her hand out."

He's right. I'm not looking forward to seeing her (or trying to get my wardrobe back). The person I want to see is Margo, which is why I feel bad for not tweeting her back this week. Finishing the London Blue video gave me a great high, but still not knowing where we stand in the contest is killing me. Courtney says Hitch said the camps were told to be on standby for the next two weeks. Once London picks a winner, she'll be here within days to shoot the video. I can't believe Hitch hasn't let it slip about us entering. He was so ecstatic when he saw the video.

It feels weird knowing I won't be here when they find out if they've won. If they do, maybe I'll come back up to see everyone when McDaddy shoots the video. Coming back so soon might be weird, though.

"I'm not going back for Kate," I tell Ethan and Lina. "I'm going back because it's time. I made it through four weeks at sleepaway camp, something I never thought I could do. I zip-lined, I mud-wrestled, I made the whole camp french toast and realized I loved to cook. There is nothing left for me to do here."

"Yes, there is." Ethan folds his arms across his chest. "You can stay and enjoy the rest of your summer with me...I mean, us."

That's pretty sweet. My cheeks burn. "With you guys, yes, but the rest of the camp still sees me as the Barbie doll who ruined their chances of meeting a pop idol."

"They wouldn't think that if you let them know we whipped out a new entry," Lina says. "A brilliant entry. Whether or not we win, everyone should know how you stepped up."

The breakfast bell rings. We're going to be late if we don't start walking. "No, it's too late for that. Besides, the damage is done. I don't want to buy their trust. Let's just go to the mess hall and enjoy breakfast together one last time."

Ethan purses his lips, but he doesn't say anything. The three of us walk the short distance in silence, and I find myself taking snapshots of the campus in my mind. I took photography as an elective this week, and every picture I took was of the scenery. A close-up of a pine tree. My favorite rock that I liked to sit on at the lake (when I'm trying to get out of free swim—you still can't get me to swim in there). The new porch on the theater, which I've been helping to build. Some of the shots were blurry, but still.

The mood is sadder than I'd like it to be by the time we get to the mess hall. Thankfully it's hard to stay upset when you're in this place. Having the whole camp under one roof is loud and distracting. By the time we get inside, even Lina has cheered up a bit. Ethan, however, has walked off to his table without even saying good-bye. Part of me was hoping he'd sit with us this morning. I've seen campers sit at other tables on a special occasion. But maybe my leaving isn't as special to him as I thought.

"Barbie, it's a bummer you're leaving today," Melody mumbles with her mouth full, "but I have to say, the french toast Beaver made to send you off is amaze." Addison nods since her mouth is full. Vickie and Trisha mumble in agreement.

I catch Jeanie glaring at them, trying to will them back to the Anti-Harper team. "Beaver's french toast is always amazing," she says and looks at me. "But I'm sure the french toast you get on Long Island is way better. Have fun at home."

Well, as long as we're both being fake... "Thanks. Have a great second session."

Suddenly the lights dim. Power outage? "I had nothing to do with it," I say to Lina, and she laughs.

"Good morning, Whispering Pines!"

Hitch is in the front, megaphone in hand, and he doesn't seem alarmed by our darkened hall, so I guess all is okay. "I hope you're enjoying your breakfast. Let's give a warm round of applause to the kitchen staff—volunteer and otherwise!"

"What's with the lights?" someone yells. It's Heath.

"Ah, I'm glad you asked, Heath," Hitch says. "I don't normally like movies during breakfast, but for this I'll make an exception, especially since it's so important."

I get a sinking feeling in my stomach. Where is Ethan? I don't see him anywhere. Lina looks pretty pleased with herself though. "You didn't."

"*I* didn't do anything." She takes a big piece of french toast and pops it in her mouth. Her expression doesn't leave me entirely convinced. "It was Ethan's idea. He figured if you were leaving, anyway, who cared if you got mad?"

"As you know, almost two weeks ago our camp entry for the 'Win a London Blue Video Shoot' contest was accidentally destroyed in a fire." The room is so quiet I can hear birds chirping outside. The fire is still a topic no one likes to talk about.

"The person responsible for that fire felt so bad about what happened that she decided to try to get a new contest entry in on her own," Hitch says. "I didn't tell any of you about it because I wasn't sure she could pull it off, but she and a few fellow campers shot a video entry that is pretty darn spectacular."

My bunk stares at me. Jeanie looks like her food just went down the wrong pipe.

"So what I'm saying is, Whispering Pines was able to enter the contest after all!" A screen drops down as the room erupts in cheers. "Watch the video for yourselves."

"He's *playing* the video?" I am shocked. "Now?"

Lina nods. I put down my fork. I can't eat while they're watching this. What if they hate what I've done even more than they hate me for ruining their first entry?

The first image is of Ethan standing with a big group of pez. "Good morning!" they yell. I shot them standing at the edge of the dock by the lake. "Welcome to Whispering Pines sleepaway camp in the Berkshires," Ethan says, being careful to leave out London's name so the other campers don't know what we're up to. He starts walking toward the camera. "We're happy to show you around the Pines. First stop—our beautiful lake, where you can start your day by paddleboarding, which is an amazing cardio workout, or on a sailboat, which we know you love, since you learned how to sail at the age of eight." The next image is of Beaver in the kitchen. "Next, let's head to the mess hall for breakfast. No need for catering when you have Beaver at your service." Our cook looks nervous but smiles brightly and points to his frying pan. "I heard you like bananas Foster!" he says. "We'll have it waiting for you!"

Addison turns to me. "When did you make this?"

"When you guys left for the overnighter in Boston," I say.

"But you only had a few hours to get it done," says Trisha in awe. "And you did all this? That's...pretty cool." Jeanie stares at her plate while Camilla swirls her cereal with a spoon.

"Thanks," I say. I strain my neck looking around the room for Ethan. Then I spot him leaning against a back wall with Kyle. He gives me a satisfied look and a little wave.

"I think I won!" Kyle mouths. I can't help but grin.

The last scene is still my favorite, maybe because of what happened after the camera was turned off. It's Ethan and Lina in the canoe on the lake at sunset. "Hey, London," Ethan says in his smoothest voice. "We hope you enjoyed your day at Whispering Pines with us. We've saved the best moment of the day for last." He motions to the sky. "The sunset. If you shoot your video here, you'll definitely want to spend time on our lake and maybe even shoot at this exact time of day. With the right person, this lake can be pure magic." I have chills just hearing it all over again. "Until then, have a great summer and enjoy the sunsets."

When the video ends, Justin is the first to whistle. Dirk, Heath, and Kyle follow suit, and then Ethan joins them. Before long, most of the mess hall is banging forks on the table,

234

stomping their feet, and getting the rowdiest I've ever seen them outside of All-Camp Night. They're all looking at me and smiling! Trisha and Vickie are actually cheering. Ethan motions for me to go up and take a bow, but I shake my head. Just hearing how happy they are with the video is enough for me. I guess that's why I don't see Ethan blow right past our table. He goes straight to the front and takes the microphone from Hitch.

"Let's hear it for Harper McAllister," he yells, and I jump as everyone cheers louder. Jeanie keeps her hands on the table. The two of them have been kind of icy with each other after Ethan confronted her about what happened after bunk karaoke. "I know a lot of us are really going to miss her when she leaves today." His eyes find mine. "I know I will."

Heath whistles, and then everyone starts to clap again. Ethan just stands up there, not looking embarrassed at all.

"Wow, it's gotten hot in here," I say to Lina, who laughs.

"All right, everyone." Hitch gently nudges Ethan aside. "Let's calm down because I still have more to say." I watch as two people join Hitch on the stage.

McDaddy? Mom? Why are they up there? "That's my parents," I tell Lina.

"This is a good friend of mine—a former bunkmate, actually," Hitch starts to say.

From the back of the room I hear Kyle call out, "Hot Pants McAllister!" and I start to laugh. McDaddy's brow furrows as he searches the crowd for my brother so he can kill him. My mother bites her lip.

"He and his lovely wife have brought me a message that I think you'll all want to hear," says Hitch. The screen behind him gets bright again, and a grainy video appears. I can see an unmade bed and clothes thrown everywhere. It looks like a hotel room. Then a face comes into view, and people start to scream.

"Hi there, Whispering Pines. London Blue here." The biggest pop star in the world is doing a shout-out to my camp! She looks like she just woke up because her hair is frizzy and her skin is free of makeup. Of course, she somehow still looks luminous (lucky!). The dyed streak in her hair is now a royal blue, and she's changed her nose ring from a sapphire to a diamond stud. Her blue eyes practically fill the entire screen.

The room erupts in craziness at the sight of her. Lina is yanking on my arm so hard I'm sure she's going to rip it out of its socket. Jeanie's jaw drops, and she looks at me as if she's seen a ghost. If London is sending us a video, then...

"I have seen a lot of entries for this contest—poems, songs, poster boards with lots of pictures, and even some food entries." She makes a face. "Note to you all for the future: Do not send food through the mail. But none of those entries held my attention like your video. How could I say no to a place that has zip lines and the best background singers around?" More screams are heard around the room followed by a loud "shush!" "Whispering Pines reminded me of my own summer camp days, which were not always easy! I was a bit of an outcast." She scratches her nose. Or is that her nose ring? "I had no clue how to start a fire with two sticks, and I hated swimming in the lake, but what I did have were some great friends who made the whole experience worthwhile. Their friendship is what inspired my next single, 'Summer State of Mind.' See you guys in one week for our shoot. We're going to have a blast!"

Everyone is screaming like we won the Super Bowl. I'm happy, but suddenly I feel wistful. I wish I wasn't just driving up to watch the video shoot. I want to be a camper in the video, too!

"We won," Lina says, still stunned.

"We won," I repeat, and the two of us giddily hug.

Lina's eyes focus on mine. "You made this happen, Camping Barbie. If we had handed in that spirit board, we would have lost. We won because of you!"

"We won because of all of us," I correct her. "I couldn't have done it without you guys."

"I can't believe you pulled this off." Jeanie looks as stunned as I feel. She looks at Lina. "So that's why you weren't on the overnighter," Jeanie says, putting the pieces together. "You, Ethan, and Kyle helped her with the video."

Before I can say anything, I am lifted off the ground. I feel Ethan and Kyle pushing me up onto their shoulders like a quarterback who just scored a touchdown.

"Let's hear it for Harper!" Justin crows, and everyone cheers. They parade me around the room, finally depositing me near the front where Hitch, Pam, Beaver, Courtney, Mom, and McDaddy are waiting for me.

Beaver grabs me first. "You did it! I can't believe London is coming here." He shakes his head. "I get to make bananas Foster for London Blue!"

"I can't wait to hear all about it." I feel a little sad as I say that. The reality is I won't be here to see him do it.

"Way to go, kiddo," McDaddy says as he and Mom whisk me away from Beaver and my own thoughts. "I had no idea you shot the video till Hitch told me himself this morning."

"So you had nothing to do with the judging?" I ask as we walk over toward Hitch and the counselors. Please say no.

"Nope." McDaddy grins. "The Pines won on its own with your help."

"Maybe you have a career in video production ahead of you," Mom says.

"Who knows?" Camp has taught me how to dabble in a lot of areas. There's nothing I can't see myself trying now. Well, as long as it doesn't involve rock-climbing and zip lines, or anything else athletic.

"You should be here for the shoot," Ethan says. I didn't even notice him come over. "You're the whole reason it's even happening. Tell her to stay," he says to Courtney and Hitch.

"Who's this?" Mom asks, and I wave her off. I don't want her embarrassing me in front of everyone.

"She's a big girl," Courtney says. "If she wants to stay, I'm sure all she has to do is ask. But if you stay, I'll have to hold on to this." She pulls my iPhone with its bedazzled case out of her pocket. "I know you've missed your old friend."

She hands it to me, and I turn the jeweled case over in my

hands. Somehow I thought I'd be happier to have my phone back. I push power, and it lights up. Within seconds, a bunch of alerts fill up my screen. Then a new text comes in.

> **Kate's Cell: Are you on your way home??? Can I hang on to your Blumarine dress? I'm having dinner with my friend Amber and I want to wear something trendy. Come! (Just don't tell Margo. She's been such a pill!) We can hit Intermix!**

The thought of spending the next month of summer with Kate exhausts me. I would never go out to dinner with her and leave Margo out. I realize I'm not ready to deal with that drama. Not when I have Lina and the others here who want to hang out with me for me. Not my AMEX. I miss Margo, but she'll understand. And when I get back, she and I are going to make some changes.

They're all still looking at me. I think for a moment. "If I stay, there might be some backlash. I mean, I did set fire to the theater porch."

"You did what?" McDaddy's head nearly spins off. "I performed in *You're a Good Man, Charlie Brown* in that theater!"

"Harper," Mom says, looking supremely disappointed.

I look at Hitch. *McDaddy and Mom really don't know?* "I figured the punishment you had here was enough," Hitch said. "Plus I already had the extra wood and man hours, so it didn't cost me a dime. I never told him."

McDaddy looks at me sternly. "Did this happen because of your aromatherapy obsession? You can't bring candles to camp!"

Hitch puts his arm around McDaddy. "Come on, Hot Pants. Why don't we take a walk over to the theater to see how the new porch looks?" Hitch winks at me and then takes my mom by the other arm. "Harper, I hope I'll see you at the mess hall tonight for the Mardi Gras dinner. You've more than proven you're a true Pines camper to me."

McDaddy softens. "I don't mind driving home without a backseat passenger."

"The world of Brookville will still be there when you get home," Mom agrees.

"Stay," Kyle begs.

"Stay," Lina echoes.

"Please stay," Ethan says. To me, the words sound like *I want you to stay.* I feel giddy.

"I know you have friends at home who miss you, but your friends here will miss you just as much," Lina says. "I can't imagine the rest of the summer without you."

"What do you say?" Courtney asks. "Want to hang around this place with us?"

I look at my friends and the Pines staff who have become like family. The All-Camp Nights, the cookouts, the early morning kitchen duty, and the time spent by the lake. Sure, camp's been tricky sometimes, but do I really want to leave all this in the middle of the summer?

I smile at them. "I guess it would be silly for me to leave before London Blue gets here."

Lina grabs me and doesn't let go.

FROM: HarperMc15@gmail.com
TO: MargoisDivine@gmail.com
SUBJECT: See you soon

I sent my parents home this afternoon because I wanted
to stay at Whispering Pines. You must think I'm crazy! After
all my tweets about roughing it out here, I would think I'm
crazy, too, but the truth is, even when I was complaining
about camp, I was starting to like it. Then in the last week
or so I really started to like it. Not "I love Prada" like it, but
enough that I want to stay and see what happens next. We
won a contest with London Blue, and she's coming to camp
next week to shoot a music video! Mostly, though, I don't
want to leave the people here who I've gotten to know. One
is Ethan (remember? From Intermezzo?), and if things
go the way I hope they will, we will have lots to talk about
when I get home.

　　Not sure how much tweeting I will be doing the next
few weeks, but I'll be home the week of August 17. I can't
wait to see you. XO, Harper

Harper McAllister @HarperMc
Long Island will have to survive the summer without
me. I'm staying for another session at Whispering Pines!
#campconvert

EPILOGUE

FOUR WEEKS LATER

"HEY, HARPER! WHERE DO YOU want me to put these torches?"

"Harper! Beaver wants to know if the pineapple smoothies are too frozen to be drunk from a straw."

"Harper, is it true we're roasting a pig tonight? Because I think that's inhumane, and I have issues..."

After a rocky start to the summer, I'm suddenly in demand.

I was worried people would be annoyed if I stuck around Whispering Pines for a second session (Cough, Jeanie. Camilla, cough.), but some people really surprised me. Most of my bunk was excited, and the guys in Ethan and Kyle's bunk gave me props for singularly destroying and resurrecting a camp dream all in one session. It didn't hurt that I agreed to have McDaddy take a picture of London with all the marshmallows when she was here. That shoot was the longest two days of my life—we had to be on set from six a.m. to eleven p.m., and it gave me a newfound appreciation for McDaddy's job.

Handling a pop star is hard work.

London was pretty great. She signed autographs, posed for pictures, and even ate in the mess hall. She loved Beaver's bananas Foster so much she asked him to come to New York City this fall and make it for a dinner she's having! Anyone who wasn't already a fan of London is definitely a fan now. That's why they've changed the traditional last-night-of-camp sleepover on the great lawn into a London Blue video party. Beaver and I came up with a Hawaiian theme that goes with the one London has in her video.

I guess I'm still trying to make up for the fact that I almost ruined everything here a few weeks ago. Plus, who doesn't love a good party? I love throwing them and spending people's money to put them on.

Just kidding! (Sort of.) I *am* going to try to scale back my spending when I get home. That's why everything at tonight's bash is stuff we already had on hand at Whispering Pines. Beaver and I came up with a menu that showcases all the campers' favorite foods and desserts, plus staples like s'mores and sundaes.

"Harper, do you want everyone to put the leis on when they get here, or should we drop them off at the cabins beforehand?" Lina asks me. She has one around her neck that is pink like her hair. Kyle is wearing several in the same color.

"What do you think?" he asks. "I'm going for the Harper— a little over the top, but fun."

"You're just saying that because *I* won our bet," I say. When I decided to stay and we won the London contest, my points in our bet skyrocketed. It helped that Kyle began spending so much time with Lina that his competitive streak fell apart for once. He's been really cute with her. "I hope you like hot pink because I have a Prada dress that is going to look adorable on you the first day of school."

Kyle looks pale. "You're kidding, right?"

Lina laughs. "Please send me pictures of that!"

"And the second day you can wear an electric-blue tulle skirt that I've been saving for just the right occasion," I add, enjoying myself.

"Please," Kyle begs. "If the guys see that, I'm done for. I'll do anything."

I smirk. "I'm just messing with you. You're off the hook. We both kind of won this bet, didn't we?" I think of Ethan.

"I guess we did," Kyle agrees and hugs me. "Thanks, Camping Barbie, although I don't think I can call you that anymore."

I shrug. "You can. The nickname's grown on me."

I see the giant blow-up screen beginning to inflate near the bottom of the hill as the lights start to come on in cabins and on walkways. The last bits of daylight are beginning to disappear and the final night of camp is really here. A light shines on the massive London Blue banner Lina created. I had it sent out to Staples so we could make a wall-sized version.

Okay, so I spent a teensy bit of my own money on this party, but I'm proud of my friend's work. London liked Lina's original drawing, too. Apparently she's thinking of using it on her website. Lina practically died when London told her that.

Kyle takes Lina's hand. "Come on, Adventure Barbie," he says. "Let's give the zip line one last run."

She swings his arm. "I thought you'd never ask. Race there?" Kyle doesn't even stop to answer her. He turns around and breaks into a run. "Hey!" She takes off after him.

Kyle starts running backward and yells to me, "If I had won our bet, you wouldn't have gotten off so easily!"

I laugh. "I figured!"

"Next summer!" he challenges.

Next summer. Everyone here is already talking about next summer. Half the marshmallows are discussing whether or not they're going to try to be CITs. Kyle, Ethan, and Lina want to. They'd be great at it, too. And me...all I know is that I'm going home with a new attitude about everything. Next summer is wide open.

"Where are those two running?" Ethan asks as Kyle and Lina race by him. He walks toward me with a sweatshirt. By mid-August the air at night has a bit of a chill to it. It's depressing how fast summer has gone. Faster than most summers I can remember.

"They couldn't resist one more sports challenge before they go home." I frown. "I'm worried about what's going to happen to them after tomorrow. They really like each other, and now they're going to be two states apart."

"They'll figure it out." Ethan pulls me close. I feel warmer just being close to him. "I'm glad we don't have that problem." He leans in for a kiss.

Every time he kisses me, I get goose bumps. His lips, the smell of his shampoo, how he puts his hand on my back when he leans in to me...I could get used to this.

"You know what I'm excited about?" he asks.

"What?" I ask.

He smiles. "Now that we're together, I'll be able to keep a piece of summer with me all year long."

This time I kiss him. How could I not when he says something like that?

The campers arrive, dragging rolled-up sleeping bags and chatting a mile a minute with their bunkmates and friends. Some are already misty. One of the peeps is inconsolable, and I see her counselor motion to Pam to try to help calm the girl down.

"What do you think of the party?" I ask Ethan. I step out of the way as one of the campers lays their sleeping bag at our feet.

"It's very you," he says. "I don't think I've ever been at a Whispering Pines party that had a smoothie bar. You really do have Beaves wrapped around your finger."

"We're meeting up in New York for a Food Network cooking class this fall," I say excitedly. "And I'll have you know, the smoothie station was his idea."

Just then Sam and Courtney walk by us. "This place looks great!" Courtney says. "I don't think we've ever had a party quite like this."

"Is that good or bad?" I ask.

"Good," Sam says. "Just try to keep Hitch off the megaphone tonight. I have a feeling he's going to want to do a London Blue sing-along. He's been watching the video over and over all afternoon since your dad sent a copy up here."

"Harper! Ethan! Over here!" Justin calls. He and a few of the other guys have set up camp a few feet away from the screen. It will be a while before Kyle and Lina make their way back. I don't see Jeanie and my other bunkmates, but we already said our good-byes at the cabin. I'm not sure we'll write or anything, but if I'm their bunkmate again as a CIT, I don't think they'll protest (as long as I don't bring a dozen beauty appliances that cause a power outage). Sam and Courtney have taken a seat with Cole and Thomas and a few other counselors nearby. For a while all of us just catch up on what we have planned for this fall. It feels weird talking about the things we'll do without one another.

By the time we're ready to view the video, the sky is a deep shade of purple. I stare out at the lake wistfully. I'm going to really miss that view. Thankfully I took about a hundred pictures of it in the last week alone, so I can blow it up as wallpaper if I want.

"I hope they show my face in this video," Heath says.

"I was one of the dancers in the dock scene. I hope your dad captured my good side." Justin turns so I can see his profile.

"I have no pull in that department," I say with a laugh.

Lina and Kyle run over, sounding out of breath. "Did we miss it?"

"Nope!" Courtney tells them. "And even if you had, I have a

247

feeling Hitch is going to play this thing ten times in a row." Lina and Kyle plop down and chug from water bottles.

"Good evening, Pines!" Hitch says. Despite Sam's wishes, he still has his megaphone. The screen lights up behind him. "Are you ready to watch your debut?" The camp cheers. "Here is London Blue's new video with a special message just for you."

"Hi, Whispering Pines! London here." She's wearing a glittery minidress. "Thanks for hosting me for two terrific days. I hope you're as happy with how the video turned out as I am! As a thank-you, I've sent copies of the video for all of you to take home. Have a great year!" More cheering.

"Your idea?" Ethan asks.

I shrug. "I might have suggested it to McDaddy..."

Ethan puts his arm around me. "You are a girl of many talents, and I can't wait to see what you think of next." I settle into his chest as the screen casts a glow over the audience.

Lina looks over and smiles. I reach for her hand and squeeze.

"Oh, don't worry," I say. "I'm just getting started."

Harper McAllister @HarperMc
The key to having the best summer of your life? Just let go and have fun! Till next year... #summerstateofmind

ACKNOWLEDGMENTS

What would sleepaway camp be without a few end-of-season (or end-of-book in this case) awards?

A shiny, red, first-place ribbon goes to sleepaway girls, librarians, and readers everywhere who have sent me countless e-mails begging for another *Sleepaway Girls* book. You guys are a dedicated group! I hope this companion book is as fun for you as an outing to Nordstrom with an AMEX is for Harper. I'm so glad you've decided to spend another season at camp with me.

Top Dog honors go to my fabulous editor, Pam Gruber, a former sleepaway girl herself, who let me return to Whispering Pines. Thanks, too, for giving me the terrific idea of building a tree house in the woods for Harper to sleep in. (By the way, this is exactly where I would sleep if I was forced to camp outdoors, too.)

A big gold trophy goes to my agent, Laura Dail, for championing a *Sleepaway Girls* reunion from day one! Tamar Rydzinski gets a medal on a pretty blue ribbon for always making sure the whole world knows about my books.

Most Impressive Teamwork goes to the folks at Little, Brown Books for Young Readers and the Poppy imprint for letting me publish my twelfth novel with them. I'm forever grateful to all of you who give my books a home—Elizabeth Bewley, Farrin Jacobs, Andrew Smith, Kristina Aven, Melanie Chang, Tracy Shaw, Wendy Dopkin, and incredible jacket designer Liz Casal.

Most Likely to Win Color War goes to librarians Larissa Simonovski, Kelly Rechsteiner, Jess Tymecki, and Pat Gleiberman—otherwise known as my fellow Beach Bag Book Club creators—for always being up for another event, writing workshop, and breakfast!

If I could bunk with anyone at sleepaway camp, it would be this group of writers that would win Best Bunk. Thank you for always helping me stay on track: Elizabeth Eulberg (cheerleader and official tour buddy), Kieran Scott (sounding board), Julia DeVillers (fairy godmother), Jennifer E. Smith (nicest person I know and also a great person to fly with even if you accidentally get booked in the same seat), Katie Sise (new friend and confidant), Sarah Mylnowski (voice of reason), and Courtney Sheinmel (most enthusiastic friend).

I'm also passing out gold stars to Elpida Argenziano (for working alongside me at Panera Bread and Starbucks); lifelong friends Lisa Gagliano and AnnMarie Pullicino (for never missing one of my local book signings); my parents, Nick and Lynn Calonita (for babysitting so I can write); Marcy Miller, a voracious YA reader and terrific friend who reads my first drafts; Aimee Berger of Camplified, who answers all my sleepaway girl questions in about thirty seconds; Lori Levine Waldman (for all the up-to-the-minute camp insight); and Miana Delucia, who is always willing to let me bounce book ideas off her, offer advice, and get her husband, Rick, to take my author photos (all but the one in this book, which is from my own camp counselor days!).

And finally, the biggest trophy goes to my incredible family—my husband, Mike; sons, Tyler and Dylan; and even the Chihuahua, Captain Jack Sparrow—for supporting me through it all and for making home always the sweetest place to be.

More juicy novels by
Jen Calonita

Secrets of My Hollywood Life

The fabulous (and not-so-fabulous) sides of being a hot teen star in Hollywood.

Sleepaway Girls

Turns out you can't hide from high school drama—even in the wilderness!

Reality Check

A TV exec picks four normal girls as THE next big thing in reality TV. Can their friendship withstand the spotlight?

Belles

A brand-new series about two very different girls and the secret that will change their lives forever.